APACHE BASIN

OTHER FIVE STAR WESTERN TITLES BY RAY HOGAN:

Soldier in Buckskin (1996)

Legend of a Badman (1997)

Guns of Freedom (1999)

Stonebreaker's Ridge (2000)

The Red Eagle (2001)

Drifter's End (2002)

Valley of the Wandering River (2003)

Truth at Gunpoint (2004)

The Cuchillo Plains (2005)

Outlaw's Promise (2006)

Fire Valley (2007)

Panhandle Gunman (2008)

Range Feud (2009)

Land of Strangers (2010)

Desert Rider (2011)

Apache Basin

A Western Duo

Ray Hogan

FIVE STAR
A part of Gale, Cengage Learning

GALE
CENGAGE Learning

Detroit • New York • San Francisco • New Haven, Conn • Waterville, Maine • London

GALE
CENGAGE Learning

Set in 11 pt. Plantin.

LIBRARY OF CONGRESS CATALOGING-IN-PUBLICATION DATA

Hogan, Ray, 1908–1998.
    Apache Basin : a western duo / by Ray Hogan. — 1st ed.
        p. cm.
    "A Five Star western."
    ISBN 978-1-4328-2563-8 (hardcover) — ISBN 1-4328-2563-1 (hardcover) 1. Sheriffs—Fiction. 2. Robbery—Fiction. I. Hogan, Ray, 1908–1998 Lynchers. II. Title.
    PS3558.O3473A63 2012
    813'.54—dc22   2011049908

First Edition. First Printing: May 2012.
Published in 2012 in conjunction with Golden West Literary Agency.

Printed in Mexico
1 2 3 4 5 6 7 16 15 14 13 12

CONTENTS

★ ★ ★ ★ ★

THE LYNCHERS

★ ★ ★ ★ ★

I

Ben Coe, three weeks' growth of black beard masking his hard face, pulled to a halt on the outskirts of Salvation and stared moodily at the brightly lit, jammed street. That was what Kilgore's letter had said they wanted him to do. And Tom Kilgore, the United States marshal for that area was the one who called the shots.

There had been but little more information contained in the summons. Explanation would come later, the lawman had stated. Coe was to report in Salvation, arriving unseen and unnoticed by anyone. The importance of that could not be overstressed. He was to present himself immediately at the home of Judge Frank Abraham. He was to be there on the 14th. The trial of the killer, Turk Duret, was set for the morning of the 15th and he had just made it. This was now the night of the 14th.

Now the long and lonely ride from Kansas was over. The noise and activity of the surging town were a welcome change and most inviting. For several minutes he sat there in the darkness, watching and listening, a wide-shouldered, slightly hunched figure on a weary buckskin horse. It would appear that almost the whole territory had turned up to witness the trial of Turk Duret. He must be a man well hated, Ben thought as he scratched idly at a scar tracing along his neck. It was an old habit of his, stroking that seared, white bullet path when he was concerned or thinking deeply. What could Duret have done to

9

warrant such attention? Something more than the usual murder, undoubtedly.

He stirred. The sound of approaching horses coming to him through the warm, soft night. They were coming up the trail he had just covered. Quietly he drifted back into the thick brush, a dozen feet to his left. He was remembering Kilgore's orders about remaining unseen. He waited out the moments while the riders, two slouching cowboys on range-worn horses, came into view. They drew alongside and passed. More customers for Duret's trial, he guessed. Kilgore and the local lawmen would likely have their hands full. He had a moment's wish that he, too, might ride into town. It had been a dry, dusty day and the July heat had been a fierce, withering blast since sunup. A cool glass of beer certainly would taste good. But he would have to forget that. Perhaps the judge could provide something wet and cold when he checked in.

He reckoned he should be getting there. Kilgore and the judge probably were beginning to worry about his arrival. He reached for the star pinned inside his shirt pocket. Better get it out of sight, just in case. For a moment he stared at its dully shining surface, the worn black letters proclaiming him a deputy U.S. marshal barely legible. This would be the first time in almost five years he would not be wearing his badge. With a faint sigh he half turned, and, taking the nearly empty sack of coffee from the left saddlebag, he buried the star in its depths. It would be safely hidden there.

Touching the buckskin lightly with his spurs, he cut across the trail and headed for the west side of town. As they moved deeper into the brush, Coe half rose in the stirrups, having one more look at the teeming town. His last good one, most likely, for tomorrow, if his guesses were correct, he would be seeing it through the barred window of a cell. And he would be the most hated man in the territory.

A woman's anguished cry suddenly shattered the stillness of the grove. It seemed to come from the trail, back where he had been. Coe halted, listening. The cry reached him again.

"Help! Please somebody, help!"

The words ended in a muffled sob. He wheeled the buckskin about sharply and drove hard for the sound.

In only moments he was on the scene. The two cowboys he had seen earlier had dismounted and were standing before a girl who they had backed against a thick cottonwood tree. One of the pair was holding the girl and had her arms pinned back. The other, a bottle in his hand, was attempting to force a drink down her throat. The girl was twisting about and struggling wildly to break free. Her dark hair had come loose and was now flowing about her shoulders. Her face, cleanly cut as a cameo in the pale light, reflected her stark fear.

"Go away! Leave me alone. Please, leave me alone!"

"You hear that, Keno?" the man with the bottle asked, pausing. "Wants us to leave her be!"

"She sure ain't very sociable. Go on, give her a drink or two. Maybe that'll sweeten her up a mite."

Coe, jerking his hat lower over his face, pointed the buckskin straight for the two cowboys. The pound of the horse's hoofs brought them unsteadily around. The one holding the girl let his hands fall away and stepped back. The other, bottle still in his fingers, wheeled to make a stand. Coe's down-sledging fist caught him high on the cheek and knocked him to the ground.

From the corner of his eye Ben saw the first rider reach for his pistol.

"Don't draw!" he warned, bringing the buckskin around in a tight circle. "Make a move to pull that gun and I'll put a bullet in your belly!"

The cowboy hastily lifted his hands. "We didn't mean no harm," he muttered thickly. "Was just havin' us a little fun."

11

"Wrong kind of fun, seems to me," Coe said coldly. "Now load your partner onto his horse and ride out of here. You come back this way again and I'll use this gun. That clear?"

"It's clear," the man grumbled. He turned to his friend, now stirring dazedly on the ground. Taking him under the armpits, he managed to get him on his feet, and then into his saddle. Mounting up himself, he started off down the trail, leading the other horse.

Keeping his face tipped, Coe glanced at the girl. She was standing in the open, her eyes upon him. She was pretty, he noted, and well-fashioned.

"You all right?" he asked.

She nodded. "Thank you for coming when I yelled. They slipped up on me."

"Not a very good idea, you being out here alone like this, Miss . . . ?"

"Bracken. Laurie Bracken."

"Miss Bracken. There'll probably be a lot of rough characters passing this way tonight. You live close?"

"We have a camp down near the river. My father and brother and a couple of friends. We're here for the trial." She paused, adding a moment later: "It's only a little ways and I could make some fresh coffee if you would like."

"I'm obliged," Coe said, wishing he might accept the invitation. But he was already late. "I've got to be pushing on. Some business that has to be tended to. I'll remember that offer, though, if it's all right with you."

He could see her smile. "The offer stands," she said.

"Fine. Now, I think you ought to be getting back to your camp. I don't think that pair will come back, but there will be others."

"I'm going," she said, turning off the trail. "Thank you again."

"My pleasure," Coe replied courteously, and watched her

disappear into the darkness.

II

Coe located Abraham's ornate residence and drew to a halt in the tamarack windbreak bordering its south side. Light shone through a lower-floor window.

Movement beyond the window brought his attention up sharply. The figure of a man crossed in front of the green-shaded lamp. That would be Abraham, most likely.

There was a second man in the well-furnished parlor. He, and the one who had moved across the window, sat at opposite sides of a heavily scrolled and carved table, playing some sort of card game in which neither seemed greatly interested.

The one on the left was Tom Kilgore, a huge man, somewhere in his early fifties. The other man would be Frank Abraham, the judge. He was older, well up in his sixties. He wore his snow-white hair shoulder length and his spade beard, also white, set off his florid, narrow features. A pair of steel-rimmed spectacles sat near the tip of his hawk-beak nose, and despite the warmness of the night his shirt was cuffed at the wrists and closed at the collar with a black string tie.

That the pair were impatiently awaiting him Coe realized when he saw Kilgore glance at his turnip watch for the third or fourth time in as many minutes. He moved in closer to the window, taking care not to silhouette himself against the block of light. He tapped lightly upon the glass. Kilgore flicked a glance at the window. The judge did not move. After a few moments the marshal rose and casually walked to a door facing him. A short time later Coe heard a sound in the shrubbery alongside the house.

Kilgore's deep voice asked: "Coe?"

"Right."

"Good," the lawman grunted. "Figured it was, but had to be

sure. Come back this way."

Ben ducked below the ledge of the window and moved to where the marshal waited. He accepted Kilgore's strong handshake and followed him then to a rear door. Once inside the house, they crossed a room, a kitchen, and entered a short hallway.

"That shade down, Frank?"

"It's down. Come on in."

Coe trailed Kilgore into the room where the jurist waited. The lawman made his introductions and Abraham at once asked: "You sure nobody saw you come here, Coe?"

Ben nodded. "Met nobody this side of the town. Had a little ruckus when I first rode in. Only people I've seen closer than a hundred yards."

Kilgore came alert at once. "That ruckus . . . anybody get a good look at you?"

Coe said: "No. Too dark for them to see much. Kept my face down anyway."

"What happened?"

"Couple of drunks trying to rough up a girl, that's all."

Kilgore again displayed his relief. He turned to the table. "Ticklish business," he murmured. "You cut things a little fine. Expected you a couple of days ago."

Coe shrugged. "Your letter took a bit of time running me down. I came fast as I could when I read it. What's this all about, anyway?"

Abraham broke in: "I expect you're a little dry and hungry. Can't do you any good on the food end. I live here alone and do my eating in town. But I've got plenty of good, cold water. The marshal can fix you up with a meal after you're safely locked in a cell."

The judge moved to a richly carved, ebony black sideboard. He poured a tall glass of water from a crockery pitcher.

"Sit yourself down, son," he said, handing the glass to Ben. "Make yourself comfortable and we'll explain."

Coe settled himself into one of the deep, leather-covered chairs.

"Don't like to ask a man to do what we've got in mind," Kilgore said, taking his place at the table, "but we've got us a situation that calls for some unusual methods."

"First time anybody ever asked me to take the place of a man about to get hung," Coe said with a wry grin.

"Just about what it amounts to," Abraham admitted, "short of the hanging part, of course."

"This Turk Duret must be a mighty important prisoner," Ben said.

"More than you'd guess," Kilgore answered immediately. "A lot rides on that jasper getting properly hung. That's why I sent for you. Can't have anything go wrong."

"Why can't you just hang him here, like you would any other killer?"

"The job's got to be done in Capital City. That's the governor's orders. Wants it done there on the scaffold inside the prison yard to prove a point. And Capital City is a two-day ride from here."

Coe frowned, considering the words. "You figure to have trouble getting him there, that it?"

"Plumb sure of it!" Kilgore said heatedly. "The way people all over this territory are feeling, we're bound to have plenty of hell, right from the start."

"Which means we'll have the same hell getting me there in his place."

Kilgore nodded. He let his eyes meet those of the deputy marshal. "Like I said in my letter, Coe, you've got a choice. You don't have to go through with it. It'll be risky. Could get us both killed. But there'll be no hard feelings if you want to pull out."

"Reckon a man dies when his time comes," Coe said, taking a deep drink of water. "Don't figure my time has showed up yet."

"Good," Kilgore answered with a hard grin. He nodded to Abraham. "Told you he was our man, Frank."

Abraham said: "I'm sure of it. But I still think he ought to hear the whole thing before making up his mind."

Kilgore laid his thick arms across the table and rested himself on his elbows. "Turk Duret was serving a twenty-year term in Capital City for a stage robbery. He did about two years of it and broke out. We don't know yet just how he managed it for the territorial prison is a hard place to get out of if they don't want you to leave. Anyway, he pulled it off. And he killed two guards doing it, one of them needlessly. We lost him completely for about a week. Then he showed up in a town south of here. Walked into a bank, shot down the clerk and a rancher who was there doing some business, and walked back out with about thirty thousand dollars. Naturally the shots attracted the town marshal and some other men down the street, and, when he stepped into the open, they caught on quick what was going on and started blasting at him.

"There was a woman, not much more than a girl actually, with her baby, sitting in a buckboard right next to the bank. Duret saw he was outnumbered so he jumped up into the buckboard and grabbed the baby. Everybody stopped shooting then, of course. Duret, using the girl and her baby as shields, drove out of town."

Coe revolved the words about in his mind. No wonder Turk Duret was so important! Four murders plus the crimes that had sent him into a prison cell in the first place. And topping those off with the kidnapping of a mother and her child.

"What happened next?"

"Worst thing of all, I guess you would say," Frank Abraham replied in a low voice. "He drove the buckboard into the hills, taking the girl and her child with him. He holed up with them in a cave. Both of them died." The jurist halted, studying the heavy ring on his left hand. "The baby from neglect and starvation, the woman from mistreatment. Nobody," he added slowly, "will ever know the hell that poor girl went through at the hands of that brute."

Coe felt his scalp crawl. Duret was more than a killer—he was a fiend, a depraved monster. The reason for the huge crowd gathered in Salvation for the trial was clear now. "How long did he hold them in that cave?" he asked.

"Almost two weeks."

"Two weeks," Coe echoed. "Looks like he would have needed supplies. Wonder somebody didn't spot him when he went after them."

"Just what did happen," Kilgore explained. "Reckon he must have had that cave all set up beforehand. Probably was what he was doing in that week when he dropped out of sight. But his store of grub finally did run out and he went to a little settlement on the far side of the mountain where he figured he wouldn't be recognized, I guess. Only thing, the storekeeper got suspicious and put the sheriff on his trail. They hemmed him up and took him without firing a shot."

"Girl and baby dead by then?"

Kilgore nodded. "Doc says he figures the baby died the first week. Girl had been dead only a couple of days."

Coe shook his head. "What gets into a man and makes him do things like that? I can understand robbery and maybe a killing during an argument. But to take a woman and treat her that way or let a baby die . . . hard to believe any man could do it."

"Lucky thing there are not many Durets in this world,"

Abraham said. "Usually you find some good in the worst criminal, but this Duret, well, I don't believe there is one single spark of decency in him."

Coe put down his water. "Can't say as I'm going to enjoy being him much, even if it is for just a short time. One thing I am wondering . . . why me? Must be plenty of men closer than Kansas you could have called in."

"Maybe so," Kilgore said promptly, "but we can't take any chances. You're a stranger around here, for one thing. Nobody ever saw you before. Anyway, we're hoping that's true."

Coe shrugged. "Might be a couple of drifters out there in town that have been up Kansas way. Doubt if they would recognize me, however. This beard makes for a good mask," he added, fingering the stiff growth covering his chin and the sides of his face.

"You're about the same build as Duret," Kilgore went on. "You see, nobody around here ever really saw Duret up close, either."

Coe frowned. "Not even the girl's folks? Her husband?"

"None of them saw Duret. What they and all the rest of the people around here don't know is that Duret's already been tried in court and sentenced to hang. It was done in secret, at a town near the border."

That made little sense to Coe. "Then why the trial tomorrow?"

"One reason only. We want people believing you are Turk Duret. This trial, or hearing, is purely to set up our plan. If the crowd or anybody in it gets ideas about handing out their own brand of lynch law, it will be you they'll be after."

"And the real Duret?"

"Marcelino Baca, the sheriff, will be taking him to Capital City by a different road."

Coe studied the high ceiling of the room. The plan was an

ingenious one, but dangerous for him. "Where's Duret now?"

"Right here in town. In jail."

Coe's attention dropped quickly to Kilgore. The big lawman grinned. "Locked up on a robbery charge. At least, that's what we're letting everybody think."

"But, isn't he liable to start shooting off his mouth? Don't you think he might tell somebody he's Turk Duret?"

Kilgore cast a sidelong glance at Judge Abraham. "Reckon he's the only prisoner in history that the law has kept dead drunk ever since he was thrown into a cell."

"Who all is in on the plan?"

"Four people. You, the judge, myself, and Marcelino Baca, the sheriff. No more."

"Good," Coe said. "Less chance of a slip-up if there's only a few knowing about it."

Judge Abraham nodded. He leaned forward, looked more closely at Ben. "From what you just said, I take it you're agreeable to helping us?"

Coe said: "Sure. I thought you understood that. I was just getting filled in on the details. What's the next move?"

"I'll ride in with you," Kilgore replied. "Like we were just hitting town. Nobody knows I'm around, either. Been holed up in this damned house for three days. Sure will be good to get outside and moving around."

Abraham gave him a sardonic glance. "You better be appreciating all this privacy while you've got a chance. Once you show up in town with Turk Duret in tow, there'll be somebody breathing down your neck every minute. You ready to go?"

"Guess you're right about the privacy," the older lawman said. "Reckon we're ready to make our move."

"I'll go get Marcelino and a couple of deputies. Got to escort our prisoner in style."

"Style, the devil!" Kilgore snorted. "If we don't have an

escort, we won't have a prisoner long. Tell the sheriff he better bring three men with him."

"Three it is," Abraham said, and passed through the doorway.

III

"Won't take him long," Kilgore said as Abraham's footsteps faded down the brick walk. "We'd better be getting set."

He took a pair of handcuffs from his pocket and tossed them to Coe. "Put these on. I'll go round up the horses. The idea is to make everybody think we just rode in."

Ben snapped the steel cuffs about his wrists. "I left my buckskin in the tamaracks."

Kilgore nodded, and left the room. Coe settled back again in the chair. The house was quiet, warm. It had been a long, hard ride down from Kansas and now, just sitting in the deeply cushioned chair, thinking of nothing, was good.

Kilgore was back a few minutes later. He came through the doorway brushing his hands. "Now, that part's done. That buckskin of yours looks pretty much beat. I may have to dig up another horse for you to ride."

"When do you figure to start for Capital City?"

"Trial is tomorrow morning. Everything goes right, we'll pull out the next day."

"The buckskin will be all right by then. Give him a couple of nights' rest and some grain, that's all. He's strong. Besides, I'd rather have my own horse under me in case we run into trouble."

"I know what you mean," Kilgore said, nodding. "And we sure might have plenty of it."

"Anybody in particular?"

"Look for a lot of hollering from everybody when they learn Duret's to be hung in Capital City. People don't trust politicians much in this territory and they're going to want to do their own hanging right here in their own back yard. And the girl's own kinfolks sure ain't going to like it. Add to that C.J. Preston's angle and you get a fair picture of what's ahead for us."

"C.J. Preston . . . who's he?" Coe wanted to know.

"The owner of the bank Duret held up. That thirty thousand dollars was never found. Duret hid it somewhere."

"And you figure Preston will try to get to Duret and make him talk?"

Kilgore nodded. "He'll try anything to get that money back." The lawman paused, listened. "Sounds like the escort has arrived. Just keep quiet. No need for you to do any talking."

Coe signaled his understanding. Noting then the gun belt still about Ben's waist, Kilgore stepped forward quickly, unbuckled it, and tossed it into a chair. He grinned at Coe.

"Dang' near forgot that! Where's your badge?"

"In my saddlebags. Hid in a sack of coffee."

"Good," Kilgore said. There was a knock at the front door. He moved toward it. Pausing there, he ran his gaze over Coe once more, giving him a final inspection. Satisfied all was ready, he swung back the panel.

" 'Evening, Sheriff, boys," he said, stepping back to admit the men.

Marcelino Baca, the sheriff, was a large man, almost the size of Kilgore. He had the dark hair and eyes, the heavy features, the broad, white teeth of the Spanish. He nodded, flicked Coe with a cool glance as he entered the room. Only his eyes conveyed a greeting to Ben Coe.

The man behind him wore a deputy's star. He was tall, blond, perhaps thirty years old. He carried a carbine in his hands as did the two special deputies who were at his heels. They ranged up before Coe, their features portraying their disgust and hatred for Turk Duret.

Kilgore shook hands all around. To Baca he said: "How's that crowd?"

"Not too wild yet," the sheriff replied. "Mostly getting liquored up tonight. Don't think we'll have much trouble."

Kilgore said: "Good. Let's get him down there and locked up. I suspect he's a mite hungry, same as I am."

The blond deputy snorted: "Let him stay hungry! I had my way, he could starve!"

Baca's big shape wheeled on the man swiftly. "You aren't having your way, Halvers! You get this straight. This man might be a killer, but he's going to have protection as long as he's in my custody. Remember that! Makes no difference how you feel about him, he's got the protection of the law. Understand?"

Halvers's eyes were fastened to Coe's. "I understand," he replied in a low voice. "But I'm not saying I like it."

"I don't care whether you like it or not," Baca said softly. "You just do what you're told. Any time you decide you don't want to, just lay that badge on my desk and get out. I won't have any deputies around who figure the law doesn't work both sides of the table." He lifted his attention to the other lawmen. "How do you boys feel about it?"

"You're ramroddin' this deal, Sheriff," one said. "Whatever you say goes with me."

"Me, too," the other added.

"Good," Baca said. "We're ready to go, Marshal. You and your prisoner will ride in the center. We'll space out around you. In case of trouble," he added to his deputies, "we'll do no shooting unless forced to. Use your rifles as clubs."

Kilgore took Coe by the arm and guided him to the doorway. Baca and his men fell in behind. They entered the yard where the horses stood at the hitching rail. Kilgore assisted Coe to mount and swung onto his own animal. With Baca and Halvers slightly ahead and the remaining two lawmen at the rear, they left Abraham's and started for town.

It was a short ride. Down a dark and quiet lane, deep in shadows, to the main street of Salvation, ablaze with lamplight and pulsing with an overload of humanity. They breasted it head on, Halvers and Marcelino Baca clearing the way before them with shouts and drawn guns. The crowd parted reluctantly. Coe felt the eyes of many upon him, sensed the hatred they bore. It would have been better for them to have arrived by a less conspicuous route. Yet he knew there was sound reasoning behind Kilgore's movements. He must establish Coe as Turk Duret in the minds of all who were in Salvation. This was the best way to accomplish that. Coe flinched as a small rock, thrown from the depths of the gathering, struck his arm and glanced off. A man, somewhat unsteady from drink, lurched in from the side, clawing at Ben's leg. One of the deputies moved up quickly, placed his foot against the drunk's shoulder, and sent him sprawling back into the crowd.

"Keep back! Keep back!" Baca shouted. "Don't want anybody hurt here tonight!"

The shuffling, swaying throng had stirred the loose dust into thick, billowing clouds. It hung now over the street in a choking, yellowish blanket. Their progress was slow but they pushed on. More hands reached for Coe but Halvers had dropped back to his side and crowded them out. Kilgore, on the left, gave him protection at that point. Ben glanced ahead. He was bathed with sweat and he would be glad when the trip was over. The jail was now only a dozen yards distant. A few more minutes and they would be safely inside. It was an uncomfortable feeling, having several hundred persons glaring up at him, all thirsting for his blood.

Baca pulled to a stop at the rail at the rear of the jail. Dismounting, he hurried to unlock the door. Kilgore and Coe followed him to the inside. Closing the thick panel and dropping the bar into place, the sheriff mopped at his swarthy face and grinned.

"A little close, eh, *amigo?*"

"Too close," Kilgore grunted, shoving his pistol back into its holster. "Thought for a minute I'd made a bad guess. But I think we've convinced them. Sorry we had to put you through that," he added, looking at Coe.

Ben shook his head. "Mighty glad this jail wasn't at the other end of the street."

He walked deeper into the room, halted in front of the two cells. One was empty, the other contained a man. He was stretched out full length on the cot, sound asleep, his mouth blared open, one arm and leg hanging off and touching the floor. A half empty whiskey bottle was nearby.

Coe glanced to Kilgore. "Duret?"

The marshal said: "That's him. A real pretty sight." He hesitated as someone knocked at the door. "Reckon you'd better be getting inside that cell. Halvers and the others will be coming in."

Ben walked into the barred cubicle. He moved to the cot and sat down, watching as Kilgore slammed the heavy cell door and snapped the lock. After a time there was a second rapping on the door. Baca, drawing his pistol, stepped forward and opened it cautiously. It was Halvers.

"Left the other boys to keep an eye on things," he said, pushing inside. "Most of the crowd's moved on. Only ones still hanging around is the Bracken bunch."

Bracken. The name sounded vaguely familiar to Ben Coe. He revolved it through his mind, trying to recall where he had heard it before.

"We'll have trouble with them," Baca said, wagging his head.

"Can't blame them much," Halvers declared, glaring hotly at Coe. "If a man did to my wife and baby what he did to Todd

Bracken's, I'd be honin' for a chance to even the score, too."

Bracken—Laurie *Bracken!* It came to Ben Coe in a sudden burst of remembrance. A heaviness settled down upon him. Sometimes nothing worked out right for a man.

IV

Ben Coe was awake with the sunrise. He had slept well despite the precariousness of his position and for the first time in weeks he felt rested. It was around 7:00, and the sheriff, followed by Deputy Halvers, entered. The lawman carried a tray.

"Get back away from the door," Halvers ordered, coming to a halt in front of Coe's cell.

Ben sat down on his cot. The deputy opened the door and cautiously slid the tray inside. "If that ain't enough, just let me know," he said. "We always give a man a big feed before we hang him."

Standing behind Halvers, Marcelino Baca winked broadly at Coe.

It was 8:30 when Tom Kilgore made his appearance. He greeted the other lawmen, cast a sidelong glance at Coe, and studied the motionless figure of Turk Duret for a moment. He then sat down in a chair next to the sheriff's desk.

"Crowd's already gathering at the courthouse. Expect we'd better be getting our prisoner over there."

Baca nodded. He turned to Halvers. "Carl, walk down the alley and see how things look. We'll take Duret the back way. No sense tempting anybody now."

The blond deputy left. Kilgore's glance swung to the other two lawmen. "How about you two taking a little stroll down the street. See what the talk is. Might hear something we ought to know. But be back in ten minutes."

The pair moved out at once. When the door had closed behind them, Kilgore arose and, taking the cell keys, released

25

Coe. Handing the deputy his handcuffs to place about his wrists, he said: "Figured we ought to get things straight. Now, about this trial. It will be short. We'll all go in the courtroom. The judge will have the charge read and ask you how you plead. All you say is . . . guilty. He'll pass sentence, and after that we'll get up and leave. Crowd gets a little wild, we'll stay a bit in the anteroom behind the courtroom until things quiet down. Then we'll come back here."

"Here comes Halvers," Baca announced. He stepped to the rear of the room and lifted the bar lock. The deputy entered. He gave Coe a swift appraisal.

"Nobody along the alley," he said. "What can't get inside the courthouse is standin' out in front. We won't have a better chance to get him there."

"We ought to wait for the other boys," Kilgore said. "Should be back by now."

Baca moved to the front entrance. Opening it, he glanced down the street. He called to the two men who were just returning. In a moment they were inside.

"Same orders as last night," Baca said then. "No shooting unless it's absolutely necessary. Use your rifles like clubs. But the prisoner gets *there* safely and gets *back* the same way. Am I making myself clear?"

The deputies nodded. The sheriff walked to the rear and checked the alleyway once more. "All clear," he said, and stepped outside. Coe, Kilgore, and the others filed out. Baca stopped the last man.

"Turner, you better stay here with the other prisoner. He might have a friend that would try and break him out. Just keep the doors locked and don't let anybody in to talk to him."

Turner started to protest then, shrugging, turned back into the jail. Carl Halvers called to him.

"Don't fret yourself, Bob. This won't take long. And you can

26

sure watch the hanging."

They passed quickly down the narrow passageway and entered the rear of the frame courthouse without incident. A small fringe of the crowd saw them as they crossed the street and a shout went up but there was no move to intercept them. At the moment it appeared everyone was more interested in getting inside the building to witness the affair than in taking the law into their own hands.

They walked along a short, dark hallway and stopped at a door. Kilgore rapped twice upon it. Coe heard its lock grate and watched it swing back. It led into the main courtroom.

It was packed with noisy spectators and already breathlessly hot. A shout went up when they made their appearance. Kilgore motioned Coe to one of the dozen or so chairs placed in the small area separated from the spectators by a belt-high railing. Halvers and the other deputy took up a position directly behind him. Kilgore settled down in a place at the right and near the judge's table.

Smoke hung from the ceiling in boiling, shifting clouds and the stench from sweaty, unwashed bodies was like a thick blanket in the room bulging with four times its intended capacity. Ben allowed his gaze to slide over the room. It was jammed tight, even the aisles having disappeared. He saw Laurie Bracken then. She was sitting in the first row beyond the railing. The younger man on her left would be her brother, the husband of the woman Turk Duret murdered. The older man, likely was her father. All three were watching him with a cold, unforgiving hatred.

"Everybody get up!" the man who had been posted at the locked door yelled his command.

There was a general clatter of confusion as those who were seated arose. Judge Abraham entered, walked to his bench. He glanced out over the crowd, nodded to the bailiff, and sat down.

"Hear ye!" the bailiff shouted, facing the assembly. "Everybody quiet now. This here court of Judge Frank Abraham is in session. Let's don't have no more of this racket!"

Abraham's frosty brows pulled down into a firm line. He let his hard eyes again sweep the room. "Let this be understood," he said in a cold voice, "this is a court of law and it will be respected as such. Any unseemly behavior on the part of any man or woman will call for immediate action on my part. I will clear this courtroom instantly."

There was a complete silence on the heels of his words. He allowed it to ride for a full minute and then turned his attention to the bailiff.

"I do not see the prosecutor or the court clerk present. Where are they?"

Before the deputy could make a reply, a voice shouted from the audience: "You won't be needin' them, Judge! We all know this Duret's guilty. Why you botherin' to try him, anyway?"

Abraham's florid face colored a deeper shade. He rapped on the table sharply. "Deputy!" he shouted, half rising. "Get that man out of this courtroom!"

One of the lawmen standing near the entrance hurriedly shouldered his way through the pack to the offender. Clamping his hand upon the man's arm, he hustled him out.

"The next outburst like that and everybody will leave," Abraham warned. "I'll have no such foolishness."

Two men entered the room from the side door at that point—a balding, well-dressed man with a sheaf of papers under his arm and a small, thin, shabby individual with a face like a ferret. The first halted before the judge.

"Mister Allison," Abraham said, recognizing the man.

"I apologize for being late, your honor. Our clerk, Mister Conley, misplaced some of the necessary papers. We were delayed while he located them."

Abraham threw a withering look at the small man. He nodded to the prosecutor. "Very well, Mister Allison. I assume we are now ready to proceed."

Allison said—"Yes, Your Honor."—and moved to an empty chair next to the court clerk.

The judge cleared his throat. "I would like to have it understood that this is not a trial. It is a hearing at which the prisoner will learn of the charges placed against him. He will then have the opportunity for lodging his plea."

There was a murmur through the audience. Abraham pounded on his table. He swung his attention to Kilgore. "Is the prisoner represented by counsel?"

The marshal stood up. "No, Your Honor. The prisoner says he doesn't want a lawyer."

Abraham nodded. His gaze came back to Conley. "The clerk will read the charge."

Harvey Conley got nervously to his feet. Adjusting his silver-rimmed glasses, he fumbled a moment with the papers in his hands and then began.

"That the accused, Turk Duret, who, while serving a term in the territorial prison, did break out and escape and kill two guards in so doing. That he later robbed the Cañon County Bank at Junction City of the sum of thirty thousand dollars and in the doing did kill Oscar Brewer and James Mattingly. And while further escaping he did seize, kidnap, and carry off as hostages one Molly Bracken and her child, Christine Bracken, both of whom died while being held captive in a cave where the accused was hiding." Conley stopped. He mopped at the beaded sweat on his forehead and peered over his spectacles at the judge. "That's it, Your Honor."

"Prisoner, how do you plead? Guilty or not guilty to the charges made?" the judge asked.

Ben Coe rose slowly. Keeping his head tipped down, he said: "Guilty."

There was no sound in the breathlessly hot room. Outside, in the street, the faint rumble of voices could be heard. Abraham said: "Guilty of all charges?"

The prisoner nodded and sank back into his chair. A man in the back of the room turned and pushed his way through the doorway, his voice shouting the news to those in the street. Abraham studied the backs of his heavily veined hands. He was apparently framing his next pronouncement.

"In that case," he began, his voice stentorian, "I have but one more duty to perform. To declare sentence. Are you ready, Turk Duret?"

Ben Coe again nodded.

"Then stand up."

Coe pulled himself upright, his tall, wide-shouldered frame outlining darkly against the morning sunlight.

"Since you plead guilty to all charges, it will not be necessary to hold a trial by jury. I, therefore, sentence you to death, Turk Duret, for your crimes. You will be hanged by the neck until you are dead and I will ask God to have mercy on your soul. This sentence will be carried out four days from today on the gallows in the yard of the territorial prison in Capital City."

There was a long moment of stunned silence. Then sudden, wild yells of disappointment ripped through the quiet. Several men leaped to their feet, their chairs overturning and clattering loudly to the floor. Cries of—"No! No!"—echoed through the crowd. Abraham began to pound on his desk with his gavel. Kilgore came to his feet, his hand resting on his gun while Sheriff Baca, who had been standing sentry at the hall door, moved up beside his deputies, a shotgun cradled in his arms.

"You ain't gettin' away with that, Judge!" a man in the front row shouted. "He'll never hang if you send him up there!"

"You bet he won't!" another voice agreed. "He'll cook himself up a deal with them politicians. He'll tell them where the money's hid and they'll turn him loose!"

The courtroom was bedlam. Abraham rapped on his bench but the sound went unheeded. The judge motioned to Kilgore, and, when the marshal had stepped to his side, he said something to him. The lawman drew his pistol and fired it into the floor. The shocking blast in the small area brought an immediate quiet.

Abraham held a letter over his head and waved it. "It's not necessary that I explain the actions of this court," he stated, "but in this instance I shall do so. I will tell you why the sentence of Turk Duret must be carried out in Capital City."

He waited until the murmur of voices had again ceased. He began: "This letter is from the governor. It directs me, upon finding Duret guilty and sentencing him to be hanged, to deliver him to the prison authorities in Capital City for execution. No wait . . . ," he added hurriedly as the protests started anew, "the governor continues . . . 'Outlaws in this territory have been having their way for years. They have flaunted our laws, ridiculed our lawmen, and done pretty well as they pleased. The public execution in the prison yard of an outlaw as famous as Turk Duret will prove to all the day of the outlaw is over. It will serve as a lesson and a warning to all others of like caliber that this territory is no longer a refuge for killers and wanted men. It will prove that, at last, we have a strong law, one big enough and able enough to cope with and punish the Turk Durets.' "

"Nothin' but a lot of talk!" a voice cried, almost before the jurist had concluded. "Just a way of gettin' Duret out of our hands so's they can turn him loose."

"He won't be turned loose," Kilgore said flatly.

"He got loose before, didn't he?" the speaker countered. "Man ain't supposed to escape from the pen but he sure did. I

31

figure he had a little help."

Ben Coe was watching Kilgore closely, awaiting instructions from him. The crowd had turned from one of almost festive mood to one of sullen anger bordering on violence. It would take very little to incite them to mob action.

"That's just what'll happen again! He'll tell them where he hid Preston's money and next thing we'll be hearin' is that he escaped!"

Kilgore half swung about to face Baca. "Better get the prisoner out of here, Sheriff. Take him into that anteroom. Lock the door. I'll join you soon as I can get the courtroom cleared."

"Look out!" Halvers yelled.

Coe had a fleeting glimpse of Todd Bracken's shape lunging over the railing at him. He tried to duck away but he was too late. Bracken struck him head on, the force of it carrying him over backward to the floor. With his hands manacled Coe could do nothing to defend himself. He sought to roll away. Bracken's fingers closed about his throat. He felt the man's knees dig into his back, pinning him down.

The room was a madhouse as spectators surged forward, yelling encouragement and advice to Bracken, seeking to get in their own blows. The sharp toe of a boot drove into Coe's ribs. His face slammed into the floor as someone struck the back of his head. Feet were churning about him, stepping on him, colliding with his body. A gun exploded again but it seemed to have little effect.

The fingers about his throat suddenly slackened their pressure; the knees left his back. Twisting about, he looked upward. Tom Kilgore was standing, spraddle-legged, over him. He had pulled Todd Bracken off him. At the same moment Coe saw what had happened, the big lawman had taken Bracken by the shoulders and hurled him straight into the crowd.

Kilgore bent swiftly. "You all right?"

Coe said: "Out of wind, about all."

The marshal helped him to his feet. Reaching out, Kilgore laid his hand on Marcelino Baca's wrist. The sheriff, standing beside his deputies, keeping the crowd at bay with slow, sweeping movements of their guns, swung about.

"Your chance," Kilgore said. "Get him into that back room and lock the door. We'll clear out this bunch and join you in a few minutes."

V

They reached the anteroom without incident. Entering, Baca was about to turn the lock behind them, when Abraham and the court clerk, Harvey Conley, who scurried along at the heels of the jurist with a fistful of papers clutched in his hands, hastened to be admitted. The clerk settled down at once at a low table and began to work over his papers while the rest found chairs.

It was a full half hour before Kilgore and the two deputies had dispersed the restless crowd and knocked at the door. The small quarters, often referred to by the judge as his chambers, were stifling with its dead, dry air and by the time the lawmen arrived, those who waited were sweating freely.

Kilgore, hands on hips, halted in the center of the room. His face was taut and he showed the strain of the past minutes. "Hard to keep somebody from getting hurt in a deal like that," he said. "Some people are just plain damn' fools."

"The crowd is plenty worked up," Halvers observed.

Abraham glanced at the marshal. A wry smile twisted his mouth. "Think you can keep Duret alive for a public hanging, Tom?"

Kilgore shrugged. "Not thinking about it, just figuring on doing it."

"You'll never leave town with him," Halvers said. "That's a

33

mean mob out there. Man," he added, "I never thought one man could make so many people hate him!"

Kilgore was not listening. "Might have been better if we'd rushed him straight back to jail. Got him there before the crowd got out of the building."

Baca turned to one of the deputies. "Take a look down the alley, Cal. See if there's anybody hanging around."

The deputy left the room. Abraham asked: "When you figure to leave with him, Marshal?"

"Daylight, tomorrow morning."

"Means you'll spend the rest of this day and tonight here. You think that's smart?"

"No choice. Got to get things set. And I sure don't want to pull out with that crowd the way it is now. Wouldn't get a half a mile. I figure the safest place for the prisoner is in Marcelino's jail until morning. Things will have cooled down a little by then, I hope."

"Maybe," Halvers said in a doubtful voice. "The woman's family, the Brackens, and some of their friends are hatchin' up something. I been watchin' them. We'll sure hear from them sometime. Probably tonight."

"No doubt," the marshal replied. "Take a look out in the street, Carl. See what's happening out there now."

The deputy moved out, going down the hallway to the courtroom. In a few moments he was back. "Crowd's thinned out a mite. Most of them have drifted down to Sandalman's place. Big bunch out in front of the hotel, too."

"Cal ought to be back soon," Baca said, thinking of the other deputy.

The steady scratching of Conley's pen was loud in the room. Abraham studied the sloped shoulders of the clerk for a moment. Then: "Which way you taking him to Capital City, Tom?"

"Up the old Diamondback Trail," Kilgore answered. He

pulled a thin, misshapen stogie from his pocket and thrust it between his lips. "Figure that will be the safest way to go."

The judge nodded his approval. "Good idea. Everybody will be expecting you to take the main road."

"How many deputies will you be taking?" Baca wanted to know.

"One," said Kilgore. "Halvers, here, will do fine."

Abraham frowned. "Guess you know your business but are you sure that's enough protection?"

Kilgore chewed at his cigar. "Two or ten, doesn't make much difference. With just three of us I figure we can move faster and quieter if we have to. Besides, a big bunch of deputies would sort of prove the law is still on the weak side, wouldn't it?"

Abraham considered that for a moment. "Yes, guess you're right. But don't take any chances. You know what your orders are if things go wrong."

Kilgore nodded. He swung around to Baca. "Where the hell's that deputy, Marcelino?"

Baca walked to the door at once. "I'll find out," he said. He opened the paneling. The deputy was there, just in the act of knocking. Before the sheriff could ask his question, he spoke.

"Got a wood hauler stopped back of the building, Sheriff. His wagon's loaded. We could walk alongside it to the jail without attracting much notice."

Baca said: "Good." He turned to Kilgore. "You ready, Marshal?"

Kilgore said—"Let's go."—then paused. "Everybody here understands there's to be no talk about us taking the Diamondback, I reckon. I don't want that to get out."

They all murmured their assent. "How about you, Conley?" the lawman called to the clerk.

Conley, writing busily, looked up. "Of course, Marshal. Wasn't paying you no mind, anyway."

"Good." Kilgore reached for Coe's arm. "All right, Duret. Let's get out of here while we got a chance. Might not get a second one."

VI

C.J. Preston, the banker, stood near the front of the courtroom idly fingering the heavy gold watch chain draped across his paunch. He stared thoughtfully at the door through which Marcelino Baca had hustled Turk Duret to safety. Behind him Kilgore and a couple of deputies were moving the crowd into the street, clearing the building. He had come to the trial prepared to testify as to his losses at the hands of the outlaw but Duret's unexpected admission of guilt made it unnecessary.

He turned then and moved slowly toward the exit, nodding to Kilgore and the deputies, their chore completed, as they walked by him. He came out onto the gallery fronting the building and stopped. Directly ahead of him were the Brackens and several of their friends. Two men were assisting the stunned Todd to walk. In that moment C.J. Preston wished his only desire was to see Turk Duret dead. Todd Bracken was lucky. How would he feel if he had lost $30,000, a loss destined to mean not only bankruptcy but disgrace and arrest for fraud as well? Fraud—that was a polite word for it. Those people who had trusted him would call it plain thievery. But how could he have anticipated such a thing as a bank robbery?

Had not Duret raided the bank everything would have worked out well in time. The large losses he had incurred in that New Orleans stock venture would have been covered in a few more months. Now it was too late. As soon as the lawyers and examiners checked the records, the whole thing would be out in the open. And the men in Chicago who had backed him would not be satisfied with so small a thing as an apology and explanation. Hard cash was the only thing they understood. Preston trembled. There must be a way out of it somehow.

Duret had done the job alone. He had been captured before he had time to spend even a dollar of the $30,000; therefore, it was reasonable to believe the entire amount lay hidden still, placed there by Turk Duret when he realized his capture was imminent. But where? The cave where he had holed up with the Bracken woman and child had been thoroughly searched. Under his own personal supervision every square foot had been dug into and carefully examined. And the area around the cave's opening as well. Nothing.

The marshal had been unable to get anything out of the prisoner, either. Kilgore had questioned him at length shortly after his arrest, and, while Preston had not been given an opportunity for talking to Duret, he knew the lawman had tried his best to learn the whereabouts of the stolen money. The outlaw simply refused to talk. But there must be a way to force him—there had to be. A man just couldn't allow his entire life to be thrown away by another's refusal to speak.

He let his gaze run the hot, dusty street. There was a sizeable knot of people gathered in front of Sandalman's Saloon listening to a harangue by some individual Preston could not distinctly see. Farther along, near the hotel, he saw the Bracken family again. His eyes came to a halt halfway between. Tibo Waggoner and Bill Ford. The two men were slouched against a hitch rail, looking on. They were strangers to Salvation but Preston had become acquainted with them and their unsavory reputations while he was below the border checking into some mining property a year or so past. Both were the sort who would do anything for a price. Preston's eyes began to light up as an idea came into his mind. He removed his hat and nervously scrubbed at the sweat on his balding head.

Why not? He hurled the question at the last vestiges of conscience clamoring within him. *Why not?* He could be no worse off—and, if handled properly, the plan would work. He could find out from Conley when Kilgore planned to leave with Duret and the way they would go. A few gold eagles would loosen the clerk's tongue. Waggoner and the men he would need would come higher but they would get the job done. They were the sort he must deal with now. *My own kind,* he thought with bitter revulsion, remembering his own secret crimes. Yet, that was the way it had to be. A desperate man takes desperate measures. He came off the porch and started down the street. He must see Waggoner and talk it over with him. But he would have to be careful. It would not do to be seen talking with the gunmen.

Laurie Bracken and her father were close on the heels of Orville Stelder and Pete Brookerson, who were helping her brother along the street. Todd was groggy from the treatment he had received in the fight with Turk Duret and was having difficulty in keeping his knees stiff. But now that they were outside, away from the withering heat in the courtroom, he was recovering quickly.

"This sure ain't over yet," she heard her father say. He was looking at the jail, his eyes bright and hard.

Orville Stelder moved up to stand beside her. The Stelder place was a scant five miles south of the Brackens'. For the past year Orville had been paying court to Laurie. "You're sure right, Mister Bracken," he said. "Ain't nobody going to do something like that to our womenfolk. Comes night, we'll take that Duret out of that there jail and string him up higher'n a buzzard's roost."

Pete Brookerson came into the conversation. "You believe what the judge said, about them going to really hang him in Capital City?"

"Naw," Orville answered. "That's just another way to keep

him alive until they find the money. That's the way these here politickers work. Horse tradin' all the time. I bet that's all Preston's doings."

Laurie glanced at her brother. "You all right now, Todd?"

"I'm all right," he said gruffly. He turned to Stelder. "We got enough men lined up to break Duret out tonight?"

"More'n enough," Stelder replied. "Just ready and waiting for the word. That bank clerk had some friends. And there's the cowboys who was working for that rancher, all just honin' to get their licks in. Then, I figure we can count on some of the local citizens who don't like the judge's sentence."

"Any plans made?"

"All we've got to do is pass the word. Name the time and place."

"Front of the jail, soon as it's full dark," Todd said.

Laurie shuddered at the grimness of her brother's words. He was like a stranger to her since the death of Molly and the child. Once they had been a happy family. Hard-working and poor, like almost all the settlers in the valley. Turk Duret had changed that. He had cast a blight upon their lives and now, seemingly, they existed for only one thing—vengeance. A tremor again passed through her slender body. "Todd," she said, laying her hand upon his arm, "do you think it's the right thing to do? Wouldn't it be better to let the law handle it? The judge said he would be hanged. I don't see how they can keep from doing it now. And with all those deputies around, there's going to be shooting. And more killing."

"Not much," Orville scoffed. "Them deputies are all for show. I don't figure they're going to hurt anybody protectin' Turk Duret. They just got to make it look good."

"Won't be no difference, anyhow," Saul Bracken observed. "He's going to be strung up, one way or another. Man's been

39

sentenced. Us hanging him will be just as legal as the territory doing it."

"And it sure won't make no difference to Duret," Stelder added with a laugh. "Either way, he's a dead one."

Laurie shook her head. "I still think it is the wrong thing to do," she said in a weary voice. "It can only mean more trouble for us. And more killing."

Harvey Conley waited until the lawman and Turk Duret had departed before he spoke. He said: "I'll have these papers ready in a couple of minutes, Judge, if you want to sign them. Like to get them to the marshal this afternoon so's we'll be done with the case."

Abraham settled heavily into his chair. He mopped at his florid face. "This case won't be done with until they cut Duret down from the scaffold. You know that."

"Yes, sir," the clerk replied, nettled by the jurist's sharp tone.

Abraham adjusted his spectacles and read the document slowly. "Damned if your penmanship doesn't look more like chicken scratches every day, Harvey," he muttered. "Where's the pen?"

Biting back his anger, Conley supplied the necessary item. Abraham laboriously wrote his bold signature across the bottom of the sheet.

"No pleasure," the judge said then, rising. "Sending a man to his death never is. Even a killer like Turk Duret. What do you reckon made him do a thing like killing Molly Bracken and her baby, Harvey? What gets into a man's blood and turns him into a monster?"

"Sure don't know," the clerk replied, stacking the sheets of paper together. "Money, most likely. Thirty thousand dollars is a lot of money."

"I suppose," Abraham murmured, staring at the floor. "Other

men have done much more for less. For thirty pieces of silver, in fact."

The clerk nodded his agreement. "You think the marshal will have trouble getting him to Capital City? That's a long ride and people sure are steamed up about it."

"All he can do is try. I don't figure he'll run into any trouble he can't handle. Tom Kilgore is one of the best."

"Wouldn't surprise me none if a mob don't try to take Duret away from the law tonight."

"I'm of the same opinion. So is Kilgore and Baca. That's why they swore in a half a dozen more deputies. But I think they can take care of things the rest of this day and tonight. By morning the crowd will have cooled off and most of them forgotten what it was all about."

"And nobody's going to figure the marshal will be riding the old trail."

"Now, keep that under your hat!" Abraham warned sharply. "We don't want it known they're taking that road."

"I won't say anything," Conley replied quickly in an injured tone. He reached for his hat and placed it on his small head. "Guess I'll trot these papers over to the marshal."

"All right," Abraham said. "Mind your tongue now."

Anger flooded through Harvey Conley again. A hasty retort sprang to his lips but he clamped his thin lips shut and held it back. He would be a fool to flare up now; it would spoil everything. Best to just sit tight until he was ready to make his move.

He walked out onto the gallery and halted. The street was still crowded. People stood about in small and larger clusters all along its length. *Trouble for Kilgore and Marcelino Baca,* he thought. Movement at the corner of Engleman's Bakery, just opposite, caught his attention. He squinted his near-sighted eyes at the figure standing there. It was Mr. Preston. The banker motioned for him to cross over. *Now what does he want with me?* Harvey Conley wondered, starting across the street.

VII

At last the day's wilting heat was beginning to break. Inside the cramped jail quarters Kilgore, Baca, and two of the deputies, along with their prisoners, had waited out the painful, dragging hours. On the front gallery three more special officers had maintained a shotgun vigil over the milling crowd. Kilgore rose and moved to the door. Opening it a few inches, he briefly surveyed the street. When he came about, his square face was serious.

"Not thinning out much. Thought the heat would break up that bunch some, but looks like I guessed wrong. Appears to me there's about as many out there now as there was this morning."

"It's the Brackens that's keeping them stirred up," Carl Halvers stated. "Got their minds set on swingin' their own hang noose."

"Keep that to yourself," Kilgore snapped. "We've got enough trouble without you dropping that idea into somebody else's head."

The blond deputy shrugged. He shifted his glance to the stagecoach bandit, snoring softly on his cot. "All this ruckus sure ain't botherin' that jasper any. Bet he's mighty glad he ain't the one they're after."

"He would if he'd sober up long enough to think about it," the other deputy observed dryly.

A yell went up in the street. Kilgore immediately moved again to the door and peered out. He said something to the deputies outside and then, stepping back, closed the thick panel and dropped the bar into place, securing it.

"What happened?" Marcelino Baca asked.

"Some fool with a rope," Kilgore answered. He stood for a long minute in the center of the room, a huge, square-shaped man, staring with unseeing eyes at a calendar on the back wall. Suddenly bringing his attention to Baca, he said: "When they bringing us some grub, Sheriff?"

"Six o'clock."

"Near that now. Maybe you ought to see what's holding it up. Might not get a chance to eat after it grows dark."

Baca got up at once and moved to the rear door, Kilgore trailing after him.

"Tell Homer to bring plenty of coffee!" Halvers called after them.

Kilgore followed the sheriff out into the dusk. He said something to him, glanced about the narrow alley behind the jail building, and returned.

"He hear me?" Halvers inquired.

"Hear you what?"

"Tell Homer to bring lots of coffee."

"He heard you," Kilgore assured him.

He slowly walked the breadth of the small room. The dead heat trapped within its walls was like a smothering blanket and sweat stood out on the big lawman's forehead in bean-sized beads. He halted before one of the small, barred windows. It was open but it admitted only a meager amount of air.

"Around dark," he said, thinking aloud. "That's when they'll make their play."

"You plan to stop them . . . with guns, I mean?" Halvers questioned, picking up the thread of the lawman's thoughts.

Kilgore nodded. "If we have to. My job is to get Duret to Capital City. Alive. I intend to do just that."

The deputy wagged his head. "Don't make much sense. Maybe kill some of the town's citizens to keep Duret alive so they can hang him later."

"It's not a question of Duret's life," Kilgore said patiently. "It's a question of which is stronger, the law or a lynch mob. If we're to have law and order in this territory, it will begin right here tonight in this town of Salvation. We keep Duret alive so the territory can hang him, it means law has been established. If that mob out there takes him away from us and lynches him, then we're still an outlaw frontier."

"Maybe so," Halvers continued in that doubting way of his, "but if some of those people out there get hurt tonight, there'll be the devil to pay. They'll take this jail apart, piece by piece. And us along with it."

Kilgore cocked his head, looked sideways at the deputy. "You thinking about turning in your badge now, in case that happens?"

"Not me!" Halvers exclaimed, his face reddening quickly. "Just saying what's liable to happen, that's all."

Something thudded against the front of the building, a rock, most likely, thrown by someone in the crowd. Yells lifted and there was an outburst of gunshots. Immediately afterward there came a soft knock at the back door. Kilgore moved to open it, covered by the guns of both Halvers and the other deputy. It was Baca, a tray in one hand. Behind him was the waitress from the Bumblebee Café, bringing a second.

"Inside. Quick," Kilgore said, stepping back to admit them. "Anybody see you come this way?"

Baca set his tray on the desk and motioned for the girl to do likewise. "Don't think so, Tom. We came through the hotel."

"Somebody's going to finally remember about that alley," Kilgore said, pulling the cloth off the trays. "And when they do, we got our hands full. You go back the same way you came, miss," he added to the girl. "Don't want anybody seeing you leave here."

The waitress was staring at the man she took to be Turk Duret, her eyes filled with a bright interest and fascination. "Yes, sir," she murmured, easing slowly for the exit.

"Let her out, Carl," Baca directed.

Kilgore took one of the plates, heaped with beans, fried potatoes, and meat, and pushed it under the grating to Ben Coe. "Better eat all this. You'll be needing it."

Baca thrust a second plate into the cell of the other prisoner but the man did not arouse. The sheriff left it and turned to the desk where the other lawmen were beginning to eat.

"How about Chrisman and the other boys?" Halvers wanted to know, motioning to the deputies standing guard in front of the building.

"We'll spell them soon as we're finished," Kilgore replied. He poured himself a second cup of coffee.

The glass in the street-side window suddenly shattered. A shower of sharp particles spread across the floor. Halvers, startled, leaped to his feet. His plate overturned, spilling its contents. Kilgore threw a quick glance at Baca.

The sheriff shrugged. "I guess this is it."

Kilgore got to his feet. He swung to Halvers. "Get outside with the others, Carl. It's dark now and they'll be needing some help."

The deputy immediately picked up his shotgun and moved to the door. Kilgore opened it. His appearance was met with a burst of yells and questions. The marshal hesitated a moment, and then followed Halvers onto the porch.

Lifting both hands for silence, he said: "You people go on about your business. You're wasting your time around here."

"You think so, Marshal?" a voice challenged from the crowd. "We're giving you a chance right now to turn Duret over to us. The last one we'll give you. You don't take it, we're coming in after him."

Kilgore shook his head. "Nobody's coming in after anybody.

Try it and there will be somebody that gets hurt. These deputies have orders to shoot and shoot to kill if they have to."

"We can do a little shootin', too, Marshal," another voice replied. "Don't be forgettin' that!"

"Then you will all be guilty of murder and I'll see to it that every man jack of you stands trial on that charge! Now, get away from here. Go home. Go on down to Sandalman's and get yourselves drunk. I don't want any trouble with you."

"You got it, anyway, Marshal," a man's deep-throated voice stated. "Plenty more than you can handle."

Kilgore heard the solid thud. He saw Carl Halvers spin half about and drop his shotgun. Blood streamed down the front of his face. A rock, about the size of a man's fist, clattered up against the wall of the jail.

"Keep an eye on that bunch!" Kilgore yelled to the remaining deputies. "Shoot only if you have to."

Taking the luckless Halvers under the armpits, he dragged him back into the building. A clamor had lifted in the street at sight of Halvers's falling and the lawman knew that time was suddenly running out. The mob had tasted blood and, like the witless animal it was, would press its advantage now.

"Wrap something about Carl's head," Kilgore said to Baca. "Have to stop the bleeding ourselves. Can't risk getting a doctor yet."

He wheeled about to the cell where Ben Coe sat. "Come on, we're getting out of here."

The sheriff looked up in surprise. "You going to start now? What about a deputy?"

"Have to try without one," the marshal replied. "Better you have a full force here. Give us as long as you can, but don't let things go to gun play before you open up and let them see we've gone."

Baca signified his understanding. In a low voice he said:

"Then it's my move."

"Then it's your move, Marcelino," Kilgore said quietly. "Good luck."

"The same, *amigo. Vaya con Dios.*"

Kilgore stepped to the rear door, Ben Coe close at his heels. The marshal opened the panel and checked the alley.

"Empty," he said with satisfaction. "Where will those horses be, Sheriff?"

"Fifty yards to your right."

Kilgore and Ben Coe stepped outside into the darkness, and turned down the narrow corridor. They found the horses, three of them, saddled and waiting as Baca had said. The two men mounted up, and, once in the saddle, Kilgore lifted his hand for silence. There was a steady rumble of talk broken by sudden yells, back at the jail. The sounds were growing louder, more insistent. The crowd would not be stalled much longer.

"Let's get out of here," Kilgore said. "Straight down the alley until we hit the end of town. Then we'll take the main road."

Coe lifted his manacled wrists. "How about taking these off?"

In the darkness Kilgore grinned. "Not the handiest things a man can wear, are they? Reckon we better wait. No time to spare now."

Wheeling his horse around, he started down the alley. Ben Coe was not far behind.

Todd Bracken was standing near the north edge of the pulsing, swaying mob gathered before the jail. At that moment the door had just slammed, shutting off his view of the unconscious Carl Halvers. The jam of yelling, cursing people was moving in closer. Somewhere a voice was shouting for a log, a ram of some sort with which to batter down the door. More rocks were being hurled and another deputy was struck but the stone only grazed his shoulder.

"No place here for you," Todd said then, turning to Laurie. "Things are going to get bad in a few minutes. Go on down to the hotel and wait for us there."

The girl shook her head. "I'm staying right here," she said stubbornly. "I want to be around in case you or Papa get hurt."

"But you shouldn't. . . ."

"Shouldn't *see* a man lynched? Why not? Other women in this crowd will. Why shouldn't I?"

"Not so much that, Laurie. You might get hurt. Even shot."

"The deputies won't do any shooting," she said, quoting words she had heard earlier. "That's what you all were saying this morning."

Todd Bracken started to make a reply, paused. His eyes had picked up two riders, far down the street. They had emerged from a passageway next to Canady's store. Both looked familiar. He felt his sister's fingers close about his wrist as she, too, saw the riders.

"Todd! That's the marshal . . . with Turk Duret!"

A shaft of lamplight from Canady's fell across the pair at that moment. It glittered briefly upon the star worn by the lawman, glinted sharply off the chains that linked the prisoner's hands.

"It sure is," Todd murmured. "They're sneaking Duret out of town."

He laid his finger against Laurie's lips, pressing her to silence. Better if they said nothing about it. They could handle it themselves with their own group. He reached for his father and pulled him to his side. "Just saw Kilgore ride out with Duret. We're going after them."

Saul Bracken's reply was an angry yelp. "Dang that blasted marshal! We ought. . . ."

"Hold it!" Todd snapped. "We don't want the whole town knowing about it. Let them stay here and throw rocks at the jail. We'll take Pete and Orville and do this on our own."

"Don't count me out," Laurie said firmly.

Todd glanced at her, frowning. He saw there was no use and little time to argue. "All right. Now, Pa, you and Laurie go to the wagon yard and get us some horses. I'll hunt up Pete and Orville."

"There's Pete now," Saul Bracken said.

Brookerson shoved his way toward them and halted. Todd quickly explained what had happened, what he planned to do.

Brookerson nodded. "Good. We can handle it better alone, anyway. My horse is over in front of the saloon. I'll follow up the marshal and Duret so's we don't miss them. You catch up soon as you can."

"We won't be far behind you," Todd said. "Just be damn' sure you don't lose them!"

VIII

Kilgore and Coe reached the end of the alley and halted.

"This way," the marshal said, after a moment, and swung his horse up a narrow passageway lying between two false-fronted buildings.

They reached the street, and once again paused. Several hundred yards to the right they could see the restless mass of the crowd before the jail. Except for that, Salvation appeared to be deserted. More rock throwing was in progress at that moment, and, while they watched, a half-dozen men supporting a railroad tie between them trotted into the street. A chorus of yells greeted them immediately and the crowd parted to receive them.

"Time to get out of here," Kilgore said. He touched the horse with his spurs and rode into the open, passing through a shaft of light lying across the roadway by the lamps in Canady's windows. Coe followed and they moved out at a brisk trot for the first mile. After that distance, Kilgore pulled down to a walk.

"Turn-off is just ahead," he said to Ben. "We take the right and swing toward the mountains." Digging into his pocket, he produced a key. Handing it to Coe, he said: "Better get those cuffs off. You'll be needing both hands once we're on the trail."

Coe removed the manacles, stuffing them into his saddlebags. "I'll keep them handy, in case we run into company," he said. "Think we've fooled that mob?"

"For a spell, anyway. All we need is a little head start. And a couple of days. Big job for us is to keep anybody interested in Turk Duret dogging our tracks. That will let Baca get Duret to Capital City."

"Two days' ride, somebody said," Coe answered. "Shouldn't be too tough. You got my gun?"

"Long two days," Kilgore said, and handed the deputy his weapon.

They rode on through the night, bearing due east in the direction of the rugged-rimmed Los Pinos Mountains.

"That fool lawyer!" Kilgore suddenly exclaimed. "Allison, or whatever his name was. Thought for a minute there this morning that big mouth of his was going to get us all lynched."

Coe grinned. "Hope that's the last time I'm called on to play outlaw. That crowd really had blood in its eye."

"Little close, all right," Kilgore commented.

"Sort of funny, going to all this trouble just so Duret can hang in Capital City."

"More to it than that, than what Abraham said back there in the courtroom. This territory wants statehood in the worst way. Before it can get it, it has to prove it's ready. Got to show those Eastern senators and bigwigs that it's come out of the frontier class and has established good law and order. Trying Duret and executing him through due process of law will be a mighty

50

strong argument in our favor."

"So that's it. Figured there was more to it than just some whim of the governor's. Does he know about your plan to get Duret there?"

"No. We just told him we'd have the man there for the execution. Didn't go into any details. You don't take chances on a leak in a case like this."

In the velvet blackness of the night Ben Coe scratched thoughtfully at the scar on his neck. The horses moved steadily on, covering the soft ground easily. The only sounds were the rhythmic creak of saddle leather, the breathing of the animals. Stars were out, shedding their faint, silver light. The moon was only a vagrant shadow, slipping in and out of the clouds.

"That Bracken family," Ben said then, "you know them before this all happened?"

Kilgore said: "Nope. First time I ever saw them was here in town, why?"

"The daughter, the sister of Todd Bracken, she's the one I helped that night I rode in."

"Real pretty girl," Kilgore said. "Good thing she didn't get a look at you. . . ." The marshal's voice broke off suddenly. He twisted half about in the saddle and listened. "You hear something behind us?"

Coe cocked his head to one side. "Not just now. Thought I heard a horse back there somewhere, mile or so ago."

Kilgore settled and relaxed. "That's what it sounded like to me. Hardly seems possible anybody could have got on our trail this quick."

"Unless they saw us ride out and followed."

In that next instant both men heard the telltale sound, the unmistakable click of a shod hoof against rock.

"Somebody's sure back there," Kilgore said in a low voice. "Let's lose them."

He spurred his horse into a full gallop and Ben Coe followed his example. They rode hard and fast for the next hour, keeping to the trail that circled the towering hills. They were gradually climbing, and after a time they were compelled to pull up and allow the blowing horses to rest.

"The road we want is on the other side of the mountain," the marshal explained. "When we reach it, we cut back to the north. Diamondback Trail, they call it. Runs along parallel to the valley road the stagecoach uses except the mountains lie in between. Once we get on the Diamondback, I figure we're in good shape."

They were back in the saddle in a quarter hour but the going had become steeper and traveling was much slower. Eventually they reached a crest, however, a low-running hogback, topped out, and descended to the shallow cañon on the far side. At the forks where one road bore directly on eastward toward the flat, Texas plains, they took the other, striking northward on a fairly level trail.

They kept the horses at a good pace for the better part of an hour, hoping to reach the more heavily timbered areas before halting for sleep and rest. Neither man had spoken for miles, being intent upon their purpose, but finally, as a dark band of trees drew nearer, Kilgore reined in beside Coe.

"We'll make camp in that grove. Horses can't keep going at this rate much farther."

Coe nodded his agreement. He could use a bit of rest himself. He glanced ahead. The grove the marshal had indicated was a small one, a dark, triangular patch spewing out onto the low hills from the higher mountains to the left. He could smell the clean, fresh odor of pine as they drew closer.

Quite suddenly four men stood before them. A fifth, still mounted, waited off to one side in the shadows of the trees.

Star shine glinted brightly off the rifles and pistols held by the men.

"Far as you go, Marshal," one of the four said, his voice vaguely familiar. "You and Duret just climb down off them horses. And keep your hands where we can see them."

IX

Ben Coe sat quietly on the buckskin, hands half lifted, and waited out the moments. From the corner of his eye he could see Kilgore, also with his arms up.

"What's this all about, Bracken?"

The lawman's voice was cool as spring rain. The four men facing them moved out into the open. One Coe recognized as Todd Bracken, the slain woman's husband, who had jumped him in the courtroom. The old man was his father. The other two were strangers to him, either close friends or relatives of some sort. He shifted his gaze to the fifth member of the ambush, the one yet mounted. With a start he saw it was Laurie. In the darkness of the grove she sat very still and straight on her horse, her face a pale oval in the meager light.

"Git yourself down off them horses!" old man Bracken commanded again. He waved the long-barreled rifle in his hands. "We don't want no trouble with you, Marshal. We just aim to carry out the judge's sentence and string this here killer up ourselves."

"That's a job for the territory, Bracken," Kilgore replied without moving. "And it will be done if you'll keep out of it. Only thing this will get you is a lot of grief."

"Can't see how," one of the strangers drawled. "Court said to hang Duret. That's what we figure to do. We'll just be savin' the territory all that trouble."

"You hang him," the marshal stated in clipped words, "and you'll face a murder charge."

"Now, you tell me what the difference is," the rider persisted, "if we do it or the territory does it? Either way the judge's orders will be carried out."

"Ain't no use arguing with him, Orville," Todd Bracken said, speaking for the first time. "That's all that's been going on all day . . . just talk." He stepped nearer Kilgore and Ben Coe. "You getting off those horses or do we drag you off?"

Kilgore shuttered a glance at Coe. The marshal shrugged and nodded.

"Keep them hands up!" Saul Bracken yelled in sudden alarm. "Like I said, we don't want to hurt you none, Marshal, but you try somethin' and you're a dead man. Ain't nobody goin' to keep us from hangin' Turk Duret!"

In that hot, tense moment Ben Coe swung slowly down from his horse. He could feel the pressures building up within him and he began to understand more clearly the dangers that faced him. It was one thing to confront death for your own sake— entirely different when you were doing it in another man's place. And he was helpless to do anything about it. Kilgore could not talk, nor could he. To reveal to the Brackens now that he was not the genuine Turk Duret but a decoy to draw off any who sought to capture him would upset the whole, carefully planned ruse. And they would be off at once to intercept Marcelino Baca and the real Duret almost before the sheriff and his prisoner were out of Salvation.

"Get the marshal's iron, Pete," Saul Bracken said. "Why, look there, all of you!" he added, his voice rising. "He ain't even got Duret tied up! No ropes or nothin' on his hands. You sure are trustin', Marshal."

Kilgore made no answer. He stood motionlessly while Pete cautiously drew the pistol from its holster and thrust it into his own waistband.

"Where's that rope?" Todd Bracken asked, his voice grim.

Old man Bracken turned to the girl. "Laurie, fetch us that rope."

The girl dismounted and came forward. She handed the coil to her father and returned to the shadows where she had been waiting.

"All right, Duret, come on. You too, Marshal. Both of you walk up ahead. We got a good tree all picked out."

"Laurie!" Saul Bracken called again. "Lead that buckskin over here. Reckon a man ought to go a-settin' his own horse."

Kilgore had not moved. He stared at the four men lined up before him. "I'm warning you for the last time, Bracken. You do this and I'll see you all hang for it!"

"Maybe so," Todd Bracken replied, stepping forward. "But I don't reckon there's a jury in the country that would convict us for what we're doing. Duret murdered my wife and baby. I got a right to see that he pays for it."

"Eye for a eye, tooth for a tooth," old man Bracken sang out.

"But you've got to let the law handle. . . ."

"We ain't got much faith in the law," the man called Orville broke in. "We figure, before they'd hang Duret, they'd make themselves a deal with him so's they could find Preston's money."

"That's damn' fool thinking!" Kilgore retorted angrily. "Everything the judge told you this morning was pure truth. Duret will hang just as soon as I can get him to Capital City. You can take my word for it."

There was a long, uncertain moment of silence, a hush laden with the promise of sudden violence. Ben glanced at Laurie. She wore a pair of faded Levi's and a shapeless old shirt, evidently one cast off by Todd. He wondered how she felt about the matter.

"Let's get on with it," Todd Bracken said quietly. "I can believe you, Marshal, but I can't trust those people in Capital City."

Ben caught the signal from Tom Kilgore. As one they lunged forward, straight into the four men. A gun exploded in Coe's face, blinding him momentarily. He felt the hot blast of the muzzle, heard the scream of the bullet as it sped by him. Todd was directly before him and he struck out. Bracken dodged and the blow skated harmlessly off his shoulder. Ben felt something, a rifle butt likely, come down across his back. The force was light and it merely staggered him.

Saul Bracken was yelling at the top of his voice: "Don't shoot him! Save him for a hangin'!"

Coe heard Kilgore gasp as the wind was driven from his lungs. He flung a glance at the lawman. He was down on one knee. The man named Pete was swinging at his head with a pistol butt, a second blow, apparently. In that moment Coe felt a pair of powerful arms clamp about his legs. Orville was rushing at him, fists swinging. He tried to duck away but Todd Bracken had him anchored to the spot. Orville's ham-like fists crashed into him, one high on the chest, the other just grazing his chin. He lashed out at Todd, trying to break the man's vise-like hold on his legs. His hand connected with Bracken's skull and did no damage. Orville was pounding at him again, striking at his face. Ben dodged and fought back, feeling his fists drive into yielding flesh. But he was having little effect, he knew. Trapped as he was by Todd Bracken, he could get no leverage and no power into his swing.

He cast another look at Kilgore. The marshal was trying to get to his feet. Saul Bracken was swarming in on him, rifle held, club-like, over his head. Ben yelled a warning. In the same instant Orville's balled fist found its mark. Coe felt the shock of it behind his ear, felt it streak through him and set up a sort of paralysis. His arms at once were heavy and there was no strength left in his trembling legs. Orville's grinning face began to blur. Vaguely he heard a gunshot shatter the night. It sounded hollow and distant but the flash was nearby. There were horses, and more men.

A voice called out: "Hold up there! What's going on?"

X

Coe was out only brief seconds. Even as he crumpled to earth, his brain began to clear. On hands and knees he shook his head savagely, throwing off the filmy webs shrouding his mind.

"Stand away from them!"

Faintly through the haze Ben heard the sharp command. It was followed immediately by Saul Bracken's protesting reply. "This ain't none of your business, Sergeant. Just you and your soljer boys keep right on goin'."

"Maybe it is Army business," the sergeant answered. He rode up close to Coe and the still prone Kilgore. "This the marshal and the man he's taking to be hung?"

The lawman groaned and stirred. The soldiers and the others remained silent while he struggled to a sitting position. He rubbed at the back of his head. Blood streaked down from one corner of his mouth and there was a raw, ugly scratch crossing the left side of his face. Brookerson and old man Bracken had used him plenty rough.

"You the marshal?"

Tom Kilgore lifted his glance to the sergeant. "I am," he said, studying the man. He was a husky, broad-faced individual who sat his McClellan like a partially emptied sack of grain.

"Then I reckon you're who we're lookin' for." He swung down from his horse. He threw a glance at the soldiers who remained mounted. "Keep your rifles on them people. They try something, shoot."

Kilgore had gotten to his feet, as had Coe. The sergeant faced the marshal. "Mighty glad we found you and your prisoner. Didn't have much idea where you'd be."

Kilgore grinned. "I'm glad, too. A few more minutes like we were having and you and your boys would have happened by too late."

The soldier nodded curtly and backed toward his horse. "You all right?" he asked of Coe as he moved by.

Ben shrugged. He rubbed at his jaw. "I'll get by," he said. The sergeant nodded and climbed back into the saddle. He swung his attention to the Bracken party.

"Now, you people mount up and get out of here. Be quick about it. I don't want any trouble with you!"

Todd Bracken took a quick, angry step. "Keep out of this, soldier! No call for you to butt in!"

"Got my orders," the sergeant replied coolly.

Orville Stelder laid his hand on Todd's shoulder. He shook his head. "No use trying to fight the Army. Reckon we'll have to let the territory hang Duret."

"No, by God!" Todd yelled, and lunged at Coe. "That's for me to do! They're not cheating me out of it!"

The crack of the sergeant's pistol shattered the long quiet of the grove. From nearby a startled bird whirred blindly off into the night. The bullet threw up an explosion of trash and dust at the feet of Todd Bracken. He halted.

"Next time I won't be aiming at the ground," the soldier said coldly. "Next time that bullet will go plowing into your belly."

The three remaining soldiers, at the crack of the gun, had ridden forward and now ranged out alongside their burly leader.

Laurie, too, had reacted. She uttered a low scream and ran to her brother. She threw her arms about him and held him back. But Todd Bracken made no further attempts to reach Ben Coe. He stood, spread-legged, hands hanging at his sides while a white-hot hatred burned in his eyes.

"No cause to hurt anybody, Sergeant," Tom Kilgore reproved mildly. "Just give these folks a chance and they'll be on their way. They're kin to the dead woman. Can't blame them much for how they're feeling right now."

"Best thing they can do is get out of here," the soldier observed sourly. "I won't take no back talk from people such as them. They want trouble, me and the boys can sure accommodate them."

One of the soldiers laughed. Kilgore glanced at him. And then back to the sergeant. He frowned. "Didn't get your name, Sergeant," he said, and moved nearer.

"Waggoner. Tibo Waggoner. Men with me are Bill Ford there. And George Kemm. Third one is Chancey Desmond."

The lawman nodded to each. He turned his back to them, faced the Bracken party. "I'd suggest you move out right away. Wouldn't want to see any of you hurt."

Saul Bracken grumbled his agreement and they all started for their horses, tethered just within the grove. Coe and the others watched them depart moments later. They rode westward, up one of the many long cañons that apparently would lead them to the ridge and down the opposite slope.

When they were beyond sight and sound, Tom Kilgore rubbed thoughtfully at his bruised chin. "A close one. Sure glad you happened by, Sergeant."

Coe saw Kilgore pause and deliberately await the soldier's answer, as if much depended upon it.

"What I was told to do, marshal."

"So? Told to do what?"

"Meet you and the prisoner and ride escort to Capital City."

Kilgore continued to stroke his jaw. "That right. Real thoughtful of them. Who gave the order?"

"Came straight from the governor. Seems he's right anxious for you and your prisoner to get there safe."

In the semidarkness Kilgore's face betrayed none of the suspicion Coe knew was clouding the lawman's mind. The marshal ducked his head, as if he understood and came slowly about. "Don't think it is safe to camp here the rest of the night. Never know what those Bracken people might take in mind to do." He swung his eyes to Ben Coe. "Mount up, Duret. We're moving out."

Ben knew what was passing through the marshal's thoughts, that the governor knew nothing of their plan to reach Capital City, that he had no idea of when they were even starting, in fact. It all added up to one thing. Sergeant Tibo Waggoner and his men, despite their cavalry uniforms, were fakes.

Ben saw Kilgore heave his bulk onto the saddle and rein about. He watched the lawman's face for some indication of the next move, of his plans and what was expected of him. But the darkness made it difficult to see any signal from Kilgore. Remembering then, he dropped his hand to the right saddlebag, lifted its flap, and prepared to snatch up the gun hidden there. "Let's go," the lawman said, looking at Coe straight on.

Ben kneed his horse around and Kilgore fell in beside, almost knee to knee. Waggoner and his three riders dropped into the double file a few feet to the rear. They followed the wagon track trail, barely visible by starlight, through the dense stand of pines.

"Be ready to move out fast," Kilgore murmured, leaning forward to adjust his stirrup. "I give the word, break out for the trees. Keep going north. We'll meet up later."

Coe said: "Right."

"Don't know what these jaspers have got up their sleeves, but I don't figure it's good. The thing that bothers me is how did they know we were taking this trail?"

"The Brackens knew."

Kilgore muttered. He straightened up. "Reckon that's so. But they could have seen us leave and followed. Maybe taking a short cut they knew to head us off. But Waggoner and his bunch came in from the north, like they'd been waiting along the road for us. Sure would like to have the answer to this."

"You figure they're some of Duret's gang?"

The lawman shrugged. "Could be. One thing I'm sure, they're not soldiers and the governor didn't send them."

"I don't see how they could be any of Duret's outfit, unless they had never seen Duret. They would have spotted me at once."

"I was just thinking that. Could be somebody hired them to do this job."

They rode steadily on, getting deeper into the higher mountains. The chill of the greater altitude began to make itself felt, a welcome change from the day's driving heat. Waggoner trotted his horse up beside Kilgore, his heavy face dark and shadowy in the pale star shine.

"How much farther you plannin' to go, Marshal?"

Kilgore shook his head. "Another hour maybe. You boys getting tired?"

Waggoner said: "Can't see much use ridin' all the night. Might as well camp around here somewheres."

"Good place about ten miles on. We'll stop there."

Waggoner made his grumbling reply and dropped back to his original position. Kilgore waited until he was beyond hearing distance.

"We reach the foot of that slope ahead, there's a sharp bend to the left. Trees are thick on both sides of the road. We'll make a break there. You go left and I'll go right. Good luck."

Coe nodded and said—"See you up the line."—and set his gaze on the slowly approaching turn in the road. When it was only yards away, he risked a casual glance over his shoulder, determining the location of the men behind them. Waggoner and his bogus soldiers were a scant thirty feet away. Getting quickly beyond reach of their guns was going to be a hard chore. But there was no other answer.

The slope reached ground level, dissolving into the plains and revealed a bulking knob of rock jutting upward. Ben could see the thick stand of pines flowing out to the right and assumed a similar grove lay to the left. At that moment it was hidden from his view.

"Make the turn," Kilgore said softly, "then go for it."

Coe tensed in his saddle. He drew abreast of the rocky bulge and set himself for a sudden plunge, off into the protective blackness of the pines. Together he and Kilgore made the sharp curve.

"Now!" Kilgore yelled, and drove spurs into his horse's flanks. Both mounts leaped forward, Ben only slightly behind the marshal. Coe swung hard left and drove hard for the nearest cover, only a dozen yards distant. Tom Kilgore was whirling off to the right for a similar haven.

Waggoner's hoarse yell lifted behind them. A gunshot blasted through the night. Ben clawed at his saddlebag, reaching for his own gun and found nothing. It was gone, apparently taken by the Brackens earlier. Another shot flatted through the darkness, echoing along the cañons. He heard the whine of the bullet and involuntarily ducked. A half dozen more shots rapped out after that, some coming from Kilgore. There was a pounding of hoofs off to the left, Waggoner's men closing in, trying to cut him off. If he could have another few seconds, he would make it, he would be inside the trees. That was when he saw Tom Kilgore.

The lawman's horse was curving back toward the road at an uneven trot, seemingly uncertain where to go. Kilgore was doubled over the saddle, arms dangling loosely around the animal's neck. The thought—He's hit.—flashed through Coe. Immediately he swerved from his course and rode for the marshal's side. If he could grab the reins, there might still be a chance they could reach safety.

The shooting had ceased when he changed his direction. He

raced across the open ground and snatched up the trailing leathers and thundered on toward the shelter of trees. Suddenly he was aware of riders all about him, rushing in. Ducking low, he pressed the buckskin for more speed.

"Hold it, Duret!"

Waggoner's harsh command rapped at him from only inches away, it seemed.

"Pull up, unless you want the same as the marshal got!"

XI

Ben Coe hauled the buckskin back on its haunches. Around him, in a swiftly closing noose, Tibo Waggoner's men swept in.

"See if he's dead, George," Waggoner snapped at the man nearest Kilgore.

Kemm sidled over to the lawman and grasped him by the shoulder. He pulled backward. Kilgore's body slid brokenly to the ground.

"Sure looks like it," Kemm commented, staring down at the marshal. Kilgore appeared to be no more than a pile of dusty clothing.

"Make damned sure!" Waggoner directed in the same tone. "Don't want no loose ends draggin'."

Ben watched the rider dismount, a deep and bitter anger eating through him. Hell of a way for a good man like Tom Kilgore to die—shot in the back by a bunch of hardcase outlaws. He deserved better.

"He's dead," Kemm announced. "Two bullets got him. Both in the chest. One in the heart, I reckon."

"Drag him over there into the brush where he won't be seen, in case somebody comes along," Waggoner said. "Bill, catch up that horse of his. Don't want him wanderin' back to town. Might set folks to askin' questions and lookin'."

Keeping a tight rein on his anger, Ben Coe asked: "You're

63

not going to bury him? Ought to. At least put him in a grave."

Tibo Waggoner swung to Coe. "No time for that, Duret. What difference it make to you anyway? He ain't nothin' but a John Law. For a man who took a woman and kid into the hills and let them croak, you're mighty soft-hearted all of a sudden."

Coe settled back into his saddle, acutely aware in that moment of his responsibilities, of the part he must play. He was Turk Duret to Tibo Waggoner and anyone else until Marcelino Baca had delivered the real killer to Capital City. So much depended upon it, and already Tom Kilgore's life had been sacrificed for it. He would have to watch himself. The idea of the marshal's body being callously dumped into the brush had infuriated him to such a point he had almost tipped his hand.

He shrugged, pulled his mouth down into a hard grin. "Makes no difference to me," he said. "A man just hates to think about the coyotes and buzzards getting to a body . . . any body."

Waggoner laughed. "Reckon it won't make no difference to the marshal. He ain't feelin' no pain where he is."

The two men who had dragged Kilgore's heavy figure off the road returned to their horses. Ben made a mental note of the location, determined inwardly he would return and give his friend a proper burial. That would be after Baca had delivered his prisoner and after he saw to it personally that Waggoner and his crew were under lock and key for the murder of the lawman. But first came the matter of staying alive, of coming back. He swung his glance to Waggoner, knowing the hatred he felt for the outlaw glowed through his eyes. "What's next? What's this all about, anyway?"

"You'll find out quick enough," Waggoner replied. "Me and the boys and a friend of ours have got a little business with you."

"Meaning what?"

"Meanin' just what it sounds like. Now, suppose you head right on out the way we was goin'. And don't try no tricks. We'll be watchin' you like a horny toad watchin' a bluebottle fly and the first thing you do will mean a bullet where it hurts. We don't aim to kill you 'cause we got to keep you alive, but they ain't nothin' says we can't make you feel mighty miserable."

Ben urged the buckskin into motion up the trail. He slowly sorted the bits of information he had gleaned, trying to fit them into a picture. "Who's this friend you're talking about?"

Waggoner laughed again, the sound harsh and unpleasant in the night's stillness. "You'll find out, bucko. Just keep ridin'. Your friend Kilgore didn't know it but he was headin' right where we wanted him to."

Coe considered that. "You mean to Capital City?"

"Nope. Got a little shack up here in the hills. Real quiet sort of place. Figure we won't be bothered there while we ask you a few questions."

"Questions?" Coe prodded.

Waggoner grinned, his broad teeth gleaming whitely in the half light. "Questions like where you stashed that money you hauled out of Preston's bank. We figure we'll get the answer."

Realization struck Ben Coe at once. Believing him to be Turk Duret, they planned to force him into telling where he had hidden the $30,000 the outlaw was reputed to have stolen. And they would employ any and every method to loosen his tongue. Men like Tibo Waggoner stopped at nothing. Well, he would just have to stand and take it. If Tom Kilgore could give his life for the cause, he could do his part by keeping his mouth shut, at least until he was certain Marcelino Baca had delivered his prisoner. How long would that be? *Two days . . . three at the most*, Kilgore had said. That promised to be a long time. Ben Coe asked himself the important question—could he stand it? Could he manage to hold onto his senses, keep his mouth closed under the punishment Waggoner and his men would dish out to him? A man could only try, he assured himself, could set his nerves and his will and try.

Another thought came to him then as he rode wearily along—escape. For one thing he did not like the idea of traveling northward. If Waggoner and his mysterious partner discovered somehow he was not the genuine Turk Duret, they would suspect a ruse and immediately rush to lay an ambush outside of Capital City, hoping to make an interception there. The farther north they were, the quicker they could reach such a point.

If he could manage an escape, he might be able to lead Waggoner and his bunch off into a different direction, to the south perhaps and thus gain some advantage. That Waggoner would not dare kill him was evident now; dead he could not reveal his supposed secret as to where Preston's money had been hidden.

He glanced back over his shoulders, first the right and then the left. He was well attended, being in the center of a crescent formed by the four men. Tibo Waggoner saw his move and trotted up closer.

"Gettin' ideas, Turk? Don't. You wouldn't make ten feet before you caught a half dozen slugs in your back."

"Little hard to make a dead man talk," Coe said dryly.

Waggoner only shrugged and returned to his position. Coe looked ahead. They were well into the mountains now. The brush along the trail had thinned out to more sturdy junipers and piñon trees. Beyond them were pines with the thick, triangular silhouette of a spruce making an occasional appearance. To the left he saw the ghostly, white flank of a sandstone escarpment denoting they were climbing well toward the summit of the range. To his right a narrow wedge of blackness laid its shape. At sight of that Ben Coe's hopes lifted. It would be a narrow, probably deep cañon running at right angles to the road and mostly likely well overgrown with brush. A man might dodge quickly into its depth. . . .

Back upon the ridge a coyote broke the steady clop-clop of the horses' hoofs with his lonely, fragile wail. Almost immediately his reply, coming from somewhere farther along the escarpment, echoed forlornly.

"Dang them critters!" one of the riders swore softly. "Ever' time I hear one, I get the creeps."

"Just you be glad they're real coyotes and not a pack of Apaches gettin' ready to jump us," Waggoner replied. "Ain't been so long ago, they might have been."

"You right sure they ain't now?"

"Been no Indian trouble 'round here for two, three years."

"Can always start again. Hear old Vitorio and his bunch ain't so happy on the reservation."

"They'll stay there," another of the riders said, and then added with a laugh: "Us soldiers'll see they do."

"Sure will be glad to get out of this suit and on a real saddle again! Can't figure how them cavalry boys set one of these things all day. Like ridin' a pack rig."

Ben listened idly and watched the wedge of blackness draw closer. Purposely he slanted his horse in a gradual line for the right side of the road. That six feet could mean the difference in success and failure if his chance came—in life and death, to be more honest. He glanced to the sky, soft, velvet-like black with the stars swung just out of arm's reach. A good overcast would have been a welcome advantage but the heavens were clear.

"What you figurin' to do with your share of the money when we gets it?"

Ben listened to the rider's question. *Keep talking, keep talking, get your mind on something besides me,* he thought. His gaze was fastened on the cañon, now less than a dozen yards—thirty feet—twenty. Coe kept his eyes riveted to the edge of the arroyo. If it was too deep, he would have to forsake the idea. No use breaking the buckskin's legs in a hopeless attempt, not to mention his own neck. Or if the floor was loose rock instead of sand, it would be a bad risk. Ten feet.

Ben Coe tensed in the saddle. He shortened the reins, gathering them in his left hand while he patted the buckskin's neck reassuringly. He strained his eyes to see exactly what the wash offered. It was narrow at that moment and not very deep. Four or five feet, he judged, dropping swiftly as it sliced away. It appeared to be mostly filled with brush. That was good.

"Maybe we ought to talk to . . . ," one of them was saying.

Ben drove spurs into the buckskin. He doubled forward over the saddle and yelled, as they sailed off the edge of the wash. His cry was a wild, discordant, echoing sound that split the night. But it had the desired affect; he was already plunging into the brush before Waggoner and his men had recovered from their confusion.

XII

The buckskin landed on all four, went to his knees on impact, recovered. A half dozen shots rang out and bullets clipped through the brush with a vicious, whirring efficiency.

"Don't shoot him, damn it!" he heard Waggoner shout. "Get him alive!"

Coe headed the plunging buckskin down the arroyo, thankful for the smooth, sandy bottom. But brush was there, thick and hindering. It slashed at him, clawed at his clothing, and dragged at the horse. A gnarled juniper curving over the wash almost knocked him from the saddle. They were bearing eastward, slightly north. He threw a desperate glance ahead, hoping the arroyo would double back, swing to the south. But deep in the cleavage he could tell very little about its course.

Waggoner and his men were close behind him. The crashing

their horses caused in the brush informed him of their near-
ness. The advantage was his, at least for the moment as he had
a few yards' lead and the brush effectively screened him in the
darkness. And they would not shoot, he knew that now.

"Get him! Get him!"

Waggoner's strident bellow echoed above the racket of the
horses. The rough going began to tell on the buckskin. His sides
were heaving and his willingness to leap the brushy barriers was
less eager. But their mounts also would be tiring, and if the
buckskin could not maintain the pace, neither could the horses
pursuing.

"Couple of you . . . head him off! Get out on the bank and
circle ahead!"

Waggoner's command instantly set up its worry in Ben Coe's
mind. They could easily do just that, climb out of the arroyo to
the level ground bordering either side. A horse could stretch out
there and soon overtake and pass anyone down in the impeding
brush. Coe threw a hasty glance to his left and to the opposite
side. Tibo Waggoner's men were too close for him to try a similar
plan; he had no choice but to keep on, following the floor of the
wash—and hope for a break.

The buckskin had given about all he had. He started to falter,
to stumble. A branch caught at the bridle and he shied, off balance. The stiff limb sprang free and struck Coe sharply across
the chest and he grabbed the horn to keep from falling. Another
stand of briar barred their way. He reined the buckskin to one
side, avoiding it, going partly up the bank of the wash. The
husky little horse fought gamely to keep his feet, stumbled,
regained his stride, and came into a small clearing beyond the
thorn patch. Two of Waggoner's riders, the ones he had sent to
circle ahead were waiting. The buckskin skidded to a stop.

All the pent-up hatred engendered for Waggoner and his men
by the murder of Tom Kilgore, all the personal anger and

frustration built up within Ben Coe during the past moments suddenly fused within the man and burst. He left his saddle in a low, flat dive straight at the two men, both sitting side-by-side on their horses. He struck them with animal fury. His powerful arms reached out for them, looped over their shoulders, dragged them both to the ground amid the churning hoofs of their horses. Both men yelled in surprise and fright. Heedless of his own danger, Coe lashed out at the nearest, felt the satisfying yield of flesh under his knotted fist. He struck again, missing and staggered as one of them caught him from behind.

Waggoner and the other men were there by then, piling off their horses and coming into the fray. Ben saw a face loom in close and drove it to the ground with a straight right. He felt hands claw at him, settle about his arms. He went to his knees, was dragged back up. Fury still raging through him, he struggled to break free, to drive his fists again and again into these enemies. A hard jolt to the side of the head rocked him. Another into the belly sent the wind gushing through his lips. His head swam and lights danced before his eyes.

"Get a rope!" Waggoner's voice ripped through the haze. "Just so you'll know we ain't foolin' around with you no longer, Duret!"

Coe's breath was coming in painful gasps. He tried again to break free but strong hands pinned his arms to his sides. Fingers dug into his hair, jerked his head back.

"Wind that rope around him and set him on his saddle," Waggoner ordered. "I'll take no more from this jasper tonight."

Coe vaguely felt the rope bite into his arms, cinching them against his ribs. He was half carried, half propelled to the buckskin, and hoisted aboard. As his senses slowly cleared and his breathing dropped back to normal, he heard the outlaw's voice again.

"Chancey, hang onto that buckskin's reins and don't lose

'em. He gets away again I'll bend a gun barrel over your head!"

Ben glanced at the man who reached for the leathers. He was dabbing at his nose; it was bleeding freely. He had been one of those who had blocked the way in the clearing. Coe grinned at the man.

"You won't be laughin', come mornin'," Desmond said sourly, and led the buckskin back to the trail.

"Climb out of this wash," Waggoner said when they were all mounted and together. "Too hard travelin' and we already lost time."

Coe steadied himself as best he could in the saddle while his horse followed the lead rider up the embankment onto level ground. His attempted escape had not profited him much, an hour, possibly two at the most. But two hours would put Marcelino Baca that much nearer Capital City. It had been worth it.

They cut straight across the flats until they once again were on the main road. There they swung northward, keeping at a steady pace that was not too hard on the horses and that carried them deeper into the mountains. Toward the morning they were beyond view of the mesa, with hills completely surrounding them. At a shallow cañon they turned off and climbed sharply for a quarter mile through dense pines to break, finally, into a broad clearing. Daylight was just beyond the ridge to the east when they pulled to a stop before a low-roofed cabin.

"Here's home, Mister Duret," Tibo Waggoner said sardonically, waving his hand at the poor structure.

Ben let his eyes drift over the place. Two horses, still saddled, stood at the hitch rail on the south side. A faint wisp of blue smoke trickled from the chimney. The door of the cabin swung back, setting up an overly loud creak in the early morning quiet. Two men walked out onto the sagging gallery. One Coe recognized instantly—the slight, stooped shape of Harvey Conley, Abraham's clerk. The second was an older man, much

71

larger, with balding head and a round belly that overlapped his belt.

"Here you are, Mister Preston," Waggoner said, "just like you ordered."

C.J. Preston, the banker.

XIII

Here was the answer—Conley had been the only other person to know they planned to ride the Diamondback Trail. Coe was thankful, in that moment, the jurist and the lawman had withheld their trust at that point, that Conley had not been taken into their confidence as to the real and the bogus Turk Duret. And Conley, somehow, was hooked up with Preston.

Preston walked closer, his small mouth pursed, his eyes hard glinting. He looked Coe over carefully, and then swung his attention to Waggoner. "You were a long time getting here. Have some trouble?"

"Some," Waggoner admitted. "He tried to make a break for it. Had to run him down."

"Kilgore?"

"Dead."

A frown pulled at Preston's features. "Bad, plenty bad. Couldn't you have avoided that? Don't like the idea of having a federal man's death on our hands."

"Better get used to it," Waggoner said dryly. He swung down from his saddle. "Take these horses around to the rail, Chancey."

The others dismounted, and Waggoner stepped up to Coe to assist him.

Conley said: "Well, guess my job's done, Mister Preston. You give me my money and I'll be moving on."

Preston glanced at the clerk. "Not yet, Harvey. We still have to find out where Duret hid it."

"But that wasn't our agreement," Conley protested mildly.

"You said all I had to do was tell you when Duret and the marshal were leaving town. And the road they were taking. I've done that."

Preston shrugged. "Can't pay you until I get my hands on that money. I'm broke."

Conley's thin shoulders sagged. "What am I going to do? I was figuring on pulling right out for California. Now I got to wait. And I can't go back to town."

"This won't take long," Waggoner said, pushing Ben toward the shack. "I've got a feeling Mister Duret will talk pretty quick."

Ben staggered across the porch and into the shadowy, squat room. It was a single square, four walls, dirt floor, and a ceiling through which light was beginning to leak. A broken table canted in one corner with two upturned nail kegs beside it for chairs. The only other furniture was a small, sheet-iron stove, weakly alive against the morning chill.

"Set down," Waggoner directed, shouldering Coe to one of the kegs. "Be smart now, Duret, and we'll get this over with in a hurry."

"I'll handle this, Tibo," Preston said in a low firm voice.

"Then get at it," Waggoner said, stepping away. "I'm about done in, ridin' all night. And we ain't got much time to waste."

"Shouldn't take long," Preston said smoothly, sitting down on the other keg. "Duret's smart enough to realize his best bet is to talk. Now, why don't you and the boys scrape together a little breakfast for us? Supplies are there in that sack."

Ben knew what was coming, what lay ahead for him. First the easy approach, the velvet glove tactics by the banker. Then, if that failed to produce the desired results, Waggoner's way of handling things would be used. He had a moment's wonder about Marcelino Baca. Where would he be at that daylight hour? Well on his way to Capital City undoubtedly, but not far enough along yet. Coe braced himself. It was his job to delay Preston

73

and Waggoner to the limit of his ability and strength.

He glanced at the banker. "Don't know what you got in mind," he drawled, "but I'm not talking about anything until you take these ropes off me. I can hardly breathe."

"Take them off," Preston ordered. Waggoner and George Kemm stepped up and released the knots.

"There'll be a gun on you every minute," Tibo Waggoner said. "Try and run for it and we'll shoot your legs out from under you."

"He won't try," Preston said. "He knows better."

With the binding pressure of his bonds gone, Ben felt better. The numbness began to fade as unrestricted circulation worked through his body and it was easier to take a full breath. Nor did he feel so utterly helpless.

"Maybe we ought to get him a soft blanket now," Waggoner said sarcastically. "Could be his tail end is a mite tired from settin'."

Preston ignored the remark. "Duret, I'll come straight to the point. We got you loose from the marshal for one reason . . . the money you stole from me. I want it back. Where did you hide it?"

Ben gave the man a hard grin. He shook his head. "Something you'll never know, Preston."

From out of nowhere, it seemed, Waggoner's open hand came arching downward and crashed into the side of Coe's head. It knocked him off the nail keg and into the wall. For a minute Ben lay there, shaken to his heels, caught against the rough logs. Slowly he gathered his scattered senses. After a time he managed a grin.

"Get you nowhere," he said to the glowering Tibo. "Might as well save yourself the work."

Waggoner drew back his arm for a second blow. Preston shook his head. "Don't be a jackass, Tibo. Knock him senseless

74

and he certainly won't be able to talk. There are plenty of other ways."

Full daylight now lay across the ridges and peaks and streaked through the openings in the cabin. George Kemm moved to the outside and hunkered near the fire over which Desmond and Bill Ford were frying salt pork and boiling coffee.

"You'll save yourself a lot of pain, talking now," Preston said then to Ben. "You see what Tibo's like."

Coe shook his head.

Waggoner swore loudly in disgust. "Still think the only thing this jasper will understand is a damn' good workin' over. Give me ten minutes with him and I'll sure guarantee he'll be ready to talk."

"Or never talk again," Preston said acidly. "No, we can always try that. Let's have a bite to eat and give Duret a chance to think things over."

He arose and walked to the doorway, Waggoner's hulking shape at his heels. At the opening, both men halted.

"Duret won't be eating, Chancey," the banker said in a voice meant to reach Coe. "We'll just save his plate for him until after he's talked."

The smell of the bubbling coffee filled the small room, as did the frying meat and potatoes, but Coe was not particularly hungry.

"Mighty fine stuff!" Bill Ford called, lifting his cup in a sort of salute.

Ben changed his thoughts to other matters, to the necessity for keeping his wits about him, to the death of Tom Kilgore, to the Brackens. Had that family forgotten their desire for vengeance and returned to Salvation? He thought of Laurie and the memory of her filled his mind. He hoped she had not shared the feelings of her hate-crazed brother and father. When this job was over with, he would return to Salvation and find her. He would explain what had transpired, make his position and true identity clear. She would understand, he was certain.

"Come on, come on," Waggoner's grumbling voice came through the doorway, breaking into Coe's thoughts. "Let's get this over with."

"What's the hurry?" Preston asked. "You said Kilgore was dead, so he can't give us any trouble. Nobody knows where we are and there's not enough time gone for them to miss Duret yet. We've got today and tomorrow, if we need them."

"I ought to be leaving now," Harvey Conley said in a faint voice. "I don't think it's a good idea for me to be hanging around."

"Maybe we ain't got as much time as you figure," Waggoner said, poking at the fire.

Preston glanced sharply at the outlaw. "What does that mean? Something you never told me?"

"There's the family of the woman Duret killed. The Brackens. We jumped them when they was about to string Duret up. We run them off, but it could be they're still hangin' around somewheres."

Preston studied the cup of black coffee in his hand. "Well, that's possible, but I doubt it. Might be they'd go back to town and one of them would say something about soldiers running them off. But I doubt if they will do any talking at all. Otherwise, they might have to explain what they were doing with Duret and the marshal in the first place."

He finished his drink and set the empty cup on a flat rock near the fire. Rising, he motioned to Waggoner and started for the door of the cabin. They entered, and Ben watched Preston take his place on the nail keg.

"You've had time to think things over, Duret. You ready to talk now?"

Coe looked straight into the eyes of the big man. "What

would I gain by telling you anything?"

"Only that you'll be dead by sundown if you don't."

"I'll be dead anyway, once I reach Capital City. Die one way or another, it's all the same."

"Little foolish hiding all that money so nobody will ever get any use from it. Be a sad waste."

"Anyway, you had yourself a big time with that woman," Waggoner put in. "Reckon that was better than money to a man who'd been cooped up alone for a long spell."

Ben lifted his gaze to the heavy face of Tibo Waggoner. The man was actually enjoying the thought. Holding back the angry words that sprang to his lips, he said: "Far as I'm concerned, nothing is better than money. You ought to know that."

Preston nodded his understanding. "My own sentiments exactly. Maybe we could work up a deal, Turk."

"What kind of a deal?"

Waggoner growled his disapproval. Preston ignored the man. "Lot of money involved. Suppose we split . . . ?"

"No, by God!" Waggoner exploded, and struck at Coe. "We don't split with nobody!"

Ben ducked the wild swing. He came swiftly to his feet and drove a straight right into Waggoner's face. It stopped the outlaw cold. Ben turned him around with a left that cracked when it landed, doubled him over with a right to the belly. Preston yelled and backed to the opposite wall. Coe tried to snatch the pistol from Waggoner's holster. His fingers brushed the butt of the weapon but Tibo was coming to and twisting away. At that moment Kemm and Bill Ford rushed into the room, summoned by the noise.

They crowded in upon him. Coe went over backward, off balance under their combined weight. He came up against the table and it collapsed under him. Fists lashed out, striking him in the body, in the face, on the head. His breath was suddenly gone, driven from his lungs by the crushing weight of the two outlaws, bearing him down. He felt a stinging blow, heavier than the others, and realized someone was kicking him. The sharp point of a boot drove into his ribs and the small of his back time after time. He tried to squirm away. Something smashed against his chin and he felt no more.

He came back to his senses dripping water. He was lying on the floor, atop the shattered table. Tibo Waggoner stood over him, an evil, vicious grin on his broad face as he poured the contents of a bucket onto Coe's head. Ben gasped, sucking deeply for breath.

"Feel like a little talk now, Mister Duret?" Waggoner's voice cut through the fog.

Ben shook his head, faintly aware of the outlaw's arcing boot immediately lashing out at him. He tried again to roll away. The blow missed his ribs, caught him just behind the ear. Blackness once more engulfed him.

Some intuitive, subconscious caution kept him still when he revived the second time. He opened his eyes to mere slits, making no movements with his body. Preston and Waggoner stood near the doorway. The sun was two-thirds up the morning sky and the thought reached Ben Coe that he had gained a few more precious hours by his actions. If he could hold out a while longer—at least until sundown. He heard a step, saw Preston and Waggoner move back to allow George Kemm, carrying a bucket of water, to enter.

"Pour it all on him," Waggoner ordered.

"Don't you be so damned quick to lay a hand on him this time," Preston snapped. "Give him a chance to talk."

"You ain't havin' much luck your way," Waggoner replied sourly. "Goin' to take somethin' besides jawin'."

Water cascaded down upon Ben, still feigning unconsciousness. Maybe he was a fool to take this sort of punishment but he would hold out and do his part. Somehow.

XIV

That day, wearing slowly from morning into afternoon, was a succeeding nightmare of blackness and light. A lesser man would have never survived, but Ben Coe's grim determination and animal stamina carried him through. Toward evening, however, he knew he could not last much longer. Eventually he would break, not of his own volition, perhaps, but involuntarily under the stress of pain the truth would be out. Near sundown he stared with glazed eyes through the open doorway. Preston and Waggoner, close to exhaustion themselves from frustration and their own violent efforts to loosen his tongue, were conversing in low voices. Beyond them he could see George Kemm and the other outlaws, Desmond and Ford. They had removed the uniforms they had been wearing and were dressed now in the customary range clothing. He could not see Harvey Conley anywhere and had a moment's wonder about that.

He lay there, body throbbing, eyes burning with a fever-like intensity. His ears and the bones in his head ached. Where Waggoner's descending boot had struck his jaw, a loosened tooth beat a steady cadence of pain. But he had survived the day and that was some reward. Marcelino Baca would be well out on the valley route with his prisoner by that time. Yet, he was not in the clear. There still was no good margin for absolute safety. Hard riding horsemen could circle the mountain and cut him off. More time was needed.

Coe began to cast about in his fogged mind for an idea, a plan that would keep Preston and the outlaws occupied for another day, or at least until noon of that next day.

"How about it, Bill?" Waggoner called to Ford. "Ready yet?"

The outlaw walked to the fire. Bending over, he took up the long handle of an axe, the metal part of which had been nestled in the glowing coals. "Ready," he answered.

Waggoner laughed harshly. "Reckon Mister Duret will do some talking now. A red hot axe blade on his naked belly will make him do 'most anything."

Ben Coe knew instantly this was the end of it. Such pain would turn him into a babbling madman in a few short moments. No matter how hard he fought to keep his lips sealed, the story would come out. From the depths of desperation a plan suddenly evolved, one that might gain him the night and most of the next day. It could cost him his life but he was beyond the point of caring much about that. He thought the plan through to a conclusion and decided it was worth a try.

He struggled to a sitting position. "Preston!" he called.

The banker and Tibo Waggoner heard and wheeled instantly. They came quickly into the cabin.

"Ready to talk, Turk?"

Ben nodded. "Had enough," he said thickly through bruised lips.

"Told you I knew how to open him up," Waggoner chortled. "Should have let me work him over sooner. Saved us all this time."

Preston paid the man no attention. "Glad to hear it, Duret. Hate treating a man like we've had to treat you."

"You said something about a deal," Coe began, feeling a little stronger.

"No deals!" Waggoner cut in roughly. "We don't need to make none with him now. He'll talk, anyway."

"Maybe," Ben replied. "But like I said, dying here in this shack won't be any worse than dying on the end of a rope in Capital City. Maybe easier, in fact. Now, if you want anything from me, you'll listen."

"We'll listen," Preston said. "The rest of you keep out of this and let him say what he's got on his mind. Go ahead, Turk."

Behind the pair Ben could see the other outlaws standing just outside the doorway. Harvey Conley was there, too, his narrow face drawn and anxious.

"Here's my offer," Ben said. "I want five thousand dollars of the money and a horse to get to Mexico on."

There was a long, strained minute of quiet. Tibo Waggoner suddenly laughed. "That what you want? Why, sure, we'll go for that, won't we, Preston?"

Ben saw Waggoner cast a wink at the men outside. His chances for winning in such a deal, were he really intending to try it, would be about as good as bringing Tom Kilgore back to life. He stared at Waggoner. "I want Preston to say it. He seems to be running this outfit."

"I agree," the banker answered quickly. "Five thousand and a horse. The one you were riding. And we'll go you one better, Turk. We'll see that you get to Mexico without any trouble."

Coe said: "Good. We've got a deal."

"Now," Waggoner said, rubbing his palms together, "where's that money stashed?"

Ben glanced at the big man and laughed. "Tell you now and have you sneak out of here tonight and grab it for yourself? Not much, Tibo. I'll take you to it tomorrow."

"What's wrong with goin' there right now?"

"Plenty," Ben said flatly. "Long ride, for one thing, and, thanks to you, I've got to have some rest. The way I feel, I couldn't make fifty yards. And I need some grub."

"The hell with that . . . ," Waggoner began angrily, but Preston silenced him.

"Morning will do all right. We all could use some sleep. Once we get the money, we'll have a hard ride ahead of us so we better be ready." He turned to Ben. "The place where you hid the thirty thousand, is it close by?"

Ben shook his head, thinking fast. "Like I said, it's a long ride. South of here. Back toward the town."

Waggoner thought that over for a minute. "Somewhere around that cave, that it?"

Coe said: "Pretty near. Have to see the place to find it." The plan was working well. And most importantly of all, they would be riding south, in the opposite direction to Capital City. He would be leading them away from Marcelino Baca and his prisoner.

"Are you able to walk?" Preston asked then. "Come on outside and eat. Plenty of food and coffee left. Then we can bed down for the night."

Ben got stiffly to his feet. His head spun from the effort and he staggered drunkenly when he walked, but he managed to make it to the fire. George Kemm handed him a plate of meat and potatoes and a chunk of hard tack. Chancey Desmond poured him a cup of the black, steaming coffee. He sat down on the ground and ate hungrily while the others looked on.

By the time he had finished, the sun had dropped behind the ridge to the west and night was coming on. The outlaws had removed their blanket rolls from their saddles and were spreading them near the fire. Ben stood up and started for his buckskin, intending to get his own woolen and canvas.

"Never mind," Waggoner said quickly. "I'll fix you a bed."

Taking the roll, he paused for a time and glanced about the camp. Spotting a sturdy, young pine some thirty feet or so from the fire, he walked to it. Kicking aside several branches and rocks lying beneath it, he spread Coe's bed.

"Over here's where you'll sleep!" he called to Ben. "Bill," he added, "bring me some rope."

Ben moved to the blanket and sat down. Ford, a coil of rope in his hands, followed by Preston, came up.

"Just want to be sure Mister Duret's comfortable . . . and will be here when we wake up in the mornin'," Waggoner said, taking the rope from Ford.

He cut off a short length and handed it back to the cowboy. "Tie his hands. Behind his back, now. And be damned sure he can't get loose. I'll just use the rest of this to hobble him and picket him to this here tree."

In a few minutes they were finished. Ben, lying on his side, knew there was no chance at all of escape.

Preston smiled down at him. "Sorry about this, Turk, but we can't take any chance on you changing your mind. It'll just be for tonight. After tomorrow you'll be on your own again."

Ben nodded. Tomorrow would bring other problems. But he was too tired to think about them now. He watched Preston and the two outlaws walk back toward the fire. He was asleep before they reached it.

XV

In that cold hour preceding dawn, Ben Coe came suddenly awake. He was stiff and sore and his body was a single, continuous ache. He lay completely still and let his swollen, half closed eyes study the outlaw camp. Something had roused him from his slumber. It had been none of the men near the fire for, with the exception of George Kemm who was crouched over the small flame soaking up some of its heat, they were yet asleep.

He remained unmoving, senses gradually becoming more acute as the moments wore on. Lying, as he was, on his side, he could see all of the men. Preston was near the cabin. Waggoner and Bill Ford on the far side of the fire. Chancey Desmond and the clerk, Conley, a few feet to their right. In the pale light they were barely distinct but he could make out their features. He shifted his gaze to the peaks in the east. The first flare of daybreak was shooting its long fingers into the sky.

"Don't move!"

The words wore a hoarse whisper, coming from behind him. Hope sprang alive within Ben Coe. He felt a tug at the rope binding his wrists. Cold metal touched his arms, rubbed slowly back and forth against them for a few moments, and then his hands were free.

"Don't move!" the warning came again. "Stay like you are."

He was aware of fingers working at the bonds that pinned his ankles together. And they, too, were released. Coe lay quietly, waiting.

"You got one chance," the whisper advised him. "While they're asleep, crawl back into the brush that's behind you. You'll find a horse about fifty feet away."

The words renewed Coe's sagging strength, drove the pain and weariness from his body. Help had come; he had not dared hope for any but somehow it had arrived. He tried to place the voice but could not.

"When you get the horse, follow me. I'll be waiting."

Ben heard the slight rustle of brush as the man returned to the thicket skirting along the clearing's edge. He tried to flex his muscles without making any outward movement. He must be careful. One wrong move now, one overloud sound, and this chance for escape would be gone. And if he did manage to reach the cover of the bushes, could he run to where the horse had been tethered? His body was so cramped and stiff he doubted if he could walk, much less run any distance. But he would try.

He glanced to the camp, preparing to make his first move. Kemm still hunched over the fire but he no longer was the only man awake, Ben noted with sinking heart. Bill Ford was on his feet, stretching and yawning. Keeping his eyes squeezed to only slits, he saw the outlaw throw a look in his direction, then move around to Kemm's side. Taking up the soot-blackened coffee pot, he placed it over the flames.

Coe realized he must act quickly. In only moments, the rest of the men would be awake, and then it would be too late. He moved his legs experimentally, testing their strength and response. He would have to be as quiet as a cougar to get away from the tree and into the brush. The throbbing of the many blows that hammered into his body faded as the time for action came. He tensed himself, planning each move, each foot of distance he must cover to the thicket. He would worm his way from the tree, keeping flat on the ground. When he reached the first stand of brush, he would rise. Then he would run, fast and quietly as possible. And it had to work the first time. There would be no second try.

He froze. Chancey Desmond had sat up. Ben remained motionless, keeping his body stiff and straight, as though the ropes still bound him. Desmond rubbed at his grizzled chin, scrubbed his cheeks. He said something to Kemm, and lay back down. It would be dangerous to delay any longer. They all would be awake in another minute or two. Ben began to work his way out of the clearing. The muscles in his legs complained at each move but he ignored the pain and crawled slowly on. His head throbbed with the straining effort and new aches slugged at his body but he gave no quarter and continued on.

He reached the first outcropping of taller growth and rolled into it, no longer keeping his eyes on the camp. He got to his feet and, with a fresh burst of pain shooting through him at the change, began to run. He kept low for another ten or fifteen feet, and then came upright. They had not missed him yet. Now, if he could reach that horse. . . .

He was moving at a long-legged, unsteady gait. It brought him full tilt against brush and trees alike. The impacts sent him reeling off but he drove on, heedlessly, jerking himself free of the clutching branches, stumbling over rocks and uncovered roots. He looked eagerly ahead, searching for the horse. It must be close now. Only fifty feet his rescuer had said. *Fifty feet.* It seemed like he had covered a mile already.

Back in the clearing a shout went up. They had discovered his escape. They would mount up instantly and give chase, knowing he could not have gone far on foot and was still in the nearby area. Ben tried to muster more speed but his trembling legs would not respond. His breath was coming in great, heaving gasps and his chest seemed to be filled with double-edged, sharp-pointed knives. But he drove himself onward.

He saw the horse. A broad beamed little white waiting patiently beside a gnarled and twisted juniper. The animal heard his noisy approach, shied to one side nervously. Coe attempted no soothing words. There was no time left for that. He simply had to chance it that the animal was securely tied.

He plunged into the small clearing, reaching for the reins looped into a slip knot. They came free at first jerk. One hand on the horn, one on the cantle, he dragged himself into the saddle, grateful the horse could shy no farther than the blocking juniper. Behind him he heard the crashing approach of Preston and his men, already beating through the brush for him. They were no more than moments off.

"This way!"

The same hoarse whisper reached him from the far side of the tree. Obediently he headed the white toward the sound, forcing him to break path through the brushy barrier. A short distance ahead, a rider on a buckskin was snaking his way expertly through the trees, a man, undistinguishable in the half light of the grove but somehow familiar. Ben Coe asked himself no questions. It was enough that he had been delivered from the hands of Tibo Waggoner, Preston, and the others. That their present pursuit of him was taking them farther away from Marcelino Baca was an added relief. He glanced over his shoulder, searching the forest for signs of Preston's men. He could see only the brush and the trees.

The man on the buckskin was leading him eastward. Ben kept the white on his trail, never allowing him to slacken his pace. A gunshot ripped through the quiet. A bullet clipped leaves overhead, sank solidly into the trunk of a tree some yards past. They had spotted him. He risked a hasty look. It was Bill Ford, again aiming. This time his bullet would likely find its mark in the white horse. The first shot had been a warning.

Ben turned to the man ahead. He was almost beyond view at that moment as he dropped onto a slight grade. They were entering a wide cañon, coming into it at right angles. Ben reached the lip and began his descent. He watched the rider before him. The man was now swinging sharply back to the right, as a deer will do, to shake a pursuer. In a few more moments they were climbing a gentle slope to a smooth running ridge. At once they dropped into the paralleling cañon, one of much greater depth. Faintly, off to the east, Coe could hear the shouts of Tibo Waggoner and the answers the others were making while they worked the rocky ground. It had been a clever move on the part of the buckskin's rider to double back on his own trail.

Ben glanced ahead. The crouched man was pulling his horse to a stop in the shadow of a pyramiding spruce. He urged the white toward him.

"I'm obliged . . . ," Ben began, managing a smile through his swollen, battered lips.

The words died. The rider had whirled about in his saddle. A leveled gun was in his hand. Ben took a long breath, let it out slowly. He had been following Todd Bracken.

XVI

For the time of a dozen heartbeats the two men stared at one another. Bracken's face was taut, his mouth curved down into a bitter, hating arc. His eyes burned with an insane fire and Coe knew without second thought he was facing the final moments of his life. Todd Bracken, consumed with that driving need for vengeance, meant to kill him. There might have been a chance with Preston but not so with Todd. He could count on one thing—dying. Ben stirred in the saddle. Off to the east the sounds of Preston and his crew became fainter.

There was a rustling of the brush behind Coe, more subdued noises to the right. From the tail of his eye he saw Saul Bracken ride into the clearing. He was followed by the man they called Orville. And then Laurie. An odd feeling possessed Coe when she met his glance. It was something akin to thankfulness, relief. Or possibly it was something deeper. He gave her a wry grin and watched her lower her gaze before his. Somehow his hopes lifted a little; something in her manner gave him the impression she was not as convinced he should die by their hands as were the others. And if that were true, he had at least one ally in the Bracken camp.

"You calculate you give old Preston the slip?" Saul Bracken asked, pulling up beside Ben.

Todd said: "Maybe for a spell. But he'll be back."

Old man Bracken grinned at Coe. "Like we was tellin' you, Duret, ain't nobody goin' to cheat us out of stringin' you up."

Ben glanced to the rising sun. A good six hours yet until noon. He rubbed thoughtfully at his neck. Still too soon to end the masquerade. Marcelino Baca and his prisoner should have those hours for safe margin. Somehow he must stall the Brackens—and continue to stall them. He turned to Todd.

"Don't know if I should be thanking you or not. Preston and his bunch were taking me back to where the money was hid.

88

Then I was lighting out for Mexico."

"That's what we figured," Todd Bracken said. "But you're a fool if you think Preston would have turned you loose."

Coe shrugged. "He'd have no cause to kill me, once he got the money back. Anyway, a poor chance is better than no chance at all. And I don't even have that chance with you, I reckon."

"You're right," Todd Bracken said coldly.

Ben shifted his gaze to Laurie. She was studying him closely, the tan oval of her face serious. Coe shook his head. "I still feel like it would be a mistake."

"Mistake? What would be a mistake? Hangin' you?" Saul Bracken's voice cracked with his impatience.

"No, just letting all that money lay there and go to waste." There was a complete silence. Finally the elder Bracken said: "You got some idea about it?"

"I could take you there. I'd rather see you folks have it than know it was going to stay there and rot."

"We're not caring anything about the money," Todd said suddenly. "We don't want any of it!"

"Thirty thousand dollars," Saul Bracken murmured. "Sure is a lot of money. Does seem a shame, it just goin' to waste."

"It won't be doing me any good, if you folks are so set on stringing me up. Somebody might as well have it."

Orville Stelder said: "If you feel that way about it, why didn't you tell Preston and his bunch where you hid it instead of takin' all that beatin' from them."

Ben rubbed at his neck again in that thoughtful way of his. "With Preston I had a chance, but with you folks, feelin' the way you do, why . . . ?" Ben shrugged.

"You goin' to tell us where you hid it?" Saul Bracken demanded, his voice lifting with eagerness.

"Well, like I said, somebody ought to have it." Coe paused, looked slowly about. He was taking up the minutes, allowing them to pass. "Is there any chance of my buying a ticket to Mexico if I do?"

"None," Todd Bracken snapped. "We don't want that money and couldn't keep it if we got it. If you think you can buy us off for killing my wife and baby, you got another think coming!"

Ben, once again, allowed his gaze to switch from one of the party to another—Laurie, Orville, old man Bracken. "Is that the way you all feel?"

The girl made no reply. Orville tipped his head at Todd, indicating the decision was with him. Saul Bracken lifted his hands, let them fall.

"Up to my boy, I reckon."

"Forget it!" Todd snarled, suddenly angry and impatient. "Let's move out of here. Preston and his crowd will be doubling back this way and I don't want to run into them again."

"All right," his father grumbled. "I sure think we ought to talk about that there thirty thousand dollars a little more, how-somever. Ain't right, lettin' it go to waste."

They filed out of the clearing, riding southward. Old man Bracken led the way, followed by Laurie, Coe, and Orville Stelder. Todd brought up the rear. Ben's eyes were on Laurie's slim figure directly ahead of him. Even in the shapeless, worn clothing of her brother, there was a full, sweet womanliness about her. He recalled, then, those moments earlier when he had caught her studying him. Was she trying to remember something? A man coming to her aid back along the trail just outside of Salvation, perhaps? He decided that could not be it. The night had been dark and he had taken care to keep his face concealed.

"Let's haul up and eat!" Saul Bracken called back after an hour had passed. "Ain't put no vittles inside my belly since last night."

Todd murmured his assent. "Swing up the next draw you

come to. Orville, you keep an eye on Duret. He tries to run for it, shoot him in the legs."

They rode up the narrow slash that turned off at right angles to the high hills and pulled to a halt beneath a broadly spreading cottonwood. The open space was small, confined, and it was necessary to picket the horses a few yards distant in an adjacent clearing. Laurie at once began to prepare a meal, procuring hard biscuits, dried beef, and some already boiled potatoes from her saddlebags.

"Watch that fire now," Todd warned as his father scratched up a small pyramid of dry twigs and leaves. "Don't want smoke showing for Preston to see."

Saul Bracken grunted. "Don't you be tellin' me how to pick ducks, boy. I was makin' fires with no smoke 'fore you was born."

Todd made no reply. He swung his glance to Ben Coe, the question he was asking himself apparent in his eyes.

Ben shook his head. "If you're wondering if you ought to tie me up, forget it. I'd be a fool to go chasing out there with Preston and Tibo Waggoner and all the rest beating the brush for me. Anyway, I still think you ought to listen to my proposition."

Todd said: "No, we're not listening to anything. We got one thing to do . . . get clear of Preston and then string you up to the nearest tree. You better start worrying about that."

Coe said nothing. He glanced at the sun. Now about two more hours until noon, he estimated. He cast about in his mind for more ways to delay matters, to consume the dragging minutes. If he could only persuade the Brackens to take him to the cave where the money was supposedly buried. But Todd Bracken would not listen to such a proposal. He decided then to concentrate his efforts on old man Bracken.

"How far you reckon it is to that cave where I was hiding out?" Ben asked, sitting down beside Saul.

Bracken scratched his head. "Five, maybe six hours' ride. Why?"

"Just thinking. You're wanting to keep clear of Preston. That would be a good place to go and I just might change my mind about telling you where that thirty thousand dollars is, once we were there."

The greed in Saul Bracken brought a glitter to his eyes. "You mean you'd just tell us where it was without expectin' us to make you no deal?"

Coe said: "Looks like Todd has made up his mind. But I still hate to think about that money not doing anybody some good. Kind of a sin, letting it go to waste."

Saul Bracken swung about to his son. "Todd . . . ," he began, but the younger man cut him off.

"Forget it, Pa. That money ain't for us. Quit fooling yourself and quit listening to Duret. It's some kind of a trick."

The elder Bracken got to his feet and stalked away, muttering under his breath. Ben turned his attention to Laurie, working over the low fire. Her face was flushed from the heat and a stray lock of her dark hair hung over her forehead but she seemed not to notice. The odor of frying meat and potatoes was beginning to fill the clearing. He watched her set the pail of boiling water off the flames and add a generous handful of coffee to it. When it surged up to a foaming crest, she stirred it down with a knife.

Laying out four plates, she then portioned out the meal, reserving only a small amount in the frying pan for herself. Taking up one of the plates, she walked to where Ben sat and handed it to him.

Studying him gravely, she said: "You aren't Turk Duret. Who are you?"

XVII

There was a long, dead minute of silence. Time itself became a suspended thing. Ben returned Laurie's steady gaze, conscious of the thread of gladness that marked her tone. She had, somehow, recognized him and now remembered him from that night. But how?

"What did you say?" Todd Bracken broke the hush, his voice shocked and strained.

Laurie turned to her brother. "He's not Turk Duret. I don't know who he is, but he's not Duret."

Orville Stelder had risen to his feet. Saul Bracken, scarcely pausing over his plate, scoffed. "Him not Duret? What are you sayin', girl? Didn't I see this same jasper in the courtroom with my own eyes?"

"He's the same man that was at the trial," Stelder confirmed. "I ain't wrong about that."

"Sure he is and for certain," Saul continued. He hesitated over his meal. "You gone and got yourself sot on this man, Laurie? I been suspectin' you was sweet on him ever since that mornin' when we stopped him and the marshal. Could see it in your eyes."

Orville Stelder swung a startled glance at Laurie, and then looked down. Ben, too, stared at her, the words of old Saul Bracken filling him with a strange, powerful pride. But he said nothing; Todd Bracken, in his present state of mind, was unpredictable. The next few moments would be delicate, fraught with danger.

The younger Bracken moved up closer. "What kind of talk is that?" he snarled, pulling his gun and leveling it at Coe's breast. "You're the man I saw at the trial. You're the same one I jumped. You claim that's not so?"

The time had arrived. Marcelino Baca and his prisoner were on their own. Ben sighed his relief. "That's right. But my name's

Coe. Ben Coe. I'm a deputy U.S. marshal."

Todd's face distorted as anger whipped through him. The hammer of his pistol clacked loudly as he drew it to a cocked position. Ben met the man's insane fury with a calmness he did not entirely feel and rode out the dragging moments. Laurie suddenly stepped before him, shielding his body with her own.

"No!" she said in a sharp voice. "You'll not kill him just because you've been outsmarted! You'll not have a murder on your hands!"

"Still don't believe it," Saul's plaintive voice broke the deadly tension. "I seen this here man right in the courtroom. You sayin' I didn't?"

"That was me," Ben explained, placing his hands on Laurie's shoulders and putting her gently aside. "I took Duret's place at the hearing. The real trial was held weeks ago in a different town. The law expected trouble from folks like you, and others, so I took his place. The real Duret is with Sheriff Baca, either in Capital City by now or almost there."

"You were a decoy, that it?" Stelder said, more as a statement than a question.

Ben nodded. But Todd Bracken was as yet unconvinced. He continued to glare at Coe. The gun in his hand still pointed at the lawman. "I don't believe none of it," he said finally.

"I can prove it," Laurie said at once. "I saw Ben . . . him. That night before the trial. I walked up to the hill behind our camp to look at the town. He rode up and stopped, coming from the river. He was just looking, too. When he scratched at that scar on his neck a while back, I knew I remembered something. Then it came to me. The man who was on the hill that night did the same thing. If he were Turk Duret, Todd, do you think he would just come riding in to Salvation of his own accord and turn himself in?"

Todd had no answer. Ben listened as Laurie went on telling

about the two drunken cowboys, the fight that ensued. He grinned to himself. So that was how she knew—his scratching at that bullet track on his neck. A man's habits often prove his undoing and deliverance.

"Where's the real Duret?" Stelder asked.

"Probably in Capital City by now, as I said. Sheriff Baca left with him soon after Kilgore and I rode out of town. They took the valley road while we took this trail, hoping we would draw off any ambush."

"Damn you!" Todd Bracken suddenly cried in bitter, unreasonable anger and hurled himself at Ben. "I ought to kill you for tricking me!"

Coe stepped aside. As Todd came in, he struck him hard along the side of the head. The man went down to his knees, losing the gun as he did so. Ben scooped it up quickly and moved beyond Bracken's reaching hands.

"Tricking you?" Coe echoed. "You think I've enjoyed one minute of this? You people don't realize how important it is that Turk Duret gets hung in Capital City. It's not just the fact that it will get done there. There's more to it than that. It could be that statehood for this territory depends on it." Ben paused, his own anger and impatience aroused. "This hasn't been a job I liked, I'll tell you that. And it hasn't been a joke for me. You think I enjoyed the treatment I got from Preston and Waggoner? Or from you? I gambled my life on getting Duret to Capital City and Tom Kilgore, one of the best lawmen you'll ever live to see, gave his life for it. And you . . . you talk about killing me to satisfy your need for vengeance."

"And I will!" Todd Bracken yelled, and leaped again at Coe.

Ben whirled away from the lunging man. He had a fleeting glimpse of Laurie's horror-filled eyes; she fully expected him to shoot her brother, kill him. He brought the pistol down, club-like, on Todd's head. He went down full length and lay quiet.

Ben pivoted to Orville Stelder. "I don't want any trouble with you. Or you, Mister Bracken. Both of you toss your guns out there on the ground. You, Orville, get a rope and tie Todd's hands behind him. I don't want to be dodging him all day."

Both men complied at once, Stelder procuring a short length of rope from his pocket and binding Todd Bracken's hands.

"The two of you sit down over there," Ben said, waving them to a position across the fire. "I need to think this out for a minute."

Laurie had stood quietly nearby. Her cheeks were colored from the excitement of the moment but she had said nothing. Ben faced her. "I'm obliged to you," he said. "A friend is one thing I've been needing."

Saul Bracken grunted. "Reckon you got yourself more'n a friend, Marshal."

Laurie's cheeks flamed even brighter. She dropped to her knees beside the fire and poured coffee into the waiting cups. Ben squatted on his heels beside her.

"I hope," he said softly, "what your pa said is true."

She hesitated a long moment, and then turned to him. "Since that night along the trail . . . I've hoped we would meet again," she murmured. "I thought you had ridden on. I never dreamed it would end this way."

"This is no end," Coe said at once. "This is just the beginning. I had planned to come back this way and find you, after I was finished with my job, hoping that matters might work out for us. But I didn't even know if you would be interested. I feel now like I'm the luckiest man in the world."

Laurie's eyes were on the low fire. "But the way we treated you . . . the things we've said . . . can you forget all that?"

"They're forgotten," Ben said, laying his hand upon hers. "You thought I was Turk Duret."

From across the small clearing Saul Bracken asked: "What

about this here Duret? You dead sure they'll string him up?"

"As certain as I'm here. You've got my solemn word on that."

Todd Bracken stirred, sat up. He struggled momentarily against his bonds, and then glared at Coe.

"Ain't got much faith in them fancy pants jaspers up there," old man Bracken said slowly. "Figure they'd just as soon let him go, would he tell them where he put that money, as not."

Ben Coe shook his head. "That's the wrong kind of thinking. Maybe it might have happened somewhere, sometime, but it won't happen in Capital City. Turk Duret is as good as hung right now."

"I'd believe that if I saw it," Todd Bracken said. "I got no reason to believe anything you're telling us."

"It's up to you," Coe said, dismissing the argument. "But I'll be moving on to Capital City to wind up this job. Then I'll be coming back this way. I'll bring you any kind of proof you want."

Laurie's voice was a still, small sound in the quiet. "Then what will you do?"

"Go back to Kansas. That's where I work." Ben paused. "But before I do that, I'd like to tell you about Kansas. It's a fine place to live. Lots of people moving in. While I'm gone, would you think a little about going with me?"

She gave him a quick, sweet smile, her answer in her eyes. "I. . . ."

There was the distinct crackle of a dry twig; the rustle of brush dragging lightly against cloth. It was off to the left, outside the clearing. Ben Coe came swiftly to his feet, his gun poised.

"What is it?" Laurie whispered, alarm stiffening her features.

"Somebody out there. Stand away from me."

Laurie moved back a step or two. The noise came again, much nearer. The forest about them was in absolute silence, no chirping birds, no clacking insects. But to Ben Coe the feel of danger was like a clanging bell.

"Nobody move!" a voice shattered the hush. "Preston! Over here!"

Bill Ford's voice. Coe spun. In that same instant the outlaw fired. The bullet whirred past Coe, thunked into a tree behind Orville Stelder. Ben had a glimpse of the tall outline of Ford. He snapped a quick, answering shot. He heard the slug drive home, heard the gusty explosion of the outlaw's breath as it was smashed from his lungs.

Saul Bracken lunged for his gun. "Scatter!" he yelled. "Everybody scatter!"

XVIII

There was then the racket of running horses—Preston and the others, summoned by Ford's shout, were closing in.

"Bill! Bill Ford!" Waggoner's impatient voice rode through the quiet. "Where the devil are you?"

Ben reached for Laurie's hand. Saul Bracken and the others were moving off into the brush. "Come on," he said. "We've got to get out of here."

They slipped out of the clearing and into the thick under-growth. They reached the horses. Ben freed Laurie's mare and the little white that had been provided for him. Taking the leathers, they hurried on, not mounting yet for fear their silhouettes might be more easily visible to Preston and his men.

Waggoner had ceased his yelling, which could mean only one thing—he had found Bill Ford.

Ben drew the girl and their horses to the far side of a thickly overgrown Osage orange. "I don't like this," he said. "I think the best thing is for you to wait here until some of your family shows up. I won't risk your getting hurt."

Laurie tipped her face to him. Her small chin was set stub-bornly. "I'm going with you, no matter what."

"Before this is done with there is going to be some gun play.

That's a pretty wild bunch Preston's got with him and they won't care much who they shoot at."

"I've seen shooting before. And I'm not afraid of getting hit by a stray bullet. Anyway," she added, "if I'm to be the wife of a U.S. marshal, I might as well start getting used to such things."

Coe grinned in spite of the serious mood. He reached out, took her by the shoulders, and planted a quick kiss upon her lips. "All right, you win this hand," he said. "Now, let's get out of here."

Keeping low and still on foot, they left the shelter of the orange, headed straight away from the clearing where they had last encountered Preston and his riders. They were in single file with Coe leading, but it was the girl who heard the first suspicious sound and murmured a warning.

"Ben. Off to the left. There's somebody."

Instantly Coe froze. The stop was too abrupt for the horses and there was a moment of confusion as they shied against the brush. Coe stepped quickly back to Laurie. He thrust his reins into her hand, warned her to silence with his eyes. He dropped back a few yards, faded into a stand of wild gooseberry. He had not yet heard the sound Laurie had caught. But it should be there, nearby. He took another few steps—and was face to face with Preston and the big rider, George Kemm.

"There he is . . . ," Preston started. His words ended in a gasp as Coe hurled himself at the man, drove him flat to the ground. Kemm dropped the reins of the horse he was leading and lunged. Coe saw the move and rolled free of Preston. Kemm struck the banker and drove him back to the earth. Coe, up now and coming in fast, saw the cowboy clawing at his gun. He lashed out with a booted foot. His toe met the weapon, sent it spinning into the brush. He wanted no noise at this point. He could likely handle Kemm and C.J. Preston, but Waggoner also would be too much. And a gunshot would bring the big rider quick.

"Get him!" Preston yelled at Kemm. He was pulling himself away from the center of action.

Coe, off balance from the kick he had delivered to Kemm's weapon, half fell. The cowboy grabbed at him, caught his leg. Coe fought to stay up but failed. He went down in a sprawling heap. Kemm swung at him, a long, roundhouse right delivered from a kneeling position. Coe ducked the slow-traveling fist easily. He snatched at Kemm's arm, caught him by the wrist, and jerked. The cowboy howled in pain as his shoulder wrenched.

Ben rolled to his feet. Movement behind him warned him of Preston. He lurched to one side just as the banker struck downward with a short length of wood. The limb caught him on the upper arm just above the elbow. The force of it sent pain shooting through his entire body but he knew it was momentary and not any serious injury. He wheeled then at Preston, a wild anger suddenly unleashed by the banker's blow. Preston yelled and tried to back away. He came up against Kemm, tripped, and both men went down in a flurry of arms and legs and muttered cursing.

Coe rushed in upon them. Time was getting away fast. The odds for their escape were growing less with each fleeting moment. He grasped the dazed Kemm by the shirt collar, half dragged him upright. Holding him, he drove his fist into the man's jaw. Kemm's head rolled and his body went limp. He spun to Preston but the banker was on his feet, scrambling for the brush ten feet away. Coe started to follow, thought better of it, and ran quickly toward Laurie and the horses.

"Best trail north," he said, and swung to his saddle. "Lead out."

Laurie rode off ahead of him, striking due west through the thick brush. He did not question her, knowing she was well acquainted with the country. He was more concerned with watching the trail behind them. But he saw no pursuers.

They soon broke out of the dense grove and onto a semi-open plains country. There was no road, only a long, shallow valley, lush with good grass. This continued for a mile or so, and then led into a narrow wash that one time flood water had grooved during its rushing descent from the high hills. Travel became more difficult at that point and the horses were compelled to take things slower. But they were well hidden. Only a man riding directly into the narrow slash could know of their whereabouts.

An hour later they reached the same trail that Coe had covered that previous day with Waggoner and his bogus soldiers.

"This is the road to Capital City," Laurie said. "You think it's safe to ride it or do we keep to the brush?"

Ben considered. Preston and his outlaws were behind them and to the east; they were the only problem. And they needed to travel fast.

"Let's stick to the main road," Coe said finally. "Right now we need to put a few miles between Preston and ourselves."

Around noon, with the horses showing the affects of the steady pace, they drew off the trail into a narrow wash. There, in the shade of a small cottonwood, they halted for a rest. It was a dry camp. There was no water for either the horses or themselves but just being out of the saddle was good. Ben eased the animals by loosening their cinches.

When he was finished, he sat down beside Laurie. He was still finding it hard to believe she was with him, was willing to have him, and go to Kansas with him.

"Laurie," he said, taking her hand in his, "I don't want you doing something you might later be sorry for. You made up your mind pretty fast back there in the camp. If you think now you'd like to wait a spell, it will be all right with me."

Laurie turned to him, studied his grave face for a long moment. Then, leaning forward, she kissed him on the lips.

"You men are such fools," she said with a smile. "You seem to think love is a one-sided business. Don't you think I was as sure back there of what I wanted . . . as you were? What has time to do with how much a woman loves a man? I suppose there are cases where two people can learn to care for one another. A sort of a gradual thing, I guess you might call it, and there's nothing wrong with that. But I think the best kind is the kind where you know instantly that you have met the person you love. That was the way of it with me, Ben."

Coe nodded. "And with me, Laurie. I never got you out of my thoughts after that first meeting." He put his arm about her slim shoulders, drew her against him. "I'll be glad when this job is done. Then we can start living like people should. Right now," he added, kissing her lightly and releasing her, "I expect we ought to travel. No use pressing our luck too far."

"Your luck," Tibo Waggoner's deliberate voice reached out from the brush and shocked them, "just run clean out, Duret. Now, don't make no sudden moves. Just stand up with your hands stuck out where I can see them."

Ben got slowly to his feet, anger at his own carelessness raging through him. He should have guessed one of the outlaws, at least, would have spotted Laurie and him traveling northward. He should have used more care, he reflected bitterly. Now he had dragged Laurie into his own troubles.

"Step out here into the open," Waggoner said. The outlaw moved from the brush into the small clearing, as he spoke. He watched Ben comply. "Soon as that horse of mine gets his breath, we'll all ride back to Preston and the boys. Didn't get no chance to tell them I saw you two ridin' north. They're still beatin' the brush back there in that grove."

Waggoner was alone. Ben realized that and a faint spark of

102

hope began to glow within him. He half turned his head to look at Laurie. She was standing several paces behind him.

"Reckon I better have that gun you're wearin'," Waggoner said. "Take it out, easy like, and toss it on the ground here, in front of me."

Coe gauged his chances. He had one and one only. It was slim but it might work. He glanced again at Laurie, assuring himself she was not in the line of Waggoner's gun. Satisfied, he lowered his hand slowly over the butt of his pistol.

"Don't get no notions," Waggoner warned.

Coe's expression did not change. His eyes were locked with those of the outlaw. He felt the curved handle of the gun fit up into his palm. He let his fingers close about the smooth wood. Slowly he began to lift the weapon, letting Waggoner see every move.

"Throw it down," the outlaw said, a frown pulling his thick brows together.

"Sure," Coe answered. "Just like you want it."

He brought the gun out. Holding it loosely, he started a forward motion with his arm. In the next fleeting fragment of time, he was hurling himself to one side and to the ground. Waggoner's gun blasted in unison with his own. Ben felt the bullet rip through the cloth of his shirt. He fired again, seeing the outlaw's upright shape still before him. It was a wasted shot. Waggoner, hit in the chest, was staring at him with wonder-filled eyes. He seemed more surprised than hurt. The second bullet jolted him, rocked him back a step. He wavered uncertainly for a long moment. The pistol slipped from his hand, and then he fell heavily, going down into the brush at the edge of the clearing.

Ben was on his feet instantly. Laurie ran to him, her eyes anxious. But she asked no questions. She saw he was all right and that was the answer she sought.

"We've got to get out of here," Coe said, wheeling to where the horses waited. "Likely somebody will have heard those shots."

He pulled the cinches tight and they mounted up. Riding quickly out of the draw, they came to the road.

"This time," he said, "we better keep to the brush. My guess is we'll have company right soon."

XIX

The brief rest had benefited the horses. They moved along through the hindering brush and scrubby trees at a good pace, slowing up only when they came on to a rocky slope where the footing was more difficult. Ben did not let up until a full hour had passed. Then he called a halt.

He dismounted and moved to a low hill that overlooked the trail behind them. Laurie joined him there and together they sat quietly, listening and watching for signs of pursuit. At first there was no evidence the shots had been heard. Then they heard the distinct rap of fast-running horses. The sound was far to the east, which could mean only one thing—the riders, whoever they were, had taken the valley road, were following the more open route for the sake of speed.

"Preston?" Laurie asked, alarm in her tone.

Coe nodded. "Can't figure what he's doing over there. Thought he would come swarming up to where the gunshots were. Unless . . . ," he added thoughtfully, and hesitated.

"Unless what?"

"Unless he's got some sort of idea to circle around ahead of us, cut us off."

Laurie said nothing. Fear for Ben was plain in her eyes. She looked away. "Wouldn't it just be better to face Preston, make him understand you're not Turk Duret but a U.S. marshal?

104

Maybe if he knew that, he would forget about trying to capture you."

Ben placed his arm about her shoulders. "You think I could make him believe that? Waggoner still thought I was Duret and I'm not even sure I've got your own brother and father convinced. Or Orville. Preston is going to believe what he saw . . . me in that courtroom on trial for killing your brother's wife and child. Trying to tell him he's wrong would be a waste of time. I will first have to have proof of some kind."

She shrugged wearily. "I suppose you're right. But it all seems so useless, so unnecessary. You might even get killed just because you can't prove who you really are."

"That was the idea behind this whole set-up. Make everybody believe I was someone I wasn't. At least up to a certain point. Then Tom Kilgore was to step in and clear it all up."

"Only Tom Kilgore is dead," she finished, "and there's nobody to straighten matters out, not until you get back to Salvation and see the judge. Ben, this could cost you your life."

He said—"My job, Laurie."—and stopped. After a moment he added: "But it's not quite as bad as you think. It will come out all right. Once we reach Capital City, it will all be over with. Sheriff Baca will be there to verify my story. And so will the prison officials. I don't know them but they can easily clear me."

"If we ever reach Capital City."

"We will, don't worry about that."

"I hope so, Ben. I pray nothing will happen to you. I . . . I don't think I could go on living now if anything happened to you. I wouldn't want to."

"You worry too much," he said with a broad grin.

She said: "I guess you're right. What do we do?"

"Go on, of course. Finish the job. Unless I'm wrong there's only two horses. Preston and Kemm. Maybe three if Conley's along. Might be some others back along the trail, just waiting for us. That way they've got us pocketed."

"I see," she murmured. "Either way we go, we're trapped."

He grinned at her, trying to ease her worry. "It's not all over yet. It's one thing to set up a trap, another thing to spring it. The best thing we can do, I figure, is keep moving toward Capital City."

By the middle of the afternoon, with their horses pulled down to a steady walk, they drew near to the end of the mountain range, a long, trailing backbone that sloped down until it disappeared into a far-reaching mesa. Coe, probing it carefully, was aware of one thing; once they left the brush and protective shadows of the hills, they would be out in the open, flat ground. They would be easily seen in all directions, for a considerable distance.

"Any idea how far to Capital City from here?" he asked Laurie, thinking she might be familiar with the area.

The girl shook her head. "I'm not sure. I've never been there. But I think it's twenty or thirty miles."

"Lot of open range to cross," he said, voicing his thoughts. He glanced toward the sun. "Quite a while until dark and I hate to waste that time. I think we'll just pull up there in that grove and rest the horses for a bit and then move on." He did not explain that he wanted the animals in the best possible condition when they started across the flat mesa; there was every possibility they might have to make a run for it.

They continued on and a short time later reached the scatter of trees, all thick-bodied cottonwoods clustered about a small spring. As they approached, a horseman suddenly appeared and rode forward to meet them. Ben Coe's hand dropped to the gun at his hip but Laurie's voice stayed him.

"It's Papa. It's my father."

Saul Bracken trotted his gray up beside them. "Had me a

mite worried," he said, mopping sweat off his brow with the back of a hairy wrist. "All that shootin' back there. Figured maybe you was in trouble."

"Waggoner," Coe said. "Was that you we heard coming up the valley?"

Bracken nodded. "Reckon so. Todd and me figured to catch up and ride into Capital City with you. Got a hankerin' to see Duret hang ourselves. That way, we'll know the job's been done."

"Where's Todd?" Laurie asked, looking about.

"Settin' over there in the shade. Got hisself nicked by a bullet."

"Todd's been shot?" Laurie exclaimed.

"Not bad. One of Preston's bunch."

"Where's Orville? He didn't get . . . ," Laurie faltered.

"Kilt? Nope. Orvie's all right. Last time I saw him he was tearin' off through the brush with one of Preston's buckos on his tail. Expect he led the feller down the valley a ways and then went on home."

Ben was thinking deeply. Since it had been the Brackens they had heard, Preston and his men must be behind them yet. Coming up the trail, most likely. It meant one thing. They would have to forego the proposed rest for the horses. They would have to push on at once. It would not pay to let Preston get too close.

They entered the shadows of the grove and pulled up beside the spring. Todd Bracken, a handkerchief wrapped about his left forearm, was sitting with his back propped against a tree. He watched Ben with a cold hostility and gave no greeting to Laurie as she dismounted and hurried to his side.

"How bad is it, Todd?" she asked, her fingers plucking at the stained cloth.

Todd brushed her roughly aside. "Forget it."

Saul Bracken said: "Todd still ain't so sure about you, Coe.

One of the reasons why we decided we'd just go on into Capital City. They don't hang Duret, then we got us a mighty big bone to pick with you."

Todd, never changing his hot, hating glance from Ben, said to Laurie: "You're a fool to be believing so strong in this man. Maybe he's not Duret, but I won't even bet for sure on that. And if he ain't, he's in with those other jaspers in Capital City that's running this territory. And he'll sell us out just like they're planning to do."

"You're wrong, Todd," the girl said. "I wish I could make you see it but you're all wrong. Ben isn't in with anybody, as you claim. He is just a lawman doing the job that was assigned to him. I believe that. And when he tells me the real Duret is being delivered to Capital City for hanging, I believe that, too."

Todd spat in disgust. "Sure, he can make you swallow anything he says. He's the kind who can sweet talk a woman into anything. You really think he means all those things he's been telling you . . . maybe about marrying up and such?"

Laurie made no reply. She stared at her hands.

"He's just using you as his ticket to get to Capital City. Once he's there, you'll see. He'll drop you like a hot potato, leave you flat. I know his kind."

Laurie shook her head. "I believe him, Todd."

Ben Coe, anger steadily rising within him, crossed to the younger Bracken. "You all through?" he demanded in a tight, outraged voice. "If you weren't Laurie's brother and crippled up, I'd make you eat those words, Todd. I'd take a lot of pleasure in kicking your teeth in. And when this is all finished, I'm making a special trip back down here to do just that."

Todd returned his furious gaze. "You'll never live that long, Duret. I'll kill you before you get a chance to start back."

A sudden wild fury blazed through Ben Coe. "Of all the bull-headed, knot-brained . . . ," he began, taking a long step toward the man. Laurie came to her feet at once, threw herself before him.

"It doesn't matter, Ben," she said in a low, soothing voice. "What he or anybody else says doesn't matter to me. I believe what you say."

Ben turned away, his arm going around the girl. She was right. No matter what Todd or anyone else thought, it was of no consequence. Just so long as Laurie had faith in him.

He had his hands about her shoulders, holding her before him, looking down at her. He heard then the harsh voice of C.J. Preston lash out from the brush behind him.

"Put your hands up, Duret! You're covered!"

XX

Coe moved gently away from Laurie. He let his hands remain poised, only half lifted. Saul Bracken had come to his feet but Todd had not moved. Ben gauged the approximate location of Preston; almost directly behind him, he figured. If he could get another two steps to the left of Laurie, thus removing her from the line of fire, he could whirl, drop, and shoot. And maybe bring to a close, once and for all, this problem he had with C.J. Preston. In the next moment he knew it was out of the question.

George Kemm's voice, coming from the other side of the clearing, reached out to him: "Duret, if you're gettin' one of your cute ideas, forget it. I've got you covered, too."

Coe came to a stop. He was trapped between the two men. He might get one but never the pair of them.

"Just stand quiet," Preston said. "And raise those hands higher! Turn around slow."

Ben complied. He had no choice. He came slowly about.

"Don't none of the rest of you folks get any ideas, either.

Now!" he added, glancing at the Brackens. They did as they were ordered.

"You ain't got no right to do this!" Saul Bracken protested, suddenly finding his voice.

Preston laughed. He moved farther into the center of the clearing. "Old man, I got thirty thousand rights. . . ."

"But he's not Turk Duret!" Laurie broke in, rushing to Coe's side. "He's not the man you want. He's a lawman, a deputy U.S. marshal. He was only taking Duret's place."

The words poured out in a breathless torrent. Preston listened, faint humor in his eyes. When Laurie had finished, he said: "I suppose you'll be telling me next that he isn't the man I saw in the courtroom back in Salvation. That he's not the one I saw marched in by the marshal and sheriff, and then taken out after Abraham sentenced him to hang."

"Yes, but . . . ," Laurie began, floundering with her words. "He's the man all right but he's not Duret. He. . . ."

Preston turned his back to her. He faced Kemm. "Get some rope, George. We're going to work this a little different this time. We don't have Tibo to help us loosen Duret's tongue, but I figure, if we drag him along behind a horse for a mile or two, he might be ready to talk."

"You can't!" Laurie cried. "You can't do that to him! He's not Turk Duret! I swear it!"

Laurie threw herself upon Ben Coe as if to shield him from the two men. Kemm grasped her by the shoulders and roughly shoved her at Saul Bracken.

"She's your kin," he said. "Keep her out of the way unless you want her to get hurt."

Todd Bracken had risen to his feet. He moved into the middle of the cleared area and faced Preston. "Is there any doubt in your mind who this man is?" he asked, pointing at Coe.

Preston said: "Hell, no. Why should there be? I saw him

before with my own eyes. Anybody that says he's not that same man is loony."

Todd Bracken nodded his satisfaction. "That's the way I've felt all along, but that sister of mine claims he's somebody else."

"Who?"

"Somebody by the name of Ben Coe. A deputy U.S. marshal, she says."

Preston shrugged. "That doesn't make sense. Kilgore was the marshal on this case. Why would he have a deputy, too? Lawmen aren't that plentiful."

Todd Bracken considered that statement, his face immediately showing his belief. He swung to Coe. "You still claim you're not Duret?"

"I'm not Duret," Ben replied coldly. "And anything you do to me you'll answer to the United States government for. Now, turn me loose."

"He's a real hard talker, ain't he?" Kemm said, uncoiling the rope he had procured from his saddle. "How you want to do this, Mister Preston?"

"Tie his hands behind him. Then loop that rope around his middle. Tie the other end to your saddle horn."

"No," Laurie moaned, and broke free of her father.

Todd caught her by the arm, whirled her about, and sent her stumbling back to the elder Bracken. "Hang onto her, Pa. We'll tie her up, too, if she keeps on making a fuss. Ain't no doubt in my mind now about this being Turk Duret. How about you?"

Saul Bracken wagged his head. "I surely don't know what I'm thinkin'," he muttered helplessly.

"He's not Turk Duret," Laurie said, her words ending in a sob. "You will be murdering the wrong man."

"Maybe not murder," Preston said. "Maybe he'll be smart enough this time to answer my question. He does that, he won't get hurt."

Todd Bracken said: "Mister Preston, we both been after the same man but for different reasons. You want to get your money back. I want the pure pleasure of stringing him up to a tree limb. No use of us fighting over him."

Preston said: "That's right."

"Suppose we sort of join up. I'll help you find out what you want to know. Then you turn him over to me, so's I can do what I got to do."

Preston thought for a time. He nodded. "Sounds all right to me. Don't figure I need any help, the way this is working out, but, if you want to throw in with me, I'm agreeable. When I'm finished with him, he's all yours."

Ben Coe had listened to the conversation in silence. They were taking good care of him, he thought grimly. Carving him up like a Christmas turkey. And when they were done, there would be nothing left, nothing but a body swinging from a tree for the buzzards to have their time with. He glanced at Laurie. Her father had a firm grasp upon her wrist, keeping her at his side. He was sorry she was to be a witness to the next few hours. Saul Bracken should take her and head back to Salvation. No sense in her being put through the torture he soon would be undergoing. He felt Kemm jerk at his hands, draw them down behind his back.

"Here's a strip of rawhide," Todd Bracken volunteered. "Tie his wrists with it and he won't be working loose."

His last minutes of life were facing him. Ben Coe recognized that fact. A desperate anger lifted suddenly within him. He wasn't giving in this easy. Once his hands were bound, he would have little if any chance at all remaining. Better to try now and perhaps go down under a bullet than wait and endure the tender mercies of C.J. Preston—with only Todd Bracken's lynch rope waiting for him if he managed to survive that. He drew himself taut, considering his best course of action. He felt Kemm tug at his hands, pulling them away from his body so that he might more easily wrap the rawhide about his wrists. In that instant he acted. He threw himself back against Kemm. The sheer weight of his body knocked the man against the low brush. He tripped, went down. Coe wheeled and ducked aside, knowing Preston would shoot. The gun exploded but the bullet was wide. Coe drove forward into Preston. His shoulder caught the man in the midsection. Preston's breath went out in a blast. He buckled, his pistol blasting a second time.

Coe spun away. Kemm, recovered, was coming back into the clearing, curses streaming from his thick lips. Ben wheeled to face him. He was vaguely conscious of Laurie's scream, of a dark shape moving in upon him from the side. Todd. He had ignored the man, knowing he was unarmed and had concentrated on Kemm and Preston. Laurie screamed again just as Kemm lunged at him. Something crashed down upon his head. Lights spun before his eyes and he went to his knees.

"Don't, Todd!"

He heard Laurie's voice, realized it was Todd who had hit him with a club or a rock or something solid. He saw the grinning face of George Kemm before him, felt a warm stickiness on his head. He went forward to his hands, struggling to keep from going clear down. He saw Kemm's boot rise to meet him. The shock of the impact against his jaw drove him over backward.

He lay quiet, only barely conscious. The effort to move was more than he could muster at the moment. There was no feeling in his long body, no strength. Faintly he heard Preston's voice.

"Let him be. He won't try it again. Get some water from the spring, George."

A minute later cold water dashed against his face and yanked his senses out of the fog. He gasped, came to a sitting position.

113

Kemm and Todd Bracken took him under the armpits and jerked him to his feet. He stood there, weaving uncertainly, his brain clearing. He could hear Laurie crying brokenly, could feel the warmness of blood trickling through his scalp, down the side of his face. Why didn't Saul Bracken take Laurie away? Why was he allowing her to see all this?

Kemm clamped his hands together, bound them tight with the rawhide. He walked around to face Coe. He grinned, his broad teeth yellow and large as those of a horse. "Now, bucko, let's see you try that again," he said, and drove his fist onto Coe's unprotected belly.

Ben folded, his head spinning as pain shattered his nerves again. He staggered and almost fell. Todd Bracken caught him and held him upright.

Preston said: "No more of that, George! I want him able to talk. You're as bad as Tibo."

"Owed him that one," Kemm replied.

"And I got to have him alive to string . . . ," Todd Bracken began and then abruptly stopped.

Coe lifted his eyes to the man, wondering what had checked him. Bracken, as did all the others, looked beyond him toward the edge of the clearing.

A strange voice said: "Now, just what kind of a party we got goin' here?"

Ben turned slowly around. Three hard-faced men with drawn guns stood just outside the ring of brush. A single word jarred involuntarily from his lips. "Duret!"

XXI

There was no mistaking the heavy, brutal features of the man. Ben had seen him back in the jail at Salvation, asleep on a cot. There was no doubt. Somehow the killer had escaped Marcelino Baca, probably with the help of the two men with him.

And most likely the sheriff was at that moment lying dead along the trail, victim of an ambush.

Duret and his companions moved into the clearing. Each carried a pistol in his hand. Their cartridge belts were completely filled. It apparently had been a well-planned rescue. Kilgore and Frank Abraham had labored for nothing. And Kilgore was dead, and probably Baca.

"Looks like they been treatin' you a mite rough, amigo," Duret said easily, halting before Coe. "What they got against you?"

Ben Coe thought fast. He realized he was the last hope for getting Duret to Capital City and the justice he deserved. Just how it could yet be done was not clear but so long as he was himself alive, he must try. Perhaps, if he could persuade Duret they were of the same breed, of the same mind. . . . He said: "Seems quite a few things. I was about to become the main party in a hanging bee when you showed up."

Duret nodded. "So I see." His gaze was going beyond Coe, resting on Laurie.

"Obliged to you for stepping in," Ben said. "How about cutting me loose? Rawhide's pulled pretty tight."

"Sure," Duret said. "Cut him loose, Earl."

One of the men stepped forward. He drew a knife from his pocket and sliced through the thong.

Preston, recovered from his surprise, said: "You . . . you're Turk Duret?"

The outlaw swung his attention to the banker, having his moment of pride at being recognized. "That's me."

"Then who's this man?" Preston exclaimed, plainly confused as he pointed at Coe.

Duret swung his narrow, sardonic face to Ben. "You been tellin' folks around here you're Turk Duret, *amigo?*"

"They've been telling me that," Coe said honestly. "I've been trying to convince them that I'm not."

"Who are you? I know you?"

Ben shook his head. "Don't think so. Name is Coe."

"Claims he a U.S. marshal," Saul Bracken broke in. "A deputy, anyway."

Duret stared at Coe. He grinned. "Man, you sure do swap around some. Now, even I know better than that. Only one U.S. marshal around here. His name's Kilgore and I'm mighty well acquainted with him. Ain't I, Earl?" he added, glancing at one of his partners.

Earl laughed. "And the sheriff, too."

"Who might you be?" Duret continued, turning his attention to Preston.

"I'm C.J. Preston. I own the bank you robbed."

Duret sucked at his lips thoughtfully. "What's that got to do with this *amigo* of mine, Coe?"

"We thought he was Duret . . . you."

"And you figured to make him cough up that thirty thousand dollars I stashed away, that it?"

Preston said: "Yes, that's it. But now that I know he's not, I'm ready to make a deal with you."

Duret stared at the banker, shook his head admiringly. "You sure have got a crust, I'll say that for you. Why would I be wanting to make a deal with you?"

"You still have to get out of the country. I could help you do that."

"I don't need no help," Duret said flatly, and switched his attention to Todd. "Who are you, mister?"

Todd Bracken's face was a ghostly white. His eyes were spread wide and his mouth worked convulsively. "You murdered my wife, my baby," he began, and suddenly lunged for Duret. A long-blade knife glittered in his hand.

Ben, standing beside the outlaw, moved fast. He struck out with his fist, caught Todd on the shoulder. It knocked Bracken

116

off balance. Following up quickly, Ben drove another blow into Todd's jaw. Todd reeled off, fell heavily into the brush.

Duret stared at him in silence. Finally he said: "The husband, that it? Reckon he had a call comin'. But you keep an eye on him, Earl. He makes another move like that, kill him." He came back to Coe. "You're a mighty handy boy to have around, *amigo*. *Muchas gracias*."

"We better be moving on, Turk," Earl spoke up then. "Liable to be a posse riding our tail by now."

"Sure, sure," Duret said. His glance was again upon Laurie. "Ain't met everybody here yet. Like that little filly there."

"Forget her," Earl said quickly. "Woman got you caught the last time. Let's don't be asking for it again."

"You're too scary, Earl. Might be worth the risk."

Saul Bracken bristled. He took a step forward. "Leave her be," he said, his voice different, strong and threatening. "She's my daughter. You'll have to kill me afore you can lay a hand on her."

Duret shrugged, clearly unimpressed. The moments were growing critical—and Laurie was in great danger. A harsh fear clutched at Ben Coe as he recalled the terrible fate that had befallen Todd Bracken's wife. He said: "Turk, we ought to be pulling out of here. There's a posse, a different one, loose around here somewhere. Looking for me. They might stumble onto us if we stay around much longer."

Duret's flat eyes swiveled restlessly to him. "Reckon maybe you're right, *amigo*. You figure to ride with us?"

Coe said: "It's what I had in mind."

"How far?"

"Mexico. For a spell, anyway. Soon as things cool off, I thought I'd drop back over into Arizona Territory. Nobody knows me there."

Duret said: "Good enough. Only you're on your own. You

understand that?"

"Sure," Ben said. He was watching Laurie. He saw the disbelief and shock crowd into her eyes. From the edge of the clearing Todd spoke up.

"What did I tell you, Laurie? Didn't I tell you right about him?" There was a note of triumph in his voice.

Laurie met Ben's gaze. She stared at him for a long moment, and then he saw the light go out of her eyes. She lowered her face, turned away from him. If only he could tell her the truth. That he was only pretending to go along with Duret, long enough to win his confidence and allow him to effect a recapture. But there was no way, no time. She would believe Todd was right.

"You got a gun?" Turk's voice asked.

He nodded woodenly. He walked to the brush where Kemm had tossed it. Recovering it, he thrust it into his holster.

"Are we just going to leave all these people here, standing around?" Earl asked. "Kind of risky if there's a posse off there in the woods."

"Reckon we had ought to shut them up," Duret said with no apparent qualms.

"Gunshots would be heard," Coe put in hurriedly. "Bring that posse down on us fast. How about just tying them up? Couldn't do any harm, that way."

Duret nodded. "Good idea. You boys get busy."

Earl took the rope Kemm had brought in earlier to use on Coe. He cut it into shorter lengths and handed some to Coe and some to the third outlaw who had stood silently by during all the conversation. They began at once to bind the Brackens, Preston, and Kemm. Coe managed to work his way to Laurie. He looped the rope about her wrists, not pulling it tight.

"Laurie, you've got to believe me," he said in a low whisper. "I have to do it this way. Trust me."

She did not look at him. Saul Bracken glared up into his face. "You dirty sneak!" he said. "I should have believed my boy! He knew what he was talkin' about. Maybe you wasn't Turk Duret, but you're sure one of his bunch."

Ben ignored the old man's acid words. "Laurie, please listen. . . ."

"Let's get out of here," Duret said. "Come on, Coe, if you're ridin' with us."

"Good bye, Laurie," Ben whispered. But she did not look up or make any reply.

They rode away from the clearing, the sound of Todd Bracken's curses ringing in their ears. Duret, glancing back, shrugged. "If I had the time, I'd go back and shut that jaybird up with a bullet. Put him out of his misery."

"He's sure got hisself a powerful hate for you," Earl observed.

"Guess he has a right," Duret answered. He turned to Ben, riding a step back and to one side. "You have any idea where that posse might be, cowboy?"

Coe made a show of thinking about that. Finally: "I figure we would be better off over in the valley. They've been through there. If they're keeping an eye on this trail, we'll be spotted sooner or later."

Duret said nothing but immediately swung his horse sharply left and slanted for the valley. The others followed, Ben still bringing up the rear. They traveled another mile and began to enter the heavier timber.

"I saw you talkin' to that little filly back there, Coe," Duret said. "That what all the ruckus was about? Her pa maybe didn't cotton the idea of you two?"

"Little like that," Ben answered.

He was watching the third man narrowly, alert for the first opportunity that would present itself. He could not afford a shoot-out with them. He would have small chance against their combined guns. And he did not want Duret killed. The outlaw had to live to hang. Tom Kilgore had given his life for that. And Marcelino Baca, too. For those reasons he could take no chances on losing his own life. He must stay alive to deliver Turk Duret.

They reached the grove, far enough now from the Brackens and Preston to make a move. Ahead of him the outlaws dropped into a single file as the trail narrowed because of the thick underbrush. The man called Earl was in the lead. He was followed by Duret after whom came the third outlaw, his name still unknown. Coe brought up the rear. The going became slower as the trail grew more confined. Ben could see no possibility of moving up quietly, getting the third man out of the way and capturing Turk Duret. And then quite suddenly opportunity presented itself.

They reached a wide place in the trail. Duret pulled off to the side, allowed the third outlaw to pass him by. He waited for Ben.

"Coe," he said, kneeing his horse in beside Ben's, "you know this country pretty well?"

Ben, his eyes on the backs of the two other outlaws, now several yards ahead, nodded. He came to a halt.

"What's up?" Duret asked, pulling in.

"Horse picked up a rock, I think." He dismounted and examined the horse's hoof. "Guess not," he said shortly, and swung back into the saddle. The two outlaws were well out of sight, beyond a bend in the trail.

"What did you ask me? Did I know this country?"

Duret said: "Yeah. Do you?"

"Like the back of my hand," Coe said, lying generously. "Why?"

"Well, I've got a little business to tend to when we get close to a town they call Salvation. Then I want to get into Mexico, the quickest way I can."

"I know the road," Ben said.

"You get me there fast and I'll make it worth your while."

"We got a deal," Ben said, and waited for Duret to move past him and resume his place on the trail. He watched the outlaw go by. When he was an arm's length past, he drew his gun. He brought it down hard on the outlaw's skull. Duret grunted and doubled forward in his saddle.

Coe acted quickly. He jerked off his neckerchief, bound it around the outlaw's mouth, effectively gagging him. He took a short length of soft rope that he found in the gray's saddlebags, and tied the outlaw's hands securely behind his back.

"Hey, Turk?" Earl's call came from farther along the trail.

"We're coming!" Coe shouted back. "Keep going."

He took up the reins of Duret's horse and turned about. He threw a glance to the south, to where Earl and the third man were. There was no sign of them. They, evidently, were still beyond the bend. With Duret yet unconscious, Coe started up the valley, towing the outlaw's horse behind him. If he could get a little distance between themselves and the others before they became suspicious, he might avoid a fight.

He had scarcely got that thought out of his mind when he heard them pounding up behind him. He glanced over his shoulder. They were rounding the bend, Earl in the lead, the other man not far behind him. They were coming on fast. Duret groaned and stirred in the saddle. Coe saw then a widening in the trail, a small clearing where an upthrusting of rock formed a solid shoulder. He reached it, drew quickly off to the side.

He dismounted, stepped to Duret's horse. Taking the outlaw's pistol, he stuck it into his own belt, after which he tied both horses securely to a stout cedar growing near the edge of the rock. This done, he moved back to the trail. Earl and his partner, suspicious, had halted. They waited a few yards distant. With a gun in either hand, Coe stepped boldly out into the center of the trail.

"I'm a U.S. deputy marshal!" he called out. "I'm taking Turk Duret back to Capital City to hang. I'm giving you a warning now. You try and stop me and I'll kill you. Both of you!"

Earl half turned in his saddle, threw a smirking glance at the other man. "Well, now, lawman, maybe you will and maybe you won't," he said and reached for his pistol.

Coe threw himself to one side, fired both guns fast. One of the bullets caught Earl in the chest. He went out of the saddle and fell heavily to the ground. Ben, his guns now lined on the third man, waited. "How about it?"

The outlaw raised his hands slowly, carefully over his head. "Not for me, Marshal," he drawled. "I was just along for the ride. I run into that pair up the road a few miles. Once knew Duret."

"You with Earl when he helped spring Duret from the sheriff?"

"Nope. That was Earl and some other waddy. He caught himself a bullet, I hear." He stopped, added: "I don't want no truck with the law. If it's all same to you, I'll just mosey along."

"Maybe what you're telling me is true and maybe it's not. But I don't have time to fool around with it now. What's your name?"

"Bass. Friends call me Sam."

"All right, Sam Bass. Ride on and keep riding. Don't look back."

"Yes, sir," the cowboy said. He wheeled about and started down the trail.

Coe watched him until he was out of sight. He loaded the dead outlaw onto his horse, secured the body, and returned to where Duret, now angrily conscious, waited. The outlaw greeted him with a scowling hatred and a thorough cursing but Coe ignored the man. There was one thing yet to be sure of—Sam Bass. He climbed to the top of the rock and turned his eyes to the south. Minutes later he saw a rider, little more than a speck in the long distance. Bass had done as he had been ordered; he had kept on riding.

With a sigh Coe returned to his horse. He climbed into the saddle, motioned Duret to pull out ahead of him. With Earl's horse bringing up the rear, they started off. It would be a hard ride to Capital City.

XXII

They hanged Turk Duret for his crimes that next day at high noon. It took place within the high walls of the territorial prison on a new, well-constructed gallows. It was true the execution was witnessed by only a few but word of the outlaw's death at the firm hands of the law would spread quickly throughout the country. Before another day had passed, the knowledge would be well established that a just law now existed.

It had cost the lives of two fine lawmen, Kilgore and Marcelino Baca. But the victory was won and there now was small question of statehood. Ben Coe, shaved, rested, and dressed in clean clothing, swung up to the saddle and rode slowly for the iron grillwork gate in the south wall of the yard. Kansas was a long way off. And it would be a lonely ride.

Never before had his solitary travels been a burden to him. Indeed, he had preferred it that way, going and coming as fancy suited him or the job required. It was different now. He had continually to resist the urge to glance sideward, to see if Laurie Bracken were not at his elbow. Strange how those few, short hours with her had so completely altered his life. But Laurie had made her decision; she had been faced with a difficult choice and had made it. He did not blame her for it, only himself for not making it easier for her. The trouble was, there had been no time. Things had happened so fast. If he could have talked with her, made her understand his side of it.

"*Adiós,* Marshal," the gatekeeper called, swinging back the lace ironwork. *"Hasta la vista."*

Ben nodded and thought: *Not likely.* Chances were he never again would be in Capital City. His job lay in Kansas and, besides, there were too many memories left here to plague him. He would never again look at a towering, shadowed mountain or across the broad fling of a mesa without thinking of her.

He turned his new horse, a long-legged bay, onto the east road, toward home. He pulled up short. A hundred yards off to the right three riders waited in the shade of an apricot tree. As he watched, one of them separated from the others and hurried to meet him. Laurie! She was smiling, and Ben Coe realized at once that he had been wrong, that he had underestimated her love for him, that his own faith and trust in her had fallen short.

"What's the trouble, Marshal?" the gatekeeper called after him. "Lose somethin'?"

"Yes," Ben answered, "but I just found it."

He spurred the bay forward to meet her.

★ ★ ★ ★ ★

APACHE BASIN

★ ★ ★ ★ ★

I

To Dan Selkirk, after seven days and six nights on the trail, any town would look good. Apache Basin, lying on the eastern plateau of the New Mexico Territory, was especially appealing that summer evening. The burnished sun had dropped below its western rim and the night coolness had begun to drift in. Lamps in the shops along the dusty main street were coming on, and off somewhere in the ephemeral, breathless hush a sweet-voiced woman was singing an old, familiar hymn.

He leaned against a post on the porch of the Pecos River Hotel and took his ease. He had stabled his tired sorrel gelding, seen to it that he was well cared for. He had checked into the single-storied lodging house, bathed, shaved, changed to fresh, clean clothes. A good meal of steak and potatoes, hot biscuits and milk gravy was under his belt now. With the $1,000 Tod McGowan had entrusted to him for the herd he was to buy safely hidden in his room, he was ready to spend an evening enjoying himself.

He let his glance run slowly along the street. Not many persons were abroad yet. It was that time of day when men usually settled down to their suppers. Another hour would pass before Apache Basin came alive. He sorted the small business houses through his mind, noted particularly the saloons. The Golden Eagle appeared to be the largest and certainly the most prosperous-looking. Likely it would have gambling and a dance hall in conjunction with its liquid attractions.

It would draw the largest crowd—and that is what Dan Selkirk needed most of all—people milling about, laughing, talking, having their noisy arguments. The smell of a woman's perfume, of tobacco smoke and spilled whiskey and beer, the click of poker chips, the snap of cards. Days and nights upon end get mighty lonely for a man riding a solo trail. And there was no rush to reach the Alexander Ranch where he was to look over and buy, if he so decided, the herd that was being offered. At least, there was no critical rush. Alexander, a friend of McGowan's, had agreed to give Selkirk first look-see at the stock. He had stated in his letter he would hold up a full day on the sale for that purpose. There was time for a few hours' rest and relaxation.

He moved off the hotel gallery, stepped down into the loose, powdery dust, and angled across the street for the tall-standing Golden Eagle. He pushed through the scarred batwing doors, entered the broad room well lighted by half a dozen ceiling chandeliers and wall lamps. Three or four men were at the bar. The tables were unattended, but in an adjoining area a card game was under way.

Dan ordered a drink, strolled to where the poker session was in progress. He watched for a time, and, when one of the players finally rose in disgust and stalked off, he accepted the invitation of the other men and sat down. He played for an hour, lost as often as he won, and quit when he was somewhere near even. He returned to the bar, the edge gone from his desire to gamble.

The Golden Eagle had filled steadily while he played. The counter was lined now and at least half of the tables were occupied. He purchased a bottle, selected a corner, and settled down. Almost immediately one of the house girls separated herself from the crowd, walked to his table. He watched her cross the floor, an attractive, yellow-haired, dark-eyed woman,

128

clad in a blue and yellow dress that glittered with sequins in the lamplight. She was older than she looked, he guessed, but with the application of cosmetics and her careless, jaunty air, she appeared to be in her early twenties. She paused before him.

"I'm Clella," she said, smiling down. "Welcome to the Golden Eagle."

Selkirk grinned. "Obliged to you. Have a chair." Clella sat down. Dan waved to the bartender for a second glass. When it came, he poured her a drink. "You personally welcome all the newcomers to this place?" he asked.

"Only the ones I like the looks of," she replied, and toasted him with her glass. "Usually they tell me their names, however."

"Dan Selkirk," he said, and downed his drink. "Just riding through, headed east. And from farther west."

"About covers it, except for one thing. How long you expect to favor our fine city?"

"Only tonight. Got sick of my own company. Decided I needed to be around people for a spell so I swung wide and hauled up here." He hesitated, looked around the room. "Looks like I picked the right place. Everybody in the whole country must come here."

"Sooner or later," Clella said.

Smoke was beginning to hang toward the ceiling. The man at the piano struck up a tune. Several couples moved out onto the small, cleared area in the center of the room.

"You like to dance?" Clella asked.

"Good many things I do better," Dan answered, "but I'd sure admire to take a couple of turns." He got to his feet, waited beside her chair while she rose.

"Anything I need to do?" he wondered. "Like pay somebody, or something?"

She shook her head, smiled again. "You bought a bottle. That entitles you to my company, long as the bottle holds out. You buy another when it's gone and I still stick with you . . . if that's the way you want it."

"The way I want it," Dan said. "Hope that bartender has got plenty of bottles."

They moved out into the scatter of couples who were attempting to follow the piano's thump but who were hearing little of it above the saloon's hubbub. Selkirk, tall, dark-haired, square-faced, stood a full head and shoulders above the girl. They danced until the number ended, returned then to their table.

"You're not so bad," Clella said as she sat down. "With some of the men I run into, dancing is a day's hard work."

"Got music in my soul, I reckon." Dan grinned, and poured out fresh drinks.

They sat out the next few numbers, talking of the country, the town, of themselves. The bottle emptied; Dan signaled for a replacement. The whiskey was watered, he knew, but it didn't matter. He was enjoying himself. It was just what he had needed.

"You live here . . . in the saloon?" he asked during the course of their conversation.

"Upstairs. Number Five. Why?"

He shrugged. "Just wondered. Thought maybe you might have a home, be married even, and have a family."

Clella shook her head. "No home, no husband, no family. Only myself." She studied him for several moments. "Any more questions?"

He said: "Nope. Was just wondering."

Clella sighed. "I'll say this for you, Dan Selkirk, you're different from most of the men I come up against. I don't know whether I should consider it an insult or a compliment."

Dan said: "My folks always taught me to go only where I was invited. And, the fact is, I'm enjoying things the way they are. Talking to you, and listening and watching people."

"Well, here comes a damper on the party right now," Clella broke in, looking beyond Selkirk toward the door.

Dan turned about. A thick-shouldered, husky man wearing a star had come through the batwings. He halted just inside, glanced about the room.

"Jude Wade," Clella said. "The town's deputy marshal. Since Henry Corbin got hurt, he's taken over. Thinks he's a real big man."

Wade's eyes caught those of Selkirk. Immediately he crossed the saloon to the table where Clella and the young rider sat. He halted before them, his florid face hard.

"You Dan Selkirk?"

Dan stared at the lawman, surprised at the tone. He nodded. "That's me. Why?"

"Saw your name on the hotel register. My job is to know who rides into this town. You figure to stay around long?"

Selkirk, faintly angered by Wade's attitude, shrugged. "Depends. You got a law that says a pilgrim can't stop over for a night's sleep and a few drinks?"

"Don't get cute with me," Wade snapped. "I'll take you over and. . . ."

"Leave him alone, Jude," Clella said hurriedly. "He's just riding through, not bothering anybody."

"Keep out of this, you. . . ."

Selkirk was on his feet before the deputy could finish the sentence. Conversation in the saloon dwindled, then died completely.

"You got something like that to say to the lady, come on outside and say it to me," Selkirk invited in a low, even voice. "Without the badge and gun."

Jude Wade shifted uncertainly on his feet. He looked to his left, his right. Apparently opposition was something he had not expected. He squared his shoulders, made a stab at recovering

131

his dignity. "You say you're just passing through?"

"Could be. Don't remember saying for sure."

"My job is to find out such things, take a look at all the strangers," Wade said, stumbling a little with his words.

Someone in the saloon laughed. The piano player broke into a tune. Talk immediately resumed its normal, confused flow and the dancing started again. Wade stared at Dan, his eyes angry. Suddenly he turned on his heel and stalked off toward the gambling room. Selkirk watched him for a moment, then settled back into his chair. The hard corners of his mouth relented, softened.

"Don't mind Jude," Clella said. "He's got a big bark, nothing else. I'll be glad when Marshal Corbin gets back on the job. The whole town will be, I suspect."

Selkirk took a long swallow from his glass. He wagged his head slowly. "Got nothing against lawmen, but that kind always riles me. People can sure hang a badge on the wrong kind of man sometimes."

They danced again after that but the glow was gone from the pleasurable evening for Dan Selkirk. He now became aware of the weariness that dragged at him and the thought of a good night's sleep on a real bed was inviting. Near midnight he slipped a double eagle, unnoticed, into the pocket of Clella's dress, made his farewell, and departed. He went straight to the hotel and turned in, falling asleep almost instantly.

At 5:00 A.M. he was up. He dressed, ate breakfast at the one restaurant that was open, and then went to the stable. He saddled the sorrel himself, not trusting the heavy-eyed hostler to do the job, and, an hour later, was on the road leading eastward out of Apache Basin.

It was a fine morning. Cool and crisp with only a few clouds flung across the steel-blue sky overhead. He was loping along easily, thinking of Clella and how he would like to become better acquainted, when the sound of running horses on the road behind him brought his attention about. A half a dozen riders, he noted, coming up fast.

He did not alter his pace, merely pulled to the side of the road to permit them to pass. When they were nearer, he again glanced over his shoulder. He recognized Jude Wade, the deputy marshal. The remaining five were all strangers. Each man had drawn his gun, was holding it ready in his hand.

"Pull up!" Wade yelled and fired his pistol into the air. "Keep your hands where I can see them!"

A mixture of surprise and anger swept through Dan Selkirk. He drew the sorrel to a halt, wheeled about. He waited silently while the men rode up, halted.

"Keep them hands up!" Wade snarled. "Don't want to have to shoot you. Get his gun, Shad."

A burly, freckled redhead climbed from his horse, trotted to Dan. He reached for the weapon on Selkirk's hip. The tall rider touched the sorrel lightly with a spur, sidled away a few steps.

"Just hold on," he said quietly. "Reckon I'll have to have some reasons before I give up my gun to any man."

"You got a reason . . . because I say so!" Jude Wade yelled. "You want another? The bank in town was robbed this morning . . . and I figure you're the one who done it!"

II

Dan Selkirk stared at Deputy Jude Wade. "Bank robbery?" he echoed. "And you think I did it? Mister, you're plumb loco!"

"Maybe," the lawman said. "And don't go fiddle-footin' that horse again . . . not unless you want me to put a bullet in him. Get that gun, Shad."

The redhead again reached for Selkirk's gun, and this time succeeded in procuring it. He thrust it into the waistband of his dirty, worn Levi's.

"Come off that saddle," Wade ordered.

Dan swung off the sorrel slowly. A vague disturbance now moved through him, pushing aside the first hot rush of anger. He was a stranger in Apache Basin with no friends at all except Clella, the dance-hall girl, and her word would count for little, if at all. He glanced at the circle of grim men looking down at him. He would have a hard time proving himself to anyone.

"Quint, get down there and help Shad search him."

A dark-faced, wiry little rider dropped from his horse, hastened to the redhead's side. He drew his gun, stepped in behind Selkirk, and jammed the barrel into the tall cowboy's spine. Shad began to go through Dan's pockets. His probing fingers hesitated as they touched the bulge around the waist. Quickly he removed the money belt in which Dan carried McGowan's $1,000, handed it to the deputy marshal.

Selkirk said: "That money belongs to my boss, Tod McGowan. He sent me to buy up a herd for him."

Jude Wade made no reply. He dismounted, squatted on his heels, and methodically began to count the currency. Finished, he whistled. "A whole thousand dollars! Ain't never seen that much money in one pile." He threw a knowing glance at the men still mounted. "Reckon this proves I had the right idea about the robbery." He swung his attention back to Dan. "Now, where'd you hide the rest?"

"The rest of what?" Selkirk demanded, not understanding.

"The rest of the nine thousand dollars you took out of Bishop's bank, that's what!"

"You're plain out of your head!" Dan exclaimed. "I never robbed any bank and you know it."

"Don't give me that!" Wade barked, and struck out back-handed. The blow caught Dan on the side of the head, staggered him slightly.

A wild fury surged through the cowboy. He lunged at the

deputy, drove a rock-hard fist into the man's belly. A moment later he felt Shad's arms encircle his body, pin his hands to his sides. The round, hard barrel of Quint's revolver once again gouged into his back.

"Try that once more, mister," the redhead grated into his ear, "and you'll get full of daylight."

Jude Wade, doubled forward from Selkirk's driving fist, straightened up. His face was distorted with pain and rage. He took a long step toward Dan.

"Ease up, Jude," one of the posse members said. "You asked for that." He turned then to Dan. "Better tell him what he wants to know."

"I've told him," Selkirk said crisply. "That money belongs to my boss, Tod McGowan. He gave it to me to buy cattle with."

"A man can't buy many steers with a thousand dollars," another rider commented.

"Not at fifteen dollars a head."

"The cash is for a binder," Selkirk explained. "If I like the looks of this herd I'm going to see, I'll bind the deal with the thousand, draw a draft on McGowan for the balance."

Wade said: "Pretty good yarn but you're not fooling me any. I've heard them long tales before. Now, the way I've got it figured, you got inside the bank sometime after midnight and got nine thousand dollars. You kept one thousand, hid the rest somewhere, figuring to come back later when things had blowed over and pick it up. . . ."

"That's a flat lie," Selkirk said.

"You left the saloon around midnight. . . ."

"And went to bed and straight to sleep. Got up at five."

"You prove that? Anybody see you go to bed? Anybody swear you never left your room until you got up at five?"

"No, of course not. Nobody saw me."

"And what about this boss of yours, McGowan or whatever

135

his name is? What's the name of his outfit?"

"The Circle TM. It's a spread over in the Burnt Creek country."

"Never heard of it!" Wade declared triumphantly. "And it would take a letter a couple of weeks, going and coming, to find out for sure. You're riding a lame horse, friend. You can't prove nothing."

"I was in the hotel asleep from midnight until five this morning. I wasn't near this bank you say was robbed. And you can't prove that I was."

"Oh, no?" Wade said, waving the money belt at Dan. "I figure this is plenty of proof. It's part of the stolen cash. All I got to do is make you tell where you hid the rest."

"Something you'll never do because I sure don't know anything about it," Selkirk said.

Jude Wade studied the tall cowboy for a moment. "That's the way it's going to be, eh? Well, it's up to you. I've handled your kind before and they've always come across when I get done with them. But I like to give a man his chance. Now, I'm asking you for the last time . . . where'd you hide the nine thousand dollars?"

"Maybe we ought to take him back to town," an older man on a gray horse suggested. "Seems Corbin ought to have a hand in this."

"Forget Corbin, Jonas," Wade shot back. "I'm running this my way. And if you don't like it, move out. I'm not going back until I get the answer to what I want to know." The deputy said then, coming back to Dan: "Save us both a lot of time and trouble. Speak up and tell me what I want to know."

"You've got the wrong man," Selkirk answered. "I keep trying to tell you that."

"Lousy, stinking saddle tramp!" Wade shouted, and swung a balled fist at Dan. "Only one way to handle your kind!"

Selkirk dodged to one side. The blow grazed his cheek. He drove a hard, straight right to the deputy's jaw. Jude wilted, dropped back a step, and sat down. Quint's gun dug into Selkirk's spine, sent a wave of pain coursing through his body. He throttled the urge to hurl himself onto the lawman and hammer some sense into his round, red face.

"That was your last chance," Quint murmured in his quiet voice. "Next time I start pulling the trigger."

Wade shook his head, threw aside the fog that evidently clouded his mind. He got to his feet, glared at Dan. "You're going to be mighty sorry for that," he said in a voice that trembled with rage. "It's going to be a real pleasure, making you talk."

"There's nothing to talk about," Dan said. "You just as well get that in your head now. I don't know anything about that bank, and that thousand in the belt belongs to me . . . or to my boss. You get in touch with him. He'll prove that to you."

"I ain't swallowing no yarn like that," Wade said. "I got you dead to rights with part of the bank's money. Now you're going to tell me what you done with the rest of it. I'm through fooling around. Get a rope, Shad."

"Wait a minute there, Jude!" the man named Jonas cut in quickly. "You know Corbin won't stand for any rough stuff like that!"

"The old man ain't here. Besides, I'm marshal while he's laid up. I'll handle this my way."

"Maybe this man is guilty but that doesn't call for using a rope."

"Get the hell out of here, Jonas!" Wade snarled. "Ride on back to town and keep your nose out of my business. I know what I'm doing."

Jonas leaned over, said something to the man next to him. Immediately both wheeled about and headed for Apache Basin.

"Gone for the boss, sure as shootin'," Shad commented.

"You want I should stop them?"

"Let them go," the deputy replied. "By the time they can get to Corbin and he can ride out here, I'll be done with this bucko." He shifted his gaze to the sixth member. "What about you, Eli? You want to go bawling to the marshal about how tough I am on a bank robber? Or are you backing my hand?"

"I'm still here, ain't I?" Eli answered.

Wade said: "Good thing. Come on, let's get started at it." He glanced about. "Some trees back there a ways. We'll take him there."

The dark-faced Quint nodded. "Reckon you still want the rope, then?"

"Yes, sir. This jasper is going to do some fast talking or he'll find his neck stretched out of joint."

Dan Selkirk felt the blood chill in his veins at the deputy's words. That Jude Wade would go to all lengths to prove himself was unquestionable. After their small altercation in the Golden Eagle that previous night during which his ego had suffered badly and now, today, again getting the worst of their meeting, he would stop at nothing to redeem himself and his stature as a lawman. If there were only some way to get to Marshal Corbin, he might be able to straighten the whole affair out. It sounded as though Corbin was a fair and honest lawman, one who perhaps would listen to reason. But Jude Wade was determined not to afford him the opportunity. He was dead set on extracting a confession whether his prisoner was guilty or not. He thought then of the man named Jonas, and the rider who had returned to Apache Basin with him. Maybe they would get there in time to send Corbin back.

It was not difficult to see what lay ahead for him. And thinking of it, Dan came to the decision that he was not about to become a willing participant. Perhaps, if he could cause further delay, allow more time for Corbin to arrive, he would have a better chance. He glanced at Shad, standing off to his left, then to Quint on the right. Both, with drawn guns, were silently awaiting the deputy's orders. Wade was returning the thousand dollars currency to the money belt. That done, he tied the lacings, looped it over the horn of his saddle. "Mount up," he said, and then swung onto his horse. "Let's get over to them trees."

"You heard him," Shad said, prodding Selkirk. "Get aboard that horse of yours and don't try no funny business."

Dan pivoted to the sorrel, stepped to the saddle. He heard leather squeak as Shad mounted his horse. He could not hear or see Quint. He would have to gamble on that man's attention being, at that moment, diverted. He dug his spurs into the sorrel's flanks. The big red horse, startled, lunged forward, straight at Jude Wade. The lawman was caught unawares, in the act of turning about. As they came together, Selkirk's outstretched fingers clawed at the money belt hanging on the deputy's saddle. He caught it, jerked it free as the sorrel, rubbing hard against Wade's animal, struggled to avoid a hard collision. A yell went up from Quint, or Shad. Dan did not know which. He was bent low, trying to get clear of Wade's horse and make a run for the trees.

A gunshot blasted the hot morning air. Dan heard the vicious whine of a bullet close by. He did not stop, but drove on. Wade was half out of the saddle, almost displaced by the sorrel's close contact. Suddenly he was clear of the lawman's buckskin. He ducked down over the big red horse's neck, prepared to make the short dash for the trees. Abruptly he pulled to a halt. The posse man, Eli, was before him, blocking his path with a leveled rifle.

Selkirk jerked hard on the sorrel's reins, sought to pull him aside. Something struck him from behind. He fought to stay upright but he had no strength. He felt himself fold forward, clutched at the horn. Vaguely he could hear Jude Wade shouting and cursing but the lawman's words seemed remote, unintelligible. Only one thing was getting through to his consciousness. He had failed in his attempt to break away. Now, matters would be worse for him. He again tried to sit up, fought himself to regain control of his senses. They didn't have a rope around his neck yet—and they wouldn't, if he could manage it. Maybe there still was a chance to get away. . . . That hope died as another blow to the back of his head plunged him into total blackness.

III

He was still in the saddle. The horse was his own, the sorrel gelding. Dan remained quiet, kept his head down, his eyes closed, as voices and words began to penetrate his clouded mind.

"You sure what you're doing, Jude? You know how Corbin is."

"One thing you get straight, Eli. I don't give a hootin' damn about what Corbin thinks! Or what anybody else thinks, either. People around here better get used to the kind of law I give them."

"Sure, sure. I was only thinking. . . ."

"Forget the old man! Chances are he's done for and won't never get back on the job anyway. Too old and too soft. Town's outgrowed him and needs somebody like me."

There was a long pause. Then Wade's voice continued: "Dammit, Shad! Why'd you have to hit him so hard? I wish there was some water around here we could douse him with. I ain't got all day. Reach over there and shake him up some, Quint. See if you can bring him to."

Selkirk felt the man's hand on his shoulder. He lifted his head, met the rider's small, narrow-eyed gaze.

"He's awake," Quint said. "Reckon he's been playing 'possum with us."

"Real cute, eh?" the deputy said. "Well, I'll show him what being cute really means. He'll be wishing he'd stayed asleep for good before I'm done with him. You sure his hands are tied good, Quint?"

"Just like you said for me to."

Dan saw they were at the edge of the grove. Evidently they had moved off the road and reached the trees while he was unconscious. He became aware then of the rope around his neck. He glanced up. It had been thrown over a thick limb. The loose end was being held by Jude Wade. Dan felt cold sweat break out over his body as he looked at the deputy.

"This is no joke to me," he said. "That horse of mine is a bit skittish. He's liable to run out from under me if anybody makes a sudden move. He does, you've got a murder on your hands."

Wade laughed. "Hear that boys? We've caught us a bank robber, and if he gets killed, accidental like, during the questioning, he says it will be murder. And by his own horse!"

Shad laughed loudly at the joke. The man called Quint only shrugged. Eli said nothing, merely watched in frozen silence.

"One thing you forget," Dan said, "is that those two men who were with you are riding back to town. They know what you're up to. Anything happens to me, they'll face you with a murder charge."

Jude grinned. "Anything that happens will be a pure accident. I got three men right here who'll testify to that. What good is the word of two who didn't see anything against mine and three men who were right on the spot?"

"You sure got it all figured down to a nub," Dan said. "But you're going to a lot of trouble for nothing. I don't know anything about a bank robbery."

"So you said," Wade murmured. He pulled in the rope's slack.

Selkirk felt the rough fibers tighten about his throat. The sorrel stirred between his legs.

"Whoa, boy," he said softly. "Easy now."

"Where'd you hide the rest of the money?" Wade asked, keeping the noose taut. "In the hotel? In the stable?"

"Never saw that money," Selkirk replied, having difficulty in getting the words out. "Had nothing to do with it."

"Where is it?" the deputy repeated. "I ain't fooling with you, mister! I want to know where you hid it?"

"Tell him!" Eli suddenly cried. "For the love of heaven, Selkirk, tell him! If you don't, he'll have you swinging sure as God made grass!"

"I can't . . . because . . . I don't know," Dan gasped. "He can string me up if he's a mind to, but I can't tell him something I don't know."

"Hold up, Jude!" Eli said in an urgent voice. "He's telling you the truth. Ain't no man going to let himself get that close to glory and be lying."

Wade spat in disgust. "You're bad as the old man. You don't know these hardcases like I do. They'll lie with their last breath, just to spite the law. You just watch . . . he'll talk."

"Better wait up," Quint's low voice broke in. "Here comes Corbin."

"Blast it!" Wade said feelingly. "He would come poking his nose in about now."

"How'd he get here so fast? Ain't been time enough for Jonas to tell him."

Wade said: "He saw us ride out. I expect he hitched up and followed. Who's that with him?"

"Oscar Bishop."

The rope about Dan Selkirk's neck went slack. He twisted about, looked toward the road. Two men in a light buggy were cutting across the open country, heading for the trees. He heaved a sigh of thankfulness. Now he would get a chance to state his side of the matter.

"I'll do the talking," Wade said in a low, warning voice. "All of you keep your lip buttoned. Means you, too," he added, glaring at Dan, "unless you want more trouble than you already got."

Selkirk said—"I'll talk when it's time."—and turned his attention to the approaching buggy.

The vehicle rolled up, halted. Marshal Henry Corbin, a thin-faced, elderly man with white hair and a long, drooping mustache, climbed stiffly from the buggy. His right arm was in a sling and he limped slightly. The second man, Bishop the banker, was about the same age. There the resemblance ended. He was moon-faced, paunchy, clean-shaven. He was dressed in a drab gray suit.

Corbin's bitter face betrayed the anger that sawed at him. He stalked to where Selkirk sat on the sorrel. He reached up, lifted the noose from the tall rider's neck. Taking a knife from his pocket, he opened it, cut the cord that bound his wrists. Only then did he turn to Wade.

"What's the meaning of this, Jude?"

"This is the jasper that robbed Bishop's bank," the deputy said. "Found some of the money on him. I was just fixing to find out where he'd hid the rest when you drove up."

"By lynching him?" Corbin said scornfully. "Never yet saw a dead man who could talk."

"Didn't figure to really hang him. Only meant to scare him a mite."

Bishop had climbed out of the buggy. He walked to the marshal's side. "I hear you say you found the money on him?"

Wade nodded. "A thousand dollars of it. Got it here in his money belt."

"What about the rest?"

"Just what I'm trying to make him say."

Marshal Corbin took the thick band of leather. He stared at it for a long minute. To Bishop he said: "Do you have any way of telling for sure if this is part of your money, Oscar?"

The banker shook his head. "Not particularly. The bandit took only currency. All old bills. I didn't have any numbers, if that's what you mean."

"That's what I mean," Corbin said. He looked up at Selkirk. "Where'd you get this money, son?"

Dan explained again that it belonged to his employer, Tod McGowan. that he was on a cattle buying trip. When he was finished, Corbin folded the belt, thrust it into his own pocket.

"I'll have to hold onto it until we get this all straightened out. Have you any way to prove what you say?"

"Get in touch with McGowan," Dan said. "That's the only way I know."

"As far as I'm concerned, that's just a stall," Jude Wade said. "It's part of the stolen money. He kept that much, stashed away the rest. He'll own up to that if we push him hard enough."

"Your kind of pushing could end up getting us no place," Corbin said dryly. "Glad we run into Tom and Bert Keely down the road. They told us what you were up to. And it looks like we might have got here just in time."

"Doing my job, that's all," Wade said sullenly. "Best way to handle these owlhoots."

Oscar Bishop said: "Could be Jude's right, Henry. This Selkirk's story sounds a bit far-fetched. And it'll take ten days or two weeks to prove it out, one way or another. If it turns out he's not our man, or one of the men who robbed my bank, the real outlaws will be a long ways off."

"We'll keep right on looking," Corbin said. "I ain't saying I believe this boy's story . . . or that I don't. I just figure to lock him up until I know for sure. Meantime, we'll keep on hunting for whoever might have done it."

Locked up. Ten days or two weeks. Dan Selkirk considered that, frowned. "You hold me that long, Marshal, I'll lose out on the herd I was supposed to buy. The man that owns it promised to hold it only one day for me. It's real important to my boss."

"No other way I can handle it," Corbin said gruffly. "You want to know the truth about this, I'd guess Jude here is right about you, but I ain't one to jump at a conclusion. You just better be happy that I'm locking you up so's you'll have a chance to prove him wrong." The marshal spun about to his deputy. "Take the prisoner in and put him in a cell," he directed. "Oscar and me will be right behind you so don't try any of your tricks."

Wade made no comment. He rode up beside Dan. Shad and Quint mounted up as Corbin and the banker walked back to the buggy and climbed aboard.

"You ride the middle," Jude said to Selkirk, motioning the other riders to positions on either side of the tall cowboy. "I'll be right behind you with a gun pointed at your back. I'm hoping you'll try to make a break for it."

Selkirk gave him a tight grin. "Reckon you'd like that just fine," he said, and moved out on the sorrel. When they reached the road, the two men and the buggy were not far to the rear.

"No cause to hurry," Corbin called to Wade, his meaning plain.

They reached Apache Basin a short time later, headed first for the livery barn that stood near the jail. A hostler trotted out to meet them and take over the horses. Wade, on the ground first, waited for Selkirk to dismount, then seized him firmly by the arm. They watched as the buggy rolled in, halted. The deputy maneuvered Selkirk around to where they were near the banker.

"I know this jasper's the one who's got your money, Oscar," Wade said in a low whisper. "There ain't no use in letting things drag on like the marshal wants. Could be somebody else might stumble onto the money, where he hid it, or maybe even somebody was with him who'll come back and pick it up. Then you'll be out the whole thing."

"Just what I'm worrying about," Bishop said. "But what can I do?"

"You get the marshal out of the way and I'll make Selkirk talk. . . ."

Wade ceased his hurried whispering as Corbin turned around. Oscar Bishop frowned, gnawed thoughtfully at his lower lip. Understanding came to him a moment later. He nodded slightly to Wade. "Henry," he said, circling the buggy to meet the old lawman, "come on over to the bank with me. I want to check with Horace on those bills. Could be we do have some numbers that will help me identify the money."

Corbin said: "Sure, Oscar. Something like that would mighty quick clear up this problem." He motioned to Wade. "Take care of the prisoner, Jude."

The deputy nodded, remained quiet while the two older men struck off toward the street. When they were beyond hearing, he turned to Quint. "Get Eli away from here and don't let him come back. Take him over to the saloon and buy him a drink. Me and Shad want to be alone with our friend here for a spell."

Quint disappeared into the stable, returned at once with Eli. Together they headed for the Golden Eagle. Selkirk set himself for what he knew lay ahead. He had no particular fear but a strong anger began to rise within him. He jerked away from Jude Wade's grasp. Instantly the deputy and the burly Shad closed in on him, pinned his arms to his sides.

"Not so fast, bucko," Wade murmured with a crooked smile. "You ain't going nowhere . . . not just yet."

"You heard what Corbin said," Selkirk reminded him.

"Ain't nobody going to blame me for roughing up a prisoner

146

who tried to escape," the deputy said. "Not even old Corbin."

The two men started for the stable, propelling Dan between them. They reached the wide doorway, entered. The hostler was beginning to unsaddle the horses.

"Let that go," Wade ordered. "Get out front and stay there. You hear something going on, don't come nosing back to find out what it is. Understand? And if you see somebody coming, sing out."

"Sure, Jude," the hostler said, and hurried into the yard.

Wade swung slowly about, faced Dan. His eyes glittered brightly and the corners of his mouth were pulled down to a cruel sneer. "Now, bucko, we're going to have us some fun. Get him into that back stall, Shad."

IV

Dan Selkirk's hands were free—free, that is, to the point they were no longer locked together with a cord. He had Marshal Henry Corbin to thank for that. And as long as he could use his hard knuckled fists, he held little fear of Jude Wade and the burly Shad. But getting the chance to use them was another matter. Silent, he allowed Wade and Shad to push and shove him into a wide, double stall at the rear of the barn. The deputy took no chances.

He leveled his gun at Dan. "Grab him," he said to Shad. "Hold him tight. Got some settling to do with him."

Shad slipped his thick arms through Selkirk's, pinning them back. He forced them together, thrusting Dan's head and shoulders forward.

"Help yourself, Jude," he said in a gleeful, expectant voice.

The deputy swung hard. Selkirk jerked to one side. The blow skidded harmlessly off the side of his head.

"Damn it!" Wade snapped. "Hold him still!"

Dan felt Shad's grip upon his arms tighten. Pain shot through his shoulders, down his back. He clamped his jaws together and, through narrowed eyes, watched Jude get set for a long, roundhouse blow that, if it connected, would surely belt him into unconsciousness. A thought came to him. He estimated its possibility of success quickly. Slim, but it might work. It was his only hope, anyway. He braced himself.

Jude Wade started forward, throwing all his weight into the blow. Selkirk, ignoring the pain in his shoulders, allowed himself to sag in Shad's arms. The deputy surged in. Selkirk suddenly lifted his feet, drove them forward with all his strength. The hard corners of his boot heels buried themselves in the deputy's belly. Breath exploded from Jude's flared mouth, his eyes rolled back grotesquely as a wave of pain enveloped him. He buckled forward. Selkirk churned furiously with both feet, kicked himself free of the deputy's collapsing body.

"Hey . . . !" Shad yelled, completely taken by surprise.

Selkirk's feet came down, found solid purchase on the stable's dirt floor. He dug in with his heels, threw his weight against Shad, began to drive backward. Shad, suddenly off balance, stumbled. Dan's efforts caught the big man's momentum, kept him going. Shad tripped over his own feet, recovered himself momentarily, and then crashed into the side of the stall. Dan heard Shad gasp as breath was driven from his lungs, but the vise-like grasp about his arms slackened only slightly.

He threw himself to one side, dragged Shad about. Again he drove backward. Shad, still off balance and sucking for wind, tried to halt himself. Selkirk's strength and motion were too much for him. He back-pedaled furiously, awkwardly, came up hard against the unyielding and sharp corner of the stall. A yell of pain ripped from him as his spine and head made brutal contact. His arms went limp, dropped to his sides. Like a cat, Dan Selkirk spun away from the rider, whirled, and struck. The blow carried the full power of his weight and motion. It caught

Shad flush on the chin and the man went down with a groan.

Dan moved in on him quickly. He recovered his gun, thrust it back into its holster. He turned then to Jude Wade. The deputy crouched in a corner, was being violently sick from the terrible blow he had taken in the stomach. Selkirk gave him only fleeting notice; he would be a problem to no one for several minutes. The important thing now was to escape, to get out of the stable while he had the chance. The sorrel, still saddled, was standing with the other horses near the front of the barn where the hostler had left them. Dan sprang onto the saddle. He wheeled about, rode quickly through the stable, past the still silent Shad, the suffering Jude Wade, to a rear door. It was closed. He was forced to dismount in order to open it but that took only moments, and shortly he was on the outside.

He paused then to consider his position. He needed to think, to decide what must be done next. But it was not safe to remain where he was—in an alley, it appeared, with buildings and houses close by. Directly ahead and some distance away he could see a grove of trees beyond the last structures. That would do for the time being.

He put the sorrel to a slow trot, avoiding any unnecessary hoof drumming, and passed quickly along the houses until he gained the trees. It was a small park, it appeared, showing signs of having hosted numerous picnics during the years. He chose a spot where he and the gelding would be well hidden but that would afford him a full view of the town's outskirts. The distance was such that he would have ample time to mount up and ride on if any pursuers suddenly broke into sight.

He was in a tough spot. He had to admit that. Time was growing short and McGowan's friend, Alexander, would not hold the option on the herd longer than he had promised. And it was useless to ride on without the $1,000 that Alexander required to bind the deal. That part had been made clear to

McGowan—no cash binder, no sale. Dan had a brief notion to return to town, hunt up Marshal Corbin, and take the money from him forcibly. It was a useless idea. He could never pull it off, and, besides, the money was probably now in the bank, locked away. Selkirk muttered a curse, fully realizing his hopeless position. If ever a man was between a rock and a hard place, with nowhere to turn except one way—find the real bank robber. That solution struck him suddenly, and just as quickly the size of the chore dawned upon him. He didn't know where to begin; he would have to go it alone. He could expect no help from the townspeople or from the law. Indeed, he would have to avoid Apache Basin's two lawmen completely. They would be searching for him. And Jude Wade, anxious to prove himself, would be raging like a wild man, heading up posses and passing no possibilities by. What was more, if Wade ever laid hands on him again, he could depend on never reaching the town's jail alive. The deputy would take no chance on him escaping again.

As for Marshal Corbin, he might as well forget him entirely. The old lawman had a single-gaited mind. His one solution was to lock Dan in a cell and wait. And that could mean several days, two weeks probably. And Selkirk knew he did not have that kind of time to spare. He actually had only a day, two at the most. In that time he must run down the outlaw, or outlaws, who had robbed the bank, capture them, turn them over to Corbin. He then must claim his own $1,000 and be on his way. Two days at the most and that would be cutting it mighty thin, especially when he was a stranger to the country, knowing no one and having no friends. He thought then of Clella. She was the only one he could turn to; she might have some ideas. She would likely be aware of any strangers who had appeared in Apache Basin recently, remained only briefly, and ridden on. And he could trust her. He was certain of that. But getting to her, to the Golden Eagle, and room Number 5 on the second floor, could be quite a problem. And it would have to be done at once—in broad daylight.

V

Selkirk walked to the edge of the grove and studied the irregular horizon of Apache Basin roof tops. He located the higher silhouette of the Golden Eagle. It was to his right, one fortunate thing in his favor. It would not be necessary to cross behind or go near the stable where he had left Jude Wade and the man called Shad. He gave them a moment's thought; both should have recovered by this time, be up on their feet and getting a search party under way. Keeping out of sight was going to be difficult.

He returned his attention to the Golden Eagle. He should do his moving about on foot, he concluded. There was a lesser chance of being noticed. But the sorrel should be somewhere close by in event he needed to leave in a hurry. That immediately posed a new problem. The big red gelding, familiar now to Wade and several others, would have to be hidden. He could not stand out in the open.

Between the grove and the saloon there stood a fairly large house with a barn and two or three smaller outbuildings. Someone's residence was his guess. The distance from it to the Golden Eagle appeared to be around fifty yards or so. If he could reach it, unseen, he could hide the sorrel in the barn. There, he would be handy. That assumed, of course, there was no one presently inside the barn. He considered other ideas, discarded them all, and came back to the original plan. It was worth the gamble. The barn had a rear door. He could enter from that point, look the place over before he led the gelding inside.

He mounted at once, rode the length of the grove, and then streaked across the open ground to the back of the barn. Near it, he pulled the sorrel down to a walk, approached quietly. He halted at the door, remained in the saddle, and listened for a time. There were horses within. He could hear them moving about. There were no voices.

He dropped from the gelding, tried the door. It opened easily. Hooking the sorrel's reins over the hasp, he went inside. The structure was large and he located the opposite door at the far end of a runway. A matched pair of well-fed whites occupied two forward stalls. The remaining spaces were empty. Through the open doorway he could see the front of a fringed-top surrey standing in the yard. He moved swiftly about, looked into the tack room and other shadowy areas. Except for the white team, a stock of feed, and the usual equipment, the barn was deserted. He returned quickly to the sorrel, led him inside, and tied him in the back stall. There was a quantity of hay already in the manger and the gelding made himself at home immediately.

Selkirk retreated over the same route he had come. He would not press his luck by using the door that led into the yard and was in full view of the house. He circled the barn, kept it between himself and the stable where he had last seen Wade and Shad, and finally reached the rear of the Golden Eagle. He glanced about, saw no one along the alley, and quickly climbed the outside stairs that mounted to the structure's second floor. The door was standing open and he slipped inside quietly. He found himself in a narrow hallway that ran forward a dozen paces and there intersected with a longer corridor lying at right angle. Several doors turned off its uncarpeted length. An inside stairway was directly opposite the junction. It apparently led down to the saloon below. Selkirk could hear the mutter of voices and the occasional chink of glassware.

He turned down the hallway, reading the crudely painted numbers on the doors. When he came to 5, he halted. Hesitating he listened, considered the possibility of Clella's not being alone. All was quiet within—and it was too late to change plans now, anyway. He knocked softly. There was no answer. He tried again, this time rapping harder. After a time he heard the faint screech of bedsprings.

"Who is it?" Clella's voice, thick from sleep, asked.

"Selkirk," he replied, keeping his tone low.

"Who?"

"Dan Selkirk. Let me in . . . quick."

A key grated in the lock. The door opened and he stepped inside the darkened room quickly, wondering if his voice had been heard by anyone else along the hall. Clella closed the panel, relocked it. She turned to him. She had pulled some sort of robe over her gown and her long hair, pale gold in the poor light, reached well down her back.

"Sorry to wake you up," Dan said, "but you're the only one I could come to."

She gave him a slow smile. "I'm never sure about these left-handed compliments I get from you. Is there something wrong?"

He told her about the bank robbery and his run-in with Jude Wade and the others. He told her also about the $1,000 Henry Corbin had impounded and what it all would mean to him unless he cleared matters up at once and continued on his way. "Came to you, thinking you might remember some stranger, or maybe several strangers who have been hanging around for the last few days."

The girl walked to one of the windows, raised the shade, and looked out. "Can't recall any . . . except you," she said finally. "Not in the past week, anyway. Of course that doesn't mean there haven't been others. Not all the pilgrims and drifters come to the Golden Eagle."

"Most would," Dan said. "A man on the trail looks for the biggest and noisiest place he can find."

"Unless he didn't want to be noticed."

Selkirk nodded. There was truth in that. A man, or men, planning to rob a bank, would likely take care to be seen by as few citizens as possible.

"Expect Jude really tried himself with you after you sat him down here in the saloon," Clella said. "It could be his way of getting back."

"He's a man who likes plenty of help," Dan commented. "Who's this Shad and Quint that trail with him?"

"Shad Ross and Quint Fisher. Just a couple of cowhands that hang around the marshal's office. They pick up a little money now and then delivering prisoners and such." She paused, studied him closely. "You think they might be mixed up in it?"

Selkirk shrugged. "Everybody is, far as I'm concerned. But no special reason to think they had anything to do with it. All three of them were pretty rough with me but that could have been the normal way of handling things for Jude. The only part that worried me was knowing that horse of mine. He's jumpy. If Corbin hadn't come along when he did, I sure could have got my neck stretched."

"I knew Jude was hard on prisoners but never heard of him going that far."

"He sure is mighty anxious to be a big lawman. He told Corbin he was only trying to make me own up to the robbery and tell where I hid the rest of the money. Shad and this Quint were with him in it all the way. And another man they called Eli."

"Eli's a clerk in the hardware store. Doesn't run with them usually."

"I figured he was sort of an outsider from the way Jude talked to him. Right now I'm wondering about Deputy Marshal Wade and his two *compadres*. He sure is eager."

Clella shook her head. "Shad doesn't have enough brains to rob a bank. Quint Fisher might. He's a quiet one and you never know exactly where he stands. As for Jude . . . well, he's been

154

the deputy for several years. He's real proud of that badge. I can't see him in on it."

"He's got a perfect alibi, being a lawman."

Clella moved away from the window, sat down on the edge of the bed. "Maybe they're smarter than I give them credit for. And I could be wrong about Jude. If they did do it, why would they want you dead?"

"It would end the search for the money I'm supposed to have hidden. Jude would go through the motions, of course, but he would take care never to find it. Then when it had all blown over, they'd dig it up and split it."

"And Jude would cover up your murder by saying you tried to escape and was accidentally killed, or something like that?"

"It all fits pretty well, only I've got nothing solid to go on except that Wade was mighty rough on me." Dan moved toward the door, reached for the knob. "Where's Bishop's bank from here?"

"Across the street and down a ways. Why?"

"It looks like my next stop. I want to talk to Bishop. Maybe he can give me some ideas."

She came to her feet quickly. "Dan, that's too risky. Jude will have the whole town turned out by now and looking for you."

Selkirk said: "It's a chance I'll have to take. I sure can't get anything done by just sitting back."

Her face was serious. "I wish I could have been of more help. I'll watch and listen all I can. Where can I get in touch with you if I learn something?"

He said: "No place. I'll be on the move. It's better that I find you. Just leave this door unlocked."

She shook her head. "No thanks, not in this place." She went to the door, unlocked it, and handed him the key. "Here, use this. I have a spare." She opened the panel, glanced up and down the hallway. "All clear."

He moved past her into the long corridor. "I'm obliged to you again," he said in a low voice. "So long until later."

She leaned forward, kissed him lightly on the cheek. "Take care," she murmured, and closed the door.

VI

Selkirk halted at the door at the head of the stairs. He examined the alley below, looking to his right and left. There was still no one in sight or other evidence of activity. That struck him as strange. Jude Wade and Shad should have recovered fully by this time; the alarm should be out and a search in full swing. Understanding came to him then. Undoubtedly the two men had regained consciousness and first were seeking him out on their own, doing it quietly, reluctant to admit that he had escaped. If so, it was more good luck for him. It would allow a few more minutes during which he could move about in less danger. But it would not last long. Jude and Shad, failing to find him, would be compelled to notify Marshal Corbin and get a posse formed. Dan went down the steps quickly, stopped there, and pulled back into the shadows beneath the stairs while he considered the advisability of getting his horse.

Clella had said the bank was down the street a short distance and on the opposite side. He did not relish the idea of being so far from the sorrel, in event it became necessary to make a sudden flight. Still, the possibility of the big red horse being noticed on the street was most likely. He decided to leave the gelding where he was and take his chances on foot.

He moved off then, keeping close to the rear of the buildings until he came to a narrow cross street. A woman in a buggy was approaching the town on that lesser avenue. He walked to the opposite side, hesitated there until the vehicle was abreast, and then casually fell in beside it. In that manner he crossed the main street and gained the side upon which Oscar Bishop's bank stood. He had only a partial glimpse of the jail at the far end of town, but he saw no men or horses gathered before it.

The bank building was to his left. He followed the narrow cross street until he reached the alleyway that ran behind the structures and turned into it. He found the rear of Bishop's establishment. The heavy door was closed. If locked, it posed a new problem. He scarcely dared to show himself on the street to enter by the front. He reached for the knob, turned it slowly. The door did not give. It was locked. He rode out a long minute of disappointment, then knocked softly. He heard the scrape of a chair. He was taking a big chance, he realized. There could be several men in the room; the door could open into the main part of the bank, exposing him instantly to all who might be there. There was no help for it. He drew his gun, stood close to the panel. When it swung inward, he pushed through quickly, almost knocking Oscar Bishop to the floor.

Luck was again with him. The door had let him into the banker's private office, which was separated from the front of the bank by a wooden partition. Anyone up forward in the business area of the establishment would be unable to see what was taking place in the rear.

Bishop's eyes were wide with surprise. He recovered his voice. "You! I thought you were in jail. . . ."

"Sit down," Selkirk said in a low, harsh tone.

He moved to the doorway of the partition, glanced to the front. One customer stood before the elderly teller in the cage. Selkirk closed the door quietly and returned to Bishop.

"How did you get out?"

"Never mind that," Selkirk cut in. "Keep your voice down and you won't get hurt. I'm here to ask a few questions . . . nothing more."

Bishop seemed not to hear. Desperation tinged his words.

"There's not much money left. You took about all I had on hand."

"I'm not interested in your money," Dan said, moving up close to the banker. "Never was. I tried to tell you and the marshal that I didn't rob this bank but you wouldn't listen. Now I've got to prove it."

"But that thousand dollars. . . ."

"Belongs to my boss, just like I said. Only I can't take time for you to write him and find out I'm telling the truth. Now, listen to me, and listen good. I've checked on strangers that have been through this town lately. It seems I'm the only one. And since I know I never robbed your bank, it must have been done by somebody living right here in Apache Basin."

Bishop's small black eyes were fastened upon Dan. The amazement in them grew. He wagged his head. "Why, that's impossible. Who could it be? I know every man in this town."

"Did you notice anybody hanging around lately . . . more than usual, I mean?"

Bishop thought. "No. I guess everybody drops by at one time or another. Haven't seen anyone just standing around."

Dan considered that. "Well, was there anything strange about the robbery?"

Oscar Bishop's attention dropped to the pistol, still in Dan's hand. He said: "No, nothing odd about it. The regular safe was cleaned out and the extra five thousand I kept in my private safe was taken, too. They didn't bother with silver or gold coins."

"Too heavy," Dan said, thinking aloud. "And the gold might have been a bit hard to pass unnoticed. How did they get in here?"

"Guess there was something odd, after all, the way they pulled it off. There were no windows broken out and neither one of the doors was forced. Only thing I can figure is that one of them hid inside until after we closed and then let the others

158

in . . . if there was more than one man in on it."

Selkirk looked around. "Where could a man hide so he wouldn't be noticed by you or your teller?"

"Couple of coat closets. Not used this time of year. He could have slipped into one of them."

Selkirk grunted. "You mean you don't look the place over when you lock up?"

Bishop lifted his hands, let them fall onto his chest in a gesture of resignation. "I guess we have got a bit careless. Never been robbed before. It was Horace that closed up. I was out looking over some land. But it wouldn't have made any difference, had I been here. I wouldn't have looked into the closets, either."

"Horace the man up front now?"

Bishop nodded.

"What about him? Could he have been in on it?"

Again the banker showed his amazement. "Old Horace rob the bank? Sooner suspect myself. He's seventy years old and money doesn't mean a thing to him."

Maybe, Dan thought. *Money has a way of doing odd things to a man sometimes. Horace would bear looking into.* He got to his feet, suddenly impatient. Time was passing swiftly and he was getting nowhere. "Nothing else you can tell me about the robbery . . . nothing that would help me run down the real bandits?"

He felt the banker's gaze upon him, drilling into him. Bishop was still unconvinced that he had not done the job himself. "You know as much about it now as I do," the banker said. "Maybe more."

"If that means you figure I'm the robber, you're dead wrong. You think I'd be here now if I had done it?"

Bishop shrugged. "Why not? A smart one like you might pull just such a stunt. Maybe you figure, if you can convince Corbin and me that you're innocent by doing a lot of rustling around

159

supposedly looking for the bandits, or bandit, we'll forget about you."

Selkirk said: "A man would be loco to try that kind of a stunt."

"You've got to admit it looks like you are the guilty man. All the evidence points your way."

"Evidence? The fact that I'm a stranger around here and was carrying a thousand dollars on me . . . is that what you consider evidence?"

"You can't prove that money was yours."

"I could prove it if I had time. I can't wait. I can't hang around for a couple of weeks until you get a letter back from McGowan."

"Which is something else . . . you're in a hell of a big hurry to get away from here."

Selkirk swore in disgust. "You've been told the reason for that, too. But I see it's like talking to the wind. It's got me nowhere." He stepped to the door, placed his hand on the knob. "I can see there's no point in wasting any more time on you. Now, I'm going out of here with no trouble. You sit right where you are for five minutes. Don't move."

A slyness filtered into the banker's small eyes. "Sure. Whatever you say."

"I'll be right outside, looking around for an idea. I'll know if you even get up. Remember that."

The expression on Bishop's face had changed quickly. He said: "Sure, sure."

Dan opened the door. There was no one in the alley. He stepped out into the sunlight, pulled the thick panel shut behind him. He had no intention of wasting time around the building; he had told Bishop that merely in the hope of keeping him quiet for several minutes and allow ample time for a getaway. He turned, walked hurriedly down the alley to the cross street. There he swung right. When he reached the corner of the intersection, he halted. There was no vehicle crossing over this time with which he could walk and screen his movements. And, looking toward the jail, he realized something else. Men and a number of horses were gathered before it. Jude Wade had given the alarm.

VII

Selkirk leaned back against the wall of the building beside which he stood. Several persons were on the walks, some of which had been attracted by the excitement at the jail and were turning their steps to that direction. He looked again for some means by which he could cross over, saw there was none; he would have to risk being noticed. He took a deep breath, moved away from the corner, and stepped boldly into the street. He was no more than halfway when Oscar Bishop burst from his bank and set up his cry.

"Marshal! Marshal Corbin! The prisoner's down this way! He's been in my place!"

The banker had not noticed him, Selkirk saw. He had cut sharply right when he came from the bank, and was now running down the center of the street for the jail, shouting at the top of his voice. But those who turned to look at him did see Dan Selkirk. A yell went up from Jude Wade. Instantly there was a confused milling about in front of Corbin's office. From that mêlée three men suddenly emerged on foot. One was the deputy. The other two Dan did not waste time examining. He broke into a run, gained the far sidewalk. He wished now the big sorrel was handy; on that animal's back he could quickly flee and leave the town far behind. He noted some other man's horse a few yards to his right. It stood at a hitch rail, head drooped, patiently awaiting its owner.

A gunshot smashed along the rows of buildings, echoing loudly. Wood splintered from a post just beyond Selkirk. He

161

debated no longer the advisability of borrowing the waiting horse, but continued on down the side street, running hard for the alley. He reached the corner of the building along which he fled. The alleyway, and beyond it, open ground lay before him. He located the house and the barn where he had left the sorrel. Perhaps he could reach it before anyone saw him.

Too late! That thought rocked through him in the next instant. Three men broke into the alley two hundred yards or so farther down. Other men had joined with Wade in the pursuit and the deputy evidently had split his forces, was sending part to the rear of the buildings, keeping the rest with him on the street. There was no possibility now of getting to the sorrel.

He started down the alley, ran straight and head-on for the oncoming men. They slowed perceptibly, abruptly uncertain. They expected him to use his gun, Dan realized. He had no intention of doing so. Shooting down a citizen of Apache Basin and thereby adding to the seriousness of his situation was far from his mind. A door, partly ajar, was off to his right. Without hesitation, he ducked into the opening, quickly closed it. He was at the end of a short hallway. He started along its length that led back to the street.

He reached the end of the corridor, found himself behind a long counter upon which several bolts of cloth lay. He was in some sort of dress goods store. He looked about. The place was empty. He saw the owner then, standing out on the walk, his attention drawn to something down the street. Selkirk moved to the door. He could not long remain here. The men in the alley would soon reach the building into which he had turned and be piling through the back entrance. He halted beside the door frame, careful to keep out of sight. The sound of running men grew louder. Jude Wade's voice reached him.

"He went down the side of Apperson's place. We'll box him up in the alley!"

The deputy, flanked by a half a dozen red-faced, sweating men, trotted into view. Wade had his pistol out, ready for use. Likely it had been he who had fired the warning shot earlier. Standing there, hidden just within the dry goods store, Dan Selkirk watched Wade and his men pound by. Shad was the only other one in the group he recognized. That meant Quint Fisher was one of those in the alley.

"Where's Corbin?" a voice shouted.

"Back at the jail," one of the search party answered. "Jude's in charge here."

Dan watched them turn the corner of Apperson's, heard the hammer of their boot heels as they raced along the side street. When the last man was gone from sight, he stepped through the door onto the walk. The shopkeeper caught the slight noise he made, turned, and saw him. He frowned, not certain where Dan had come from. Selkirk grinned at the man, nodded pleasantly, and continued on his way along the store fronts. Moving casually, he reached the hotel, swung through its open door. A yell lifted back at the dry goods shop. From that he knew Quint Fisher and the others had gone through the establishment to the street and found him missing. Whether anyone had noticed him enter the Pecos River Hotel or not, he had no way of knowing.

The clerk was not behind the desk. Dan walked by it, nodded to an elderly man who occupied one of the lobby chairs, and continued on toward the back. He reached the rear of the hotel, opened the door a narrow crack to listen. He could hear the mutter of voices off to his left. That would be Jude Wade and those with him, he guessed. They had joined with Quint, were talking things over.

"Must have been some other building along here." Wade's words were nearer, plainer, indicating that he and the men were coming up the alley.

163

"Split up again. Quint, you take Eli and Herb and go out onto the street. Keep your eyes open. He's in one of these buildings. We'll go through every dang' one until we flush him out."

Dan Selkirk felt a net drawing tightly about him. He could not go out into the alley, that would mean walking straight into Wade and the men with him. A similar situation now faced him on the street. Quint Fisher, Eli, and someone called Herb would be waiting there. And it was too late to move from his position at the end of the hotel hallway. It was too late for everything—except waiting.

He drew his gun, stepped back to the hinge side of the door. He would have to rely on the darkness of the corridor, and the fact that when the door swung in he would be behind it. He pulled himself into the shadowy corner. In the alley he could hear the scuff of boot heels on the dry ground, the low rumble of conversation. The party had separated now; men were beginning to make their search of each building.

The latch on the door clicked sharply. The panel swung in, going wide. It checked abruptly as it came up against Selkirk's foot. The man swore softly. He stepped into the hall, kicked the door shut with his heel. He was a stranger to Dan, a tall, hulking figure wearing a dirty, white hat. He started toward the front of the hotel, seemed suddenly to become aware he was not alone. As he wheeled, Dan caught him on the side of the head with a solid blow. The man grunted, dropped to his knees. Selkirk drove another right to his jaw, and he flattened out. Dan paused, listened to see if the scuffling sounds had drawn any attention from the lobby. He could hear nothing. He holstered his pistol, stepped over the prostrate man who lay partly against the door. He took him by the feet, dragged him a short distance down the hall. That done, he returned to the door, opened it. The alley was deserted. Wade and the others were all inside for the moment.

He left the rear of the hotel at a run. There was no point in trying to remain unnoticed now. It was more important to get across the open ground before Jude or someone else came from one of the buildings and saw him. He cut across a vacant lot, reached the first of the scattered houses. The barn where the sorrel was hidden was only fifty yards away.

"There he goes!"

The shout came from the alley. The voice was familiar—Shad Ross's. Dan flung a glance at the man. He had just emerged from the building next to the hotel, was yet standing on the steps that led up to its door.

"Jude!" Ross yelled. "He's out here!"

Dan raced through a back yard, ducked low to avoid a clothesline, and almost fell. He recovered quickly, plunged on. He reached the barn where the gelding waited. He was on its south side. He saw the black, shining surrey standing in the yard and the wide open door beyond it. He had no time to circle the barn, to use the rear entrance as before. He crossed directly behind the house, ducked into the runway. The white horses were still in their stalls. The sorrel was where he had left him. He snatched at the pigging string anchoring the gelding, jerked it loose. The red was slow to back and Selkirk yanked hard at the bit. He got the big horse into the wider runway, hurried for the rear door. Boots were thudding across the hard-packed yard and, above that sound, he could hear Jude Wade shouting instructions to his followers.

Selkirk reached the door, hazed the sorrel on through. He vaulted onto the saddle, dug his spurs into the gelding's flanks. He didn't know exactly where he was going. Only one thing was certain—he had to get away from there.

Ray Hogan

VIII

He pointed for the grove. There would be no permanent protection there but it offered immediate cover from the pursuit that was sure to follow at once. Gunshots began to racket through the noonday heat. Half turning in the saddle, he looked back, saw Wade with a dozen or so men standing at the rear of the barn where the sorrel had been hidden. They were firing at him with pistols but the range was too great to be effective. But they now were aware of the course he had taken. In only short minutes they would mount up and come swarming after him.

He reached the grove, pulled into the first outreaching stand of trees and brush. He halted, once again threw a glance over his shoulder. Wade and the men were gone. He could see no signs of them, but he knew they were running for their horses, waiting at the jail. He put the sorrel into motion, struck for the far side of the grove. He was not familiar with the country and he did not know what lay beyond the small stand of trees. Perhaps a better hiding place. A short mile later he broke out into the open, looked down upon a long slope that terminated in a wide arroyo. That gash, in turn, appeared to drain into a wild, broken area. Breaks country. It was just what he hoped for. He touched the sorrel with spurs, moved off down the gentle slope. A short time later he reached the ravine, dipped down onto its sandy floor, and loped for the maze of rocks and brush lying in the distance. He was leaving a plain trail; he realized that when he looked back to see if any riders were in sight. But there was no help for it. There was not time to halt and brush the prints of the gelding away; he could hope only for more solid ground where no telltale tracks would be visible.

At the end of the arroyo he cut right, followed along a rocky ledge that climbed slowly toward a distant line of blue hills. He could see dark shades of dense growth along the slopes, and in that a better place in which to lose himself should the breaks

166

prove unsafe. He swung off the ledge, sliced deeper into the rough country. The sorrel found the going hard and slow, disliked every foot of it. Thorn bush, gooseberry, mesquite, briar, wild rose—all clawed at him, dug into his legs and belly and made him reluctant to travel on. Selkirk kept at him constantly, prodding him on. Ahead, only a short way, he could see the crown of a tamarack stand along with the tips of other tall shrubs and lesser trees. It would be some sort of hollow, a basin, he presumed. It should offer an ideal place in which to wait out the arrival of the posse.

He reached the sink area, found it to be as he had hoped— wild, rough, badly overgrown. Water from the infrequent rains that visited the country drained into that deep bowl, sweetening the normally moisture-starved plant life and imparting a robust, abnormal growth. He located a knoll from which he could observe the surrounding area with ease and pulled to a halt on its far side. Tying the sorrel to a low cedar, he settled down to await Wade and the posse. When he saw them, determined what course they were going to follow, he would plan his next move.

A short time later he watched three riders break over the edge of the arroyo, pause there for only moments, and then come sweeping on toward the basin. He lost them in the sea of rocks and brush. Minutes later four more men appeared on the rim. They followed the trio immediately, evidently seeing them on ahead. Seven men in all. Jude Wade, Shad Ross, and Quint Fisher unquestionably would make up a part of the posse's membership. Those remaining would be men from town—men he did not know.

He picked up the riders again about a half mile below the arroyo's mouth, saw them work their way slowly through the brush and loose rock. If they continued in the direction they had taken, they would end up with him in the heart of the basin. It occurred to Dan Selkirk that that was likely their plan. They were acquainted with the wild breaks country, guessed he would head deep into its roughest part. He glanced toward the hills, remote in the west. He should have swung that way, as he had been tempted to at first. But it was too late now. To reach them he would have to cross directly in front of Wade and the posse. Such a risk would not be worth taking. Besides, with care, he could remain unseen right there in the basin. So thick was the growth, generally, that two men might pass only a short distance apart and never see each other.

He lost the posse a few minutes after that and knew they had entered the main part of the basin. From that moment on he knew he must be on the alert every breath he took, be ready to move off quickly and silently with only the briefest of warnings. He returned to the sorrel, stepped to the saddle. He did not think it was possible for Wade and his crew to trail him with any degree of effectiveness across the littered floor of the sink, but he took no chances. He rode the big red horse off the knoll, followed along a ridge of solid rock for a quarter mile, and then pulled into a thick stand of scrub oak and twisted juniper trees. From there, he judged, he could see the posse when it first came into the open.

He had made little progress in clearing himself. He admitted that to himself as his thoughts went back over the conversation he had held with Clella and the banker, Oscar Bishop. But he was more convinced now than ever that it had been no passing drifter who had robbed the bank. All things pointed to someone who was familiar with Bishop's establishment as well as with the town. Quite suddenly he knew that such a conclusion was right. Something Bishop had said, that he had heard but passed over lightly and overlooked, popped back into his mind. The bandit had taken currency not only from the regular vault but had also emptied Bishop's private safe. *Private safe!* Who but someone familiar with the bank would know of Bishop's special hiding place?

A cottontail hopped gingerly into a small clearing a few paces in front of Selkirk. The sorrel's head snapped up at its abrupt appearance but the rabbit did not flee, merely sat and watched, his flat nose twitching nervously. After a time the small animal moved out of the brush and was gone.

The outlaw was a local person, or persons—if there had been more than one. Dan Selkirk knew that now. But he was little better off for the knowledge. It did narrow the field, however, pin his problem down to one that involved Apache Basin itself. He shrugged. The disadvantage was with him. Outside of Shad Ross, Quint Fisher, and maybe Jude Wade, he had not the slightest idea of who it might be.

The rabbit scuttled across the clearing like a fleeting shadow of gray and white. Its long ears were laid back and fright brightened its eyes. Almost immediately a coyote appeared. His sharp nose was to the ground, thick brush tail, matted with burrs, hung low. He caught scent of the man and horse, leaped to one side, his yellow eyes reflecting his fright. He was gone before Selkirk could utter a sound.

Clella had discounted his suspicions of Shad Ross and Quint Fisher as possible bandits. Thinking about it now, he was not so sure. And what about Jude Wade? Was he really just a lawman with an overbuilt sense of duty or was he trying to wipe out a trail by mercilessly persecuting a handy and logical suspect to the point of murder? But if he considered Jude Wade, then it followed he must also think of Henry Corbin. Was he the honest, straight-laced lawman he pretended to be? He was quick to want Dan locked up and made no pretense of his unwillingness to listen. And what of Oscar Bishop? Could he be guilty of robbing, or engineering the robbery of his own bank to cover up some larger, more serious crime? The list could be endless, even Clella might. . . .

He saw movement off in the basin, a mile or so away. A rider heaved into view on the crown of a low mound of rock. A second man soon followed. Jude Wade and his posse were drawing nearer. Where were the remaining five? Scattered across the basin, he guessed, working their slow way through the heavy underbrush. He must watch closely, attempt to locate them all. When the time came to move, he would need to know the positions of the riders at the ends of Wade's forage line in order to skirt them and get behind. Why was Clella so certain about Shad and Quint? And Jude Wade? She gave no particular reasons . . . ?

Dan Selkirk's thoughts came to an abrupt, chilled halt. The hair along the back of his neck began to prickle and a tingling raced up his spine. The distinct, measured thud of a horse walking slowly had reached him. Off to his right, only a few yards away. He froze in the saddle, feared even to turn and look. The dry squeak of leather broke through the hush.

"Whoa up, horse," a man's deep voice said, so clear it seemed to Dan that the rider must be at his shoulder.

Selkirk turned his head slowly. Ten feet away sat a man on a dust-covered buckskin.

IX

A wild thought flashed through Selkirk's mind; he had miscalculated somehow. Wade had managed to circle around him, close in from behind. In the next breath he knew such could not have been possible. This rider was from another party, a second posse that had come in from the opposite direction. Apparently there was a trail into the basin from the south. He studied the cowboy who, at that moment, was gazing down into the sink where Dan had last seen the two riders on the mound. It was too late to move off. And the sorrel was bound to give him away any second. He let his hand slide to the gun at his hip. He would be

170

ready if his one chance failed.

"Seen anything of him?" he asked in a casual voice.

The rider started violently. He swiveled about, his eyes blazing angrily. "Damn! Man ought to grunt or somethin' afore he speaks out bold like that! Plumb nigh scared me white!"

"Sorry. Thought you saw me sitting here."

"Naw, that's the hell of this croakin' country. Man can't see nothin' for all this brush and rock."

Inwardly Dan breathed a sigh of relief. The rider did not recognize him, most likely had never before seen him. He now had accepted him, as he had hoped, as another member of the posse. "That's for sure," Dan agreed. "Wildest place I ever rode into."

"Where's Jude? You run across him yet?"

"Nope. He and the rest are down there in the bottoms, I reckon. Saw them a few minutes ago, working this way."

"That there outlaw must be between us and him, then. I sure ain't seen no signs of him. Rest of the boys ain't, either."

Selkirk asked carefully: "Where are they now?"

The cowboy shrugged. "Hard to tell. Saw Shad back there a piece. Jenkins somewheres off to the left. Others are strung out both ways."

"Looks like Jude knew what he was doing, splitting up the posse the way he did."

"Old Jude knows these here breaks like he knows the back of his hand. Say, I don't recollect seein' you around town afore."

"Just came in this morning," Dan said, feeling his nerves begin to tighten. "Sort of got roped in on this posse."

"You from around close?"

"Been punching cows for the Triangle J outfit," Selkirk answered, recalling the name of a ranch he had ridden across a few days earlier.

"Triangle J? That's a far piece from here. You quit?"

171

"No. Been feeling poorly. Rode in to see the doc. Run smack into this manhunt and got myself drafted."

The cowboy grinned. "Jude's sure set on catchin' that bank robber. Reckon he's honin' some for the old marshal's job and figures layin' that outlaw by the heels will cinch it for him. You goin' to ride on and meet up with him and the rest of the boys or you goin' to keep settin' right where you are?"

Dan thought fast. Better to get away from the man as quickly as possible. He said: "Best we keep moving, I think. That's what Jude would want us to do. I'll swing over to the left and head down for the bottom. Didn't figure you and me were riding so close."

"How's a man to know?" the cowboy complained, clucking the buckskin into motion. "Can't see nothin'. Wonder we ain't all a nudgin' one another. So long. See you down the way."

Dan allowed a short space of time to elapse for the rider to move off and disappear into the dense brush. He then swung the sorrel off at a right angle. He was breathing a bit easier now the encounter was over, but tension still clawed at his nerves and rode him heavily. Other posse riders were scattered around him. Among them was Shad Ross, who would recognize him instantly, and there could be others, Quint Fisher, and possibly Eli. He abandoned the idea of circling Wade and the posse that was in the basin proper. The best course to follow was to turn about completely, head south. That would put him quickly behind the line of the party who had come in from the lower end. Thus he would remove himself from a position between the two closing posses who sought to trap him in between them.

He apparently was abreast of Shad's crew, if he could judge from the man on the buckskin. Thus, if he pressed on southward, he would slip through immediately. He cut the sorrel to the left. He did not increase the pace but held at a slow, quiet walk. A silent passage was more important than speed, at least for the time being.

He spotted a second rider soon after that. He was a short man, dressed in a suit and looked as if he were far from being comfortable in a saddle. He had halted in a small clearing, and, while Dan watched, he removed his narrow-brimmed felt hat and mopped wearily at the sweat gathered on his balding head. He seemed to be watching something—or someone—far ahead. It was probable he had caught sight of the rider on the dust-caked buckskin, Dan decided, and rode on. The man was gone from view almost at once but immediately the soft tunk-a-tunk of another horse on the spongy humus brought Selkirk to a stop.

He had pulled up short. A vague notion that he had not been abreast the posse but just approaching it filled his mind. The man on the buckskin had been a distance ahead of the main group. He listened intently, searched the screen of brush surrounding him for movement. He could see no one, but the sound of the walking horse and the scrape of leather against shrubbery were plain. Again he laid his hand on the gun at his side. He hoped he would not be forced to use it. The sound of a shot would bring the entire posse down upon him in short order. But the horse, with his rider and the attending danger, passed on. He had waited while the thud of the hoofs drew close, became loud, and then began to recede and slowly fade. Relief once more flowed through Dan Selkirk. That had been a close one—too close.

He settled down onto the saddle, put the gelding into motion again. A bird launched itself noisily from the foliage of a nearby tree. Its rapidly beating wings set up a sudden sound in the hush. Selkirk whirled, clawed for his gun. He grinned tightly when he saw the small shadow dip and wheel and curve off through the trees. He was jumpy as a wild goat. The pressure was about to down him. But it couldn't last much longer; he should be about through the line of searchers.

"Shad?"

Selkirk froze as the summons broke through the stillness. He was out in the open at the moment, halfway across a narrow clearing. He would be easy target for any eye turned toward him. He touched the sorrel with his spurs, prodded him into the opposite wall of brush.

"Hey, Shad!"

It was the voice of Quint Fisher. Dan recognized it then. Had Fisher heard him on the gelding, assumed it was his friend who was nearby? If so, Quint likely would ride up.

"Hey, Shad, where you at?"

"Over here!"

Selkirk relaxed. Ross's reply had come from a point a distance to his right. He was behind the pair, not far, but still a safe position. He would give them a few moments to ride on, get well beyond hearing, then he would continue toward the south. They were the last of the party, he was sure. Escape from Jude Wade's pursuit lay only minutes away.

And then Quint Fisher's voice said: "Come on over here, Shad. We got some talking to do. Something tells me we better hightail it out of this country fast."

X

Selkirk waited out Shad's reply. None came. He knew he should be moving off, that he should take himself as far from the posse as possible, but something in Quint Fisher's words stayed him, held him there.

"Damn it, Shad! Answer me!" Fisher said angrily.

"I'm comin'," Ross replied. "Keep your britches on. Horse of mine's gone and got hisself all messed up in a creeper. Like gettin' caught up in a tangle of wire."

Dan heard Fisher cross over in front of him, apparently to join up with Ross. They began to converse but distance blurred their voices and he could not distinguish the words. He spoke softly to the sorrel, eased him quietly out of the brush, and moved in nearer.

"What's got you to worryin' so?" Shad Ross was asking.

"Things are getting too hot around here. There's been too much ruckus about that bank money. Now Jude's gone and got everybody so riled up 'most anything can happen. Sure as shooting somebody's going to stumble onto something."

"Aw, what could somebody stumble on?" Shad said in a jeering tone. "We covered up things powerful good. And if Jude hangs the robbery on that drifter Selkirk, we got nothin' to worry about."

"Maybe Jude ain't going to get the chance. Selkirk wasn't hid in the woodshed when they passed out brains. He's fooled Jude right straight down the line."

"Maybe, but he's sure horsed himself into a pocket now. Only two ways out of the basin and he'll have to ride right over us or Jude to do it."

"I don't know," Fisher said in a dissatisfied tone. "This is mean country to find a man in. He could slip by us, or by Jude and the others."

"You're forgettin' we got men stashed at both ends of the trail."

"I'm not forgetting nothing," Fisher declared. "I just don't figure on stacking hay until I know it's been cut. And, seems to me, this thing ain't working out right."

"You're sort of rushin' things. Appears to me we ain't got nothin' to worry about."

"I'm going to worry plenty until I get my slice of that nine thousand dollars," Fisher said. "Not much for the job, anyway."

"It'll last a man a long time in Mexico. Reckon that's where

I'll be headin' for, Quint. What you figure to do?"

"Get the money, first of all. Then I'll do my planning. Come on, let's catch up with the other boys. I ain't heard any shooting, have you?"

"Nope," Shad replied. "Why?"

"Means one thing . . . nobody's jumped that Selkirk yet. He gives us the slip, I'm sure going to shag it out of here."

There was a pause. Finally Ross said: "Never knowed you to get so jumpy before. Maybe we had ought to get together and hash it over. That is, if we don't nail this Selkirk."

"Now you're showing some sense," Fisher commented. "Let's go."

Dan Selkirk had the answer he had been searching for, or at least a part of it. He still did not know who was in on the robbery with Ross and Fisher. But that would come later. Once inside a cell Quint and Shad would open up and talk. Gun in hand, he acted. He crashed the big sorrel through the brush in a sudden explosion of sound. Ross and Fisher, just riding off, wheeled in surprise.

"Throw up your hands!" Selkirk yelled. "And don't get any idea you can run for it. I'll drop you quick."

Shad Ross's mouth hung open. "It's him . . . Selkirk," he muttered.

Dan nodded. "And I've been listening to you so I know the whole story. Better forget about Mexico, Shad, and whatever it is you got in mind, Quint. The both of you can figure on doing a few years of rock busting for the territory now. I'm turning you over to Wade."

Fisher blinked. "He around here?"

"You know where he is," Selkirk snapped. "Now, reach over with your left hand, both of you, and pull your guns. Drop them on the ground. Do it slow and easy."

The two men obeyed. When it was done, Shad said: "What's

next, Mister Selkirk?"

"We're going to join up with the rest of the posse. I'll tell the deputy what you said about the bank money. That'll clear me. The law will have to find out where you hid the nine thousand and who the rest of your partners are."

Quint and Shad listened in silence. Dan rode in nearer. He pointed toward the basin. "Head out. Keep close together. I'll be right behind you, so don't try anything."

Ross and Fisher wheeled their horses around. Dan spurred up to where he could shepherd them more easily. They rode slowly, and, when they drew near the floor of the basin a half hour later, they had made no attempt to escape.

The first man Dan saw was the rider on the buckskin. As he came into view with his prisoners, the cowboy turned. A frown gathered on his dark face. He yelled something and three more of the posse came out of the brush and joined him.

"What's goin' on here?" he demanded when Dan halted before them.

"Here's your outlaws," Selkirk replied. "There's another one somewhere, maybe more. You'll have to find out yourself. Where's Wade?"

"Shad there . . . and Quint? They robbed the bank?" one of the men said in an incredulous voice.

"According to their own words. Sort of suspected them all along, then when I heard them talking about splitting the money and leaving the country, I knew for sure."

"Who are you? Don't remember seeing you before."

"I'm Selkirk, the man you've been hunting for. Only I've been doing some outlaw-hunting on my own since the law wouldn't believe my story."

"You're . . . Selkirk?" the rider on the buckskin exclaimed.

"That's me. Now, where's the deputy? I want to turn my prisoners over to him."

"What about this, Quint?" It was the man Dan had seen after he left the one on the buckskin—the one in the dusty blue suit.

Fisher, silent up to that moment, said: "He's loco. That's why we ain't doing anything about it. We're just waiting for Jude to show up. He'll straighten this thing out. If you're smart, you'll throw a gun on him so's he'll sure wait until Jude comes."

The cowboy on the buckskin reached for his pistol, froze at Dan's sharp glance. "This some kind of a trick?"

"No trick," Dan answered. "And all of you sit quiet until Wade gets here. Don't want to use this gun, but I will if I have to."

"That's why we're here," Shad Ross said. "He's fast with a gun. Got the drop on us. And a man's a fool to argue with a cocked pistol."

"Must be something to what he's saying," the blue-suited posse member said. "He'd be a fool to ride right into all of us unless he knew what he was talking about."

"Walked right into the bank this morning, didn't he?" Fisher said. "In broad daylight with the whole town looking for him. He's got plenty of guts . . . or else he's plumb crazy."

"Or, like I said, he knows what he's talking about."

"You mean it was us that robbed Bishop? You got too much sun, Hugh? Turning your brain for sure."

From the tail of his eye Dan Selkirk caught motion, off to his left. He turned his head slightly to look into a shallow wash. Two men. One was Jude Wade; the other he did not know. He breathed a little easier. Holding the two bandits and the several posse members at gunpoint was beginning to wear at his nerves. He was glad the deputy had finally showed up.

"Here comes . . . ," he began, and stopped abruptly as a gunshot blasted through the basin.

He heard the drone of lead nearby. Another shot followed quickly. Selkirk reeled in the saddle as the bullet smashed into his left arm, just below the shoulder. The sorrel reared, backed away on his hind legs. Both Ross and Fisher, at the first report, had leaped from their horses, ducked into the thick brush. Men were yelling and Dan had a quick glimpse of Wade bearing down upon him, shooting as he came.

He dug spurs into the frantic sorrel, brought him down to all fours. Another bullet struck the horn of the saddle, screamed off into the sky. The big red horse plunged into the dense undergrowth, his long, powerful legs carrying him forward at tremendous speed. A rash of gunfire broke out as the posse members, taking their cue from the deputy, opened up.

But Dan Selkirk, carried away quickly by the frightened gelding, was deep in the screening rock and shrubbery. Crouched low on the saddle, he let the sorrel have his head. It wasn't clear in his own fogged mind what had happened.

XI

Selkirk, despite his wounded arm, got the tough-mouthed gelding back under control after the first hundred yards. Well hidden by the rank growth and rugged terrain, he swerved to his right, sought to get out from in front of the chase he knew was coming hard on the flying heels of the sorrel. They dropped into a shallow wash, thundered down its length for a short distance, raced up the opposite bank. He could now hear Wade and the others shouting back and forth, the crashing of their horses as they plunged through the brush.

"String out! String out!" Jude Wade yelled. "No sense us all riding in a bunch. If you see him, shoot him down! Don't waste no time talking!"

Taking his position from the direction of the lawman's voice, Dan rode at a sharp right angle to them, thus taking himself off to one side. If it worked the way he hoped, they would rush on by. He glanced over his shoulder. None of the posse was in

sight but any one of them could have been near. He could see
only a short distance. He allowed the sorrel to slow down. The
footing was now too dangerous for the big red to travel at any
great speed. Loose rock had begun to mar the floor of the basin
and there were deep holes where rushing water had gouged out
the sand. They were climbing steadily, he saw, headed for a long
ridge. He swung the gelding to the right. It would not do to
break out onto a barren ledge. Silhouetted upon it he would be
easily visible. Better to keep in the thick brush along the floor of
the basin.

His arm pained continually and was bleeding much more
than was good for him. He should stop and do something for it.
It would have to wait a while longer. It was too dangerous to
halt yet. He could still hear the posse beating its way through
the breaks.

A quarter of an hour later he pulled to a stop. He dismounted,
walked a short way from the heavily breathing sorrel, and
listened. He could hear nothing. He had managed to get beyond
Wade and the posse and they had by-passed him completely.
Satisfied with what he knew, he returned to the gelding.

The wound in his arm was not serious. The bullet had entered
the fleshy part, missed the bone, and passed on through. It
needed only a bandage to stop the flow of blood. Later it would
have to be cleaned and properly dressed. He took a clean
bandanna from his saddlebags, bound the wound tightly. That
would take care of it until he reached town.

The sorrel had recovered his wind by the time Selkirk had
completed his simple medical chore and was again ready to
move on. Dan stepped to the saddle and took up the reins. He
sat for a time, thinking of what should be done next.

Return to Apache Basin. That seemed the logical thing to do.
There was no use trying to talk to Jude Wade. He was so blinded
by his conviction of Selkirk's guilt, he would listen to nothing

else. The lawman was wholly unreasonable, had even issued orders to the posse to shoot on sight. Dan swore feelingly. If Wade hadn't been such a fool, two of the outlaws would be prisoners at that very moment and Dan would be well on his way to clearing himself of the charge that hung over him.

He moved out then, cutting back across the sink for the trail that would take him to the settlement. The afternoon was beginning to grow late and it would be nearly dark by the time he reached the town. That was good. Trigger happy as everyone was, it would be better if he did his traveling under cover of darkness. He could not, of course, go to the local doctor for treatment of his wound. He would have to rely on Clella. He felt a faint twinge of reluctance at that thought. He was not too sure of the girl. Perhaps it was because she had been so certain of Quint and Shad's innocence in the robbery. And now that he knew positively they were involved, it somehow reflected back upon her. It had been only a matter of opinion, he thought then, coming to her defense himself. She had been speaking only from a casual acquaintanceship and did not actually know them well.

Getting into the Golden Eagle and up to Clella's room unseen would be no simple task. He realized that and briefly considered the possibilities. But it was the only thing he could do and immediately set aside any speculation as to the dangers of the undertaking. No point in worrying now about it. He would cross that river when he came to it. He was well down into the bottom of the basin, he saw. Slicing across it as he was presently doing, he should soon intersect the trail that would take him out of the wild, rugged area to the rim and lead him back to town. He had a hunch that the route to the south, up which the second party of posse riders had come, was shorter and he had earlier thought of taking it. But he decided it was better to stick with the trail he had been over and knew to some extent. He remembered then what Shad Ross had said about a guard, or guards, being placed at that point. If so, it was likely Jude Wade had taken similar precautions at this end. He would have to be on the alert.

He was on the far side of the basin, with the now tiring sorrel plodding slowly up the steep slope, when he saw the first of the returning posse. They had ridden south, clear to the mouth of the trail, he guessed, and, failing to find him, had doubled back. He pulled to a halt in a stand of shoulder-high scrub oak and watched the riders break out of the brush and pause in a small clearing. The distance was so great they were little more than specks and therefore indistinguishable. He counted three, and after a few minutes two more showed up. The rest either had gone on out the lower end of the basin or were yet scattered elsewhere in the brush. It did not matter. His lead on them was such that he need not fear their overtaking him. When they rode on, he resumed the climb.

Near the rim of the basin, where the trail cut through a narrow gash, he halted. He tied the gelding to a clump of mesquite, well out of sight, and went forward stealthily on foot. Long before he saw the two men sitting with their backs to a large boulder, he smelled the smoke of their cigarettes. They had taken little precaution to conceal themselves, a result born of many hours spent in boring inactivity, Dan supposed. Jude Wade would have instructed them to do otherwise.

There was no possibility of passing by them. Selkirk then turned his attention to studying the surrounding country. He saw that it was possible to gain the plateau by skirting the main trail. It would be rough going—and much slower since it would be a matter of making his way through a maze of rock and cacti and other scraggly growth that littered the slope. But it could be done.

He returned to the sorrel. Taking up the reins, he cut off the worn path he had been pursuing, struck off across the rugged waste. He did not go to the saddle but led the gelding; the footing was far too treacherous to burden the red horse with his weight. Together they wound a tortuous course up the steep incline and came finally to the flats at a point a good half mile east of where the two sentries had been stationed. Selkirk was only a little worse for wear, having slipped and fallen once. The sure-footed sorrel had only a foamy coat of sweat to indicate the effort he had expended.

They rested for a short time in the cool breeze that had begun to sweep across the mesa, and then Dan Selkirk climbed onto the saddle. Far ahead in the failing daylight he could see the grove where he had paused that morning; on its far side lay the town. The sorrel broke into a comfortable lope. It would be full dark when they reached Apache Basin.

XII

The first thing to be done was again to hide the gelding. He sat there in the deep shadows behind the Pecos River Hotel and looked about for an answer to the problem. He recalled then the small corral at the rear of the hostelry's stable. It would be dark there and little likelihood of anyone making use of the pole-fenced yard at that hour of the night.

He wheeled about, circled the squat, slant roof structure, and came in to it from the back. The corral was empty. He tied the gelding to a rail, keeping him on the outside. If he were forced to leave in a hurry, he would have no time to wrestle with the gate or corner the sorrel should he be in a perverse mood.

He started to retrace his route, suddenly found himself rocking uncertainly on his heels. He wasn't in as good a shape as he thought. The loss of blood and a lack of food had combined to set up an adverse effect within him. He shook his head to clear the cobwebs. After he got Clella to dress his wound, he would see about getting a bite to eat.

He crossed the dark yard, keeping close to the shadows, and reached the stairs at the rear of the Golden Eagle. The evening was well under way. Loud voices, laughter, and piano music lifted and fell sporadically. Somewhere in the town a gunshot broke across the night.

Selkirk climbed the steep flight of stairs slowly. The door was closed. He hesitated for a moment, breathed a hope that no one was standing in the hallway just within, and turned the knob. Relief flowed through him. The corridor was a dimly lit tunnel filled only with confused sounds coming from below.

He moved inside unsteadily, closed the panel, and leaned up against a wall. He started to go on, froze. There was the dull thud of footsteps on the steps leading up from the saloon. Dan flattened himself against the rough boards. The head and wide shoulders of a man emerged in the shadowy stairwell. He climbed deliberately, methodically, eyes cast down. Selkirk's hand crept to his gun. If the man turned down the hallway off which the rooms lay, all well and good; likely he would never notice the dark figure crouched in the shadows. But if he came straight on, headed for the back entrance. . . .

The intruder reached the top of the stairs. He paused there momentarily, searched about in his pockets for something. Apparently finding it, he moved off down the hall. Dan listened. A lock clicked. A door opened and closed, and then it was quiet. Selkirk's taut frame relaxed. He swore softly. It was a hell of a feeling to be a man with no friends. Everyone you met was the enemy, represented a source of danger. Everyone, that is, except Clella.

He stalled out another weary minute to be certain the caller down the hall was not returning. When he was sure, he glided out of the corner, and, walking as quietly as possible on the barren floor, made his way to Clella's room. He took the key she had given him, slipped it into the lock, and admitted himself. Once inside, with the lock reset, he felt better.

He leaned back against the wall, glanced about. A lamp burned on the dresser. Clella's quarters were neat and clean. Starched lace curtains hung at the windows, a white spread covered the bed, and all things were in their place. He saw a bottle with several glasses on a shelf back of the washstand. He crossed over, took down the whiskey, poured himself a generous drink.

He sat down in a low rocking chair, took a long swallow of the liquor. The fire in the whiskey struck him almost at once and he began to feel better. He finished the drink but did not refill the glass. Strong liquor on an empty stomach would hinder rather than help if too large a quantity were taken.

There had been a faint hope in his mind that the girl would be in her room. It was an outside chance, he knew, but he had hoped, nevertheless. Now that he saw that she was not, he began to cast about for some way of getting her up from the saloon. Going downstairs for her was out of the question. Too many men knew him by sight now. And there was the matter of his ragged and bloody shirt. It would instantly attract attention and arouse interest.

He heard a door slam down the hallway. He listened, expecting to hear the hard, heavy tread of the man he had seen arrive earlier. Instead, he caught the light, quick tap of a woman's heels on the uncarpeted floor. He got to his feet, hurried to the door. Opening it a narrow distance, he waited until the woman was a step beyond, then called out softly.

"Lady . . . ?"

The girl stopped abruptly, half turned to him. "Yeah?"

"Do me a favor, ma'am," he said, keeping out of sight behind the panel. "Will you please tell Clella to come up? Tell her . . . her brother's here."

"Brother?" the girl echoed, as if surprised by such knowledge. Then—"Sure."—she said, and went on.

He settled back in the chair to wait. Considering all possibilities, he arose and walked to the windows, thinking of them as a quick avenue of escape should his message go astray. It was a drop of twenty-five feet or so to the hard, uneven ground. Flight by that route likely would result in injury, a broken leg at least. Out the door and down the hall to the back stairs was the only way. He shook his head. He would just have to gamble on the girl giving Clella his words and thinking no more of it.

It was a long quarter hour before he heard her key in the lock. He stepped back into a corner, drew his gun. It could be Clella—or it could be someone else, Jude Wade possibly. He saw her then slip quickly into the room, close, and lock the door. He holstered his weapon and stepped out where she could see him.

She started at his abrupt appearance. He said: "I'm sorry. I had to be sure you were alone."

Clella smiled. "I figured it was you when Theda said my brother was up here. I don't have a brother."

Selkirk glanced at her sharply, recognizing potential danger in the fact. "Does Theda know that?"

"No. And if she did, you wouldn't have to worry any about it. Sort of a rule we've got here . . . the girls, I mean. When it comes to our private lives, we never see or hear anything. You've been hurt," she added, noting his arm for the first time. She crossed over to where he stood. "Is it bad?"

Selkirk said: "Not much more than a scratch. But I would like to get it tended. Don't want it festering up on me."

She pointed to the rocker. "Sit down there. I'll take care of it. You better not try to see the doctor. What happened?"

He watched her take a strip of white cloth from a drawer, rip it into narrow strips. She reached for the bottle of whiskey.

"It's all I've got to clean the wound with. Going to burn like fury. You better have a healthy shot before I start."

Dan shook his head. "Already had all I can handle. Go ahead. I'll be all right."

She worked quickly, with sure, deft fingers; she first cleaned the wound with water, then cauterized it with the liquor. That done, she smeared the puckered holes with some sort of salve and bound the arm with the strips of cotton. While she worked, he related the incidents of the day, omitted only that part about Shad Ross and Quint Fisher. She completed her task and he his recitation at about the same moment. She stepped back, surveyed him with satisfaction.

"Good job, if I do say so myself. Arm ought to be good as new in a couple of days."

"Doc couldn't have done any better," Dan said. "I'm obliged to you."

"Forget it . . . brother. Next thing is to get you something to eat. There's cold meat and biscuits down at the bar. Would that do?"

"Be fine," he said, wondering when she would ask him the question he was sure was in her mind.

"I'll go down and get some," Clella said. "Don't worry if I'm not back right away. It's safer if I'm seen around in the crowd for a few minutes."

She left at once, locking the door after she went out. Doubt again assailed Dan Selkirk. He rose, began to pace the room restlessly. His precarious position naturally made him suspicious of all persons, but to be distrustful of Clella angered him faintly. She was his one friend, why couldn't he believe in her? Why wasn't he sure of her? He was placing some sort of meaning into the fact that she had not asked him the question he felt sure she wanted to know: *Had he learned who really robbed the bank?* It was reasonable to expect her to be curious about it since all things hinged on his finding out. Had she not asked because she already knew?

She was not gone long. Fifteen or twenty minutes. He opened the door for her, using his left hand while he held his gun with the right. She noticed that, smiled wryly at him.

"I'm not sure you trust me," she said, and walked to a small table. "You afraid I'll bring the law with me?"

He watched her set a plate of sliced beef and biscuits on the table. "Reckon I'm a little jumpy."

"You don't have to be afraid somebody will come up here, unless I bring them. Come on, eat a little. I know you must be starved."

She sat down on the edge of the bed and he pulled the rocker up to the food, began to eat. After a moment he said: "What's the talk downstairs? Wade and the posse back yet?"

"Haven't seen him, but several of the others are here. Some of them think you are still out there in the basin, dead. They believe Jude killed you."

Selkirk said: "He sure tried hard enough. I was lucky to get away from him."

"The main reason they think he killed you is because you didn't go past the men Jude had stationed at each end of the trail. How did you manage it?"

"Circled around them," Dan said. "Tough going for a ways but we did it."

"We?"

"My horse and me."

He had his fill of the food. He rose, poured himself a glass of water from the china pitcher on the washstand. After drinking it, he measured out a small amount of whiskey. "Want one?" he asked.

Clella shook her head. "No thanks."

He returned to the rocking chair, sat down. He studied the

amber liquid in the glass he held. Finally he said: "I know now who robbed the bank . . . two of them, anyway."

Clella sat up straighter. "Who?"

He swung his eyes to her. "Quint Fisher and Shad Ross."

She thought for several moments, then said: "That's what all that talk was about. Heard only scraps of conversation in the saloon but didn't know what it meant. Are you sure?"

"No doubt of it. Listened to them talk, make plans to pull out. That's how come I got this arm shot up. I threw down on them and took them back to the posse to hand them over to Wade. Only he got the wrong idea of what I was doing and opened up on me."

"Did they admit it? In front of the others, I mean."

"Denied it right straight down the line, just as I expected they would. But they're the ones. That I know. The problem now is to find out who else is in it with them and locate the money."

Clella had been surprised—and she believed him. He felt better about her now, was vaguely ashamed that he had mistrusted her. He put his empty glass aside, took his cigarette makings from his pocket, and rolled a smoke. He lit it, stared at the glowing tip.

She said: "What comes next?"

He shrugged. "Just what I'm trying to figure out. They're guilty but I can't get the law off my back long enough to prove it and find out who else helped them."

Clella was silent. From down below came the sound of a crash and the tinkle of glass as someone became involved in an accident—or a spirited discussion. "You say they plan to leave town . . . especially Quint?"

"Yes. Quint's getting nervous about it. He thinks there has been so much fuss stirred up that somebody is going to stumble onto something. He wants to get his share and pull out."

"Then I would say the man to watch is Quint. He'll have to go to where the money is hidden, or to the partner you're still looking for. Either way you could nab him and clear your name."

"I thought of that. But it seems there ought to be a faster way. Quint might be anxious, but he won't move too sudden. He's cagey. He'll be afraid of arousing suspicion. I figure he'll stall for two or three days, maybe a week. And I haven't got that much time."

Clella rose from the bed, walked to the dresser. She studied her rouged and powdered features in the mirror for a long minute. "Time is no friend to any of us, I guess. One way or another."

Dan Selkirk got to his feet. Such talk had made him more aware of the passing minutes. Another day would soon be at hand. "I expect I'd better be on the move. I'm obliged to you for fixing up my arm . . . and for the grub."

"It was nothing," the girl said, turning to him. "I wish I could have been of more help. There's one thing I keep wondering about."

"What's that?"

"Why did Jude Wade start shooting at you when he saw you with Shad and Quint? Why didn't he wait to find out what you were doing?"

"That's the way he's been ever since I first ran into him. He's trigger happy and thick-skulled."

Clella said: "I wonder about that. Jude's a fool but he's a smart fool in some things. Everybody thinks he's rushing around trying to prove what a good lawman he is so he can have Henry Corbin's job. And being hard on you like he has been is part of that."

"He's sure trying to prove something," Dan murmured.

"That's what I mean . . . is he? Did it ever occur to you that he doesn't want you to talk? That he doesn't want you to prove you had nothing to do with robbing Bishop's bank?"

The trend of her thinking registered on Dan Selkirk's mind immediately. "Which would mean that he's the other partner mixed up with Shad and Quint."

"Could be. I would never have believed Shad or Quint would have had enough brains to pull off a bank robbery, but it seems I was wrong. I could be just as wrong about Jude Wade. And like you once said, Jude's in a fine position to cover over all the tracks."

Selkirk nodded slowly. If true, it explained a lot of things, made many of the pieces fit in the puzzle. He moved to the door. "Maybe we're both wrong, but he looks like my best bet. I'm going to have a talk with him, one way or another. Was he downstairs?"

"No. You'll likely find him at the jail. Corbin usually keeps him on duty there during the evenings."

He unlocked the door, opened it. "Thanks again," he said over his shoulder.

She gave him her smile. "I'll be expecting you back."

He grinned and stepped out into the dark hallway. Ten minutes alone with Jude Wade was all he asked. Give him ten minutes and he'd have the answers.

XIII

Selkirk made his way down the corridor and to the rear door without interruption. He opened it, stepped out onto the small landing. Below, in the alleyway that ran behind the Golden Eagle and the other buildings on that side of the street, stood two men. Dan flattened himself against the wall, hoping neither man had heard him emerge, hoping also that they were not planning to climb the steps and enter the saloon by the second floor. It seemed to be some sort of an argument. He could hear the angry words, the rise and fall of their voices, but he could

191

not make out what they were saying. After what was an interminable time to Dan, they wheeled about and entered the saloon, using, fortunately, the ground-level door.

Selkirk let out his breath slowly. Almost angrily he went down the flight of steps. Being on the dodge, fearing to be seen, keeping to the shadows were beginning to wear on his nerves. It was no way of life for him and he was growing more and more impatient with the way of things.

He moved up the alley at a fast walk. It was dark along the buildings and he had little fear of being seen unless someone stepped unexpectedly from one of the various shops along the way. Nothing of that nature occurred and he covered the full length of the street and drew up alongside the jail without incident.

He could hear voices. The window that faced him was too high to permit his seeing in. He circled quietly around to the rear of the structure. The back door was open. Taking care not to allow the light that spilled into the night to strike him, he found a position in the dark shadows close by.

Marshal Henry Corbin's voice was saying: "Not much excuse letting a prisoner escape twice, Jude! If you'd done what I told you to, he'd be in that cell right now."

"You was the one who cut the rope I had around his wrists," Wade said defensively. "If you'd let it alone, he never could have jumped me."

Corbin snorted. "You had two men with you!"

"One . . . just Shad," the deputy cut in.

"Well, then, one man. Something must have been going on for him to get by both of you."

"Meaning what? That I just let him go?"

"Meaning that maybe you ain't all the lawman you think you are."

"You got ideas like that, then get yourself another deputy."

"Keep your shirt on, Jude. Time enough for that when this is all over with. Point is, you been a mite high-handed with this Selkirk. And you let him get away. . . ."

"Sure, I stood there and just let him kick me good, right in the belly."

"Then when you find him out there with a posse, you start right off shooting at him."

"Told you why. I didn't see the rest of the boys setting there. They were back behind some brush. I thought Selkirk had ambushed Shad and Quint. That's why I opened up."

"Selkirk doing that still don't make sense to me," Corbin said in a thoughtful way.

"Does to me," Jude answered promptly. "He was pure running a bluff. No way for him to get by the posse so he was trying to fool them with that cock-and-bull yarn. He'd 'a' done it, too, if I hadn't showed up.

Selkirk listened to the lawmen wrangle back and forth. A small doubt had crept into his mind now as to the possible guilt of Jude Wade. His explanation as to why he had begun shooting there in the basin was reasonable. It was possible he did not see the other members of the posse standing off to one side and that he actually had thought Quint and Shad were captives—which, of course, they were, but not in the sense that the deputy figured. He had a thought to enter the jail then, confront the two lawmen and, at gun point if need be, force them to hear him out, tell them exactly what Quint and Shad had said. Reason stayed him. He still had no proof of anything, only his word against that of the two riders, both of whom were friends of the deputy. And Henry Corbin's one answer to it all would be a cell.

"You dead sure you winged him there in the basin?"

"Sure, I'm sure. Seen him flinch when the bullet hit him. And we found blood. Rest of the boys will tell you that."

"Then where did he go? Man shot up bad ain't going far in that country. And he didn't ride out. Leastwise, the guards you had at both ends of the basin said he didn't. Funny a dozen men riding around like you all did couldn't find him."

"He's still in there," Wade declared flatly. "Crawled up under a rock and died. Got to be."

"And that big red horse of his? Suppose he's hid himself in a gopher hole, or something."

"He's around there somewheres, too. You know what it's like in there. Man can't see six foot ahead sometimes."

"Well, we're going to dig them both out in the morning. I'm rounding up fifteen or twenty men and we'll comb that brush good. We'll leave here at daylight."

"What about keeping somebody there at the ends of the trail for the night."

"Too late now. You should've done that when you pulled out at dark. If he was able to ride, he'd be gone by this time."

"He couldn't have," Wade said. "I know blamed well he was hard hit."

"We'll know how hard, come morning," Corbin said. "If you'd been smart, you'd have strung along with him instead of shooting him up when you saw him with Shad and Quint. Then later you could have turned the tables on him. You wasn't thinking much, Jude."

"Hindsight is always easier'n foresight. I was doing what I figured was the right thing."

"Which was wrong. You've been a deputy five years now and I don't think you've learned much about being a lawman. You still think the way to handle a prisoner is slap him around, treat him mean. Looks like you'd know by now that all that does is make him fight you harder."

"Different ways of being a lawman."

"That's sure right . . . and yours is the wrong one! Now, you hang around the office here. I'm going to nose around town a bit and get a posse lined up for in the morning."

"How long you want me to stay? I could use a bit of sleep."

"Reckon you can hold out until midnight. And be here by daylight in the morning. Understand?"

"I'll be here," Wade muttered.

From his position in the darkness behind the jail, Selkirk watched Corbin move into view. The thin-faced old man with his drooping mustache paused in the doorway, turned around. "I'll be riding with you in the morning, Jude. Right alongside. I'll tell you now, I won't have you flying off half-cocked again, if we turn Selkirk up. We bring him in as a prisoner, like we ought."

"Sure, Marshal. Whatever you say."

Corbin stepped out into the street. Selkirk again had an urge to talk with him, to wait until he was a safe distance from the building, confront him, and attempt to make the stubborn old officer listen.

He heard the scuff of boots. Two men emerged from the darkness, coming up from town.

" 'Evenin', boss," the voice of Shad Ross said. "You out havin' yourself a little walk?"

The three men halted. Corbin said: "Days are mighty hot. Man needs to soak up a bit of this coolness when he gets the chance."

"That's a fact," Quint Fisher agreed. "Jude in the office? Figured we'd kill a little time before going to bed, jawing with him."

"He's in there," the lawman replied. "He'll be looking after things until midnight."

"Where you headed . . . off to bed?"

There was a pause, then Corbin said: "Oh, I'll be around in town for a spell. Got some moseying about to do. Need a posse in the morning and I figure there's an outside chance that Selkirk fellow could've slipped in and be hiding out in one of the buildings."

"He's a slick one, sure enough," Ross said. "Well, see you later."

"So long," Corbin said, and strolled on.

XIV

Ross and Quint walked slowly up to the jail. Dan Selkirk did not move from where he stood in the deep shadows. A small tremor of anticipation coursed through him; perhaps now he would hear all he needed to know.

Shad said: "Sounded like the old man was chewin' on you right smart, Jude. He bad riled?"

"He ain't exactly happy," the deputy admitted ruefully.

"What the hell did he expect you to do?" Quint Fisher said. "Seems to me you was doing all you could."

"You know how Henry is. Figures I ought to have laid that Selkirk by the heels, no matter what."

"Sure is funny the way he just up and disappears," Shad said. "What you figure happened, Jude?"

"I'd say he was laying out there in the basin dead. He sure couldn't have got out of there, not with all the men I had covering the place."

"I don't know," Fisher said doubtfully. "We ought to have seen some sign of him."

"Well, we'll sure know in the morning and I expect you'll find out I'm right. Corbin wants a big posse to work the basin. Couple a dozen men, at least."

"What's to keep him from riding out of there tonight while it's dark?"

"Nothing . . . except I don't figure he's able to ride nowhere. I drilled him good and nobody can't make me believe I didn't."

33

"You drilled him for sure," Fisher said, "but I don't know how good."

"How about us ridin' over to the basin and havin' a look around?" Shad Ross suggested. "If he's alive, he just might have a fire goin'. We could spot it easy."

There was a long silence. Jude Wade said: "Might not be such a bad idea. But on the other hand, I don't figure Selkirk for a fool. He wouldn't light no fire . . . if he's still alive. For all he knows we left men there to watch."

"He could have hightailed it clear out of the country," Fisher said. "Rode out of the basin after we pulled away. We been riding him mighty hard."

"And he could be right here in town. Don't forget the marshal's got his thousand dollars."

Fisher grunted. "A man usually figures his hide is worth more than a thousand dollars. Jude, you got a bottle around here somewheres?"

"You know I ain't. Corbin wouldn't stand for that."

"I could sure use a drink, tired as I am. Think I'll trot over to Darcey's and get one. I'm tired but I ain't sleepy . . . and I feel like a few snorts."

"Could use a couple myself," Jude Wade said. "Go ahead."

Dan heard the scrape of a chair's legs across the wooden floor of the jail. Quint Fisher appeared briefly in the doorway, stepped out into the night. He walked hurriedly toward the center of town. Inside the lawman's quarters Shad Ross spoke again.

"Sure hope you nab this Selkirk, Jude. You ain't never lost a prisoner and it'd be a shame to spoil your record."

"I ain't about to lose him," Wade declared. "And I ain't so sure I have. And if he's still holed up there in the basin, like I figure he is, it's going to be the end of the trail for him."

"Meanin', this time you ain't goin' to miss, eh?"

"Meaning just that. I still figure I got him, but in case I didn't, you can bet your money he won't get away again."

Dan Selkirk listened to the run of conversation. It swung to other topics and he only half listened. A breeze sprang up, coming down from the plains to the east, cool and refreshing. So far he had learned nothing. Wade and the two men had talked only in generalities and about all he was certain of now was that Jude Wade intended he should never get out of the basin alive. He saw Quint Fisher then, returning with his bottle of liquor. He had been gone several minutes and apparently had tarried at the bar where he made his purchase to include a few drinks over the counter. Fisher entered the jail.

Shad greeted him with a shout. "Sure glad to see you back! My tongue's been hangin' out, thinkin' about that bottle."

Dan heard the scrape of chairs again. The three men apparently were drawing up about the desk. Jude Wade said something but the words were inaudible to Selkirk. At that moment the breeze caught the rear door to the jail, slammed it shut with a loud bang. Both sound and light were instantly closed off from Dan Selkirk.

He remained where he was, considered what next should be done. It seemed useless to remain near the jail any longer. He could hear nothing with the door closed and it would not be safe to hang around the front of the building. Wade and the others had lowered their voices anyway, and, even if the breeze hadn't shut them off from him, it was doubtful if he could overhear their words. Whether Jude Wade was involved with Quint and Shad was still questionable, but all indications pointed to the possibility. As to the two men, there was no doubt at all—and in that he found the key to what he should do. Stay with them. Follow them wherever they went. Eventually they would lead him to their partner.

The back door of the jail suddenly opened. Shad Ross, followed by Quint Fisher, stepped into the yard. Beyond them, in the center of the building, Dan could see Jude Wade's bulky figure.

"Be seeing you," Fisher said, hanging on to his half-empty bottle.

The deputy made a small gesture with his hand. "I'm figuring on you two now. Don't mess me up."

XV

Selkirk pulled back into the shadows. The jail door, victim of the breeze once more, closed again. Fisher and Ross moved by.

"When?" Shad asked.

Fisher said: "Midnight. We're to get over to the stables, get three horses ready to ride out. He'll meet us with the money. Just like I told you. . . ."

Fisher's voice faded into the night as the pair walked on. Selkirk remained quiet, startled and thrilled at the same time by the words he had overheard. The bank bandits were planning to run for it. Quint Fisher was having his way. Dan considered his position. As far as Corbin and the town were concerned, he was still a wanted man with the evidence that he had robbed Oscar Bishop all against him. But a man was wrong to take the law into his own hands. And if he did try to do so, something could go wrong and the outlaws might escape. Then he, personally, would be in a worse position.

If only he could convince Corbin that he was telling the truth, it would be much safer and better for all concerned. But Marshal Henry Corbin was a hard-headed old man who saw things only one way. Selkirk was his logical suspect, an escapee from jail, a wanted fugitive. To make him believe otherwise, that possibly his own deputy was one of the real bandits, would be practically impossible. But he must try. That conclusion came to him as he thought the matter through from all angles. The

199

law should be given its chance to act. Corbin, as the representative of that law, must be told about it.

He moved out of the shadows behind the squat structure of the jail. When he reached the street, he glanced back. Through the window he could see Jude Wade seated at the marshal's desk. He wondered if, at that moment, the deputy was having his dreams of Mexico, as had Shad Ross.

He continued on down the street. It was deserted at that late hour, with the residents of Apache Basin either in their homes or else visiting one of the many saloons along the way. Dan had no idea where he would find Henry Corbin. He had told the others he was going out to recruit riders for the posse and look for the escaped prisoner. The logical place to seek both was in the saloons. That meant he would have to check them, one by one, Dan realized, until he located the lawman. He would have to be careful, as always. Since the incident in the basin he was not unknown to every citizen of the town, no matter where he went there was bound to be one man who had seen him first-hand.

He halted outside the first saloon. He doubted if Corbin would be inside it as it would have been his initial stop on a route that would take him the length of the street. But Selkirk glanced over the half a dozen patrons, nevertheless, doing his observing through a dust-streaked window in the side of the building.

Corbin was not there as he had suspected. He moved on, came up with the same negative result in the following two places. The fourth stop was the Golden Eagle. It immediately presented him with a problem. There were no windows low enough through which he might peer and two men stood on the long gallery fronting the structure, thus blocking the door to him.

He thought back, endeavored to recall the arrangement of

the saloon, should a man enter from the back. There was a lower floor door, he remembered, but he had not used it; he had, instead, gone into the building at its upper story. There had been a short hallway, at that level, down which he had walked. Likely it was the same pattern on the ground floor, but it was only a guess. And a wrong guess could get him into trouble. If the lower door opened directly into the saloon, he would be noticed immediately. And there was no spare time in which to play a game of hide-and-seek with the townspeople of Apache Basin. He considered returning to Clella's room, hoping he could again in some way summon her. She could quickly tell him if Corbin were below, even arrange to get the lawman off to one side, behind the building perhaps, where they could talk. But the problem was reaching Clella. He had been lucky the last time; it might not go so well again. He would have to come up with something else.

A moment later he saw a man emerge from a small, dimly lit building, a café, as he recalled, farther down the street. The slightly stooped figure was familiar. Dan watched intently as the man turned into a saloon. It was Corbin. Selkirk heaved a sigh. The lawman had already been to the Golden Eagle, was now working his way up the opposite row of buildings.

Remembering the two men on the porch, Dan doubled back up the dusty street a short distance, then crossed over. He circled the building on the corner, came around to the alley behind it, and trotted along its dark, cluttered course until he was back of the saloon into which the lawman had gone. He quickly made his way along the narrow passageway that ran beside it, separating it from its adjoining neighbor, and there halted.

Corbin was not long inside. Selkirk heard the screen door squeak dryly as it opened, and then the lawman's slow, heavy step. He waited until Corbin was almost even with the mouth of the passageway, and then, gun in hand, stepped out abruptly.

"Through here, quick," he commanded in a low voice.

Corbin, startled, jumped visibly at the suddenness of Selkirk's appearance. But he recovered himself. In the poor light his thin face went taut, his pale eyes hardened.

"Might have known. . . ."

Dan prodded him gently with the barrel of his gun. "Forget it. We got some talking to do, but not out here." He reached out, relieved the lawman of his weapon. "Through here," he said, motioning at the passageway. "Head back to the alley."

Corbin wheeled stiffly, marched down the dark corridor. Selkirk flung a glance at the two men on the porch of the Golden Eagle. They had not moved. He stepped in behind Corbin, his pistol pressing lightly against the marshal's spine, followed him to the rear of the saloon.

"Good enough," he said when they were in the alley. "Now, Marshal, you're going to do some listening."

"With a gun pointed at me?" Corbin said. "Times like that I don't hear nothing."

"Well, this is one time you'd better hear because it's got to be that way. You don't give a man any choice. I had nothing to do with that bank robbery, and, if you'll give me a chance, I'll prove it."

"You're an escaped prisoner. A man that's suspected of a crime and you're supposed to be in jail," Corbin replied coldly. "That's all you mean to me. If you've got some yarn about why you're innocent, you can tell it to the judge when he gets here."

"Like I've told you, Marshal, I don't have time to wait around and do that. I got to do it now so I can be on my way. And if you'll listen. . . ."

"I'll listen to you when you're in a cell, not before," Corbin snapped. "Now, hand over that gun and surrender yourself before you get in even worse trouble than you're already in."

Exasperation flooded through Dan Selkirk. "Damn it, Marshal, I'm trying to tell you I know who the bandits are!"

"I've heard that . . . Shad Ross and Quint Fisher. You'll be telling me next my deputy's in on it, too. Or maybe it was Oscar Bishop, robbing his own bank."

"I've got a strong hunch Jude Wade is in it with Shad and Quint. . . ."

"You going to hand over that gun, Selkirk?"

"Not until you listen to what I've. . . ."

"Help!" Corbin yelled suddenly. "Over here behind the . . . !"

Dan struck automatically. The pistol in his hand caught the old lawman on the side of the head. He dropped in his tracks.

An answering shout came from the street. The two men on the gallery of the Golden Eagle had heard, Dan guessed. And there would be others. He reached down, picked up the marshal's slight body. He threw it over his shoulder like a sack of grain. "Stubborn old cuss," he muttered, and started down the alley at a trot.

Behind him the back door of the saloon, from which Corbin had just come, swung open. A block of yellow light dropped into the darkness. Selkirk dodged to one side.

"Sounded like it was out here," a man's deep-throated voice said.

"Who was it? Recognize it?"

"Nope. Couldn't tell. Wasn't that plain."

"Well, there sure ain't nobody here now. Could have been in the street and what we was hearin' was a sort of an echo."

The two men went back into the building, closed the door. Dan resumed his course. He glanced about, looking for a suitable place where he could deposit the lawman. He could not take him to the jail. There was no point in that now. He saw a small storage shed standing near the rear wall of one of the stores. He hastened to it, jerked back the door. It was partly filled with empty boxes and bundles of burlap sacks. Dan laid the marshal out flat, made him comfortable as possible. He would have to remain there for the balance of the night, unless someone happened along. But he would be all right. In the morning, when they opened up the store, he would be released.

Selkirk returned to the outside, wedged the door shut, and dropped the wooden peg into the hasp. He turned then, started down the alley at a run. He would have to handle Wade and the others by himself.

XVI

Selkirk crossed the street just beyond the jail. Beneath a small tree, he paused, looked through the open doorway. Jude Wade still sat at Henry Corbin's desk. On the wall behind him he could see the clock, the black Roman numerals sharp on its white face. 10:45. Slightly over an hour remained before the planned escape was to take place.

He stood there in the darkness and considered a plan of action. He must do nothing to alarm Fisher or Ross until they made their move. He must permit them to lead him to their partner, Jude Wade, if that was who it was—and they must have the money in their possession. That was most important. Apparently Wade had the cash. To prove his innocence Dan would have to capture the outlaws while they had the $9,000 on them. There was nothing he could do until midnight except wait and watch. Wade seemed to have settled down. It was best now that he look in on the other two. He faded back into the shadows, made his way cautiously to the stable where Ross and Fisher would be.

The broad, flat-roofed building was dark. Dan crossed to the far corner of the structure where office quarters had been placed. He moved quietly to the window. Faint snoring noises told him the hostler slept. That took care of him. Now to get inside without being seen by Shad Ross or Quint Fisher.

He remembered the rear door. He dropped back, walked softly around the barn until he reached it. There was no way of knowing just where inside Shad and Quint would be at that moment. They could be in one of the front stalls or somewhere at the rear; it was entirely possible they were not around at all, having taken a few minutes off to visit one of the saloons for a fresh bottle or something. Everything was left up to chance, a blind gamble that he must take.

He laid his hand on the latch lever, pressed gently. The metal clicked and the door came open. Selkirk hesitated a moment, stepped inside quickly. He left the door ajar. The latch had made more noise than he expected and he would want to use it again.

He halted a few feet inside the huge, musty building, allowed his eyes to adjust to the gloom. Two lanterns cast a yellow glow over the littered interior, one near the front entrance, the second at the end of the runway. Dan walked quietly toward the latter. He could see the heads of several horses in the line of stalls but it was too dark to tell which wore bridles and which did not. When he reached the wide runway, he stopped. He should be hearing something—sounds made by Quint and Shad, the squeak of leather on their horses. A vague alarm moved through him. The silence was too complete. He glanced about the stable, endeavored to fathom the deep, shadowed corners, the black areas. He took another step, one that put him into the runway itself.

"Stand still!"

The low, harsh voice of Shad Ross was like a knife coming out of the darkness. Selkirk felt the muzzle of a gun jab into his spine.

"Raise up your hands, mister."

Anger flashed through Dan Selkirk. After all his careful planning, he had allowed himself to walk straight into their hands. Slowly he lifted his arms.

Quint Fisher walked around and looked closely at him. The narrow-faced rider whistled softly. "Well, what do you know, Shad? We sure caught us a big fish this time."

"It Selkirk?" Ross asked.

"The same. We figured maybe you was dead, friend."

"Not yet," Dan answered. "Could be it's going to end up the other way around."

"Mighty cocky, ain't he?" Ross said. "Don't look to me like Jude's bullet did him any harm."

"Bandage on his arm," Fisher said. "This sure fixes things up good for us. We'll just truss him up nice and tight and leave him here for the posse to find in the morning. That'll give them something to stew over for an extra hour or so. We'll have more traveling time than we figured at first."

"Might be better to take him along," Shad said. "We could get rid of him down the way a piece."

"Only slow us down. No, the thing to do is leave him right here. Corbin and his posse'll be so busy asking him questions and trying to figure out whether he's lying that we'll gain a whole hour or more."

"Reckon you're right," Shad said. "Let's get him into one of them back stalls. No use making it easy for them to find him. Get that rope offen that peg, Quint."

Dan felt the gun barrel leave his back. He saw Quint Fisher wheel away to do Shad's bidding. He reacted instantly. He whirled, his elbow extended wide. It knocked away Shad's weapon, sent it spinning to the floor. He lunged at the dark, bulky shape half crouched behind him, slammed into it with both fists.

He heard Quint Fisher coming at him as Ross went to one knee. Quint lunged at him, missed with both clawing hands, and fell partly across Selkirk's body. Dan jerked to one side, dumped the man. Fisher scrambled to his knees. Selkirk caught him with a vicious right to the head that drove the man up against the side of the stall. He felt hands clutch at his ankles, felt himself suddenly going down. He tried to throw himself off, get clear of Shad. He fell flat. Ross grunted, heaved his massive body forward. Dan felt the solid, smothering weight of the man press upon him. Selkirk thrashed wildly, got a knee clear. He brought it up sharply, drove it into Shad's groin. The rider groaned, cursed. He struck out furiously. His huge fist grazed Dan's face, tore the skin but did little damage. Selkirk used his knee again and, as Shad flinched, kicked himself free and rolled to one side.

He bounded to his feet. Both Shad and Quint were up almost as quickly as he. They rushed in together, reaching for him. He leaped to the side—toward Fisher. He dodged the man's groping fingers, threw up his hands and placed them, palms flat, against Quint's body. He put all his strength into a mighty push. Fisher went stumbling off into the darkness, collided with Shad, and ricocheted into the wall of the stable.

Dan did not see him fall. Shad Ross had wheeled, unexpectedly fast for so large a man, and was lunging straight at him. There was no time to side-step, to duck away. In defense, he came up with a short, jabbing left hand. It missed Shad's chin, caught him in the neck. The rider stalled, briefly off balance. Selkirk tried to follow through. He closed, smashed home a hard right.

Ross staggered, stumbling over his own feet. Dan pursued him, drove him relentlessly, crowded him with punishment. Shad came up against the wall. He dropped into a crouch, covering up. Selkirk measured him, began a long uppercut from the floor. Suddenly he was aware of Quint Fisher behind him. A warning flashed through his mind. He tried to step aside but was too late. Something heavy and solid slashed through the stable's gloom. It caught him on the back of the head, drove him forward. There was a roaring sound in his ears and a pinwheel of lights burst in his eyes. He crashed into the side of the stall. There was a fresh explosion of color, and then total darkness.

XVII

Dan Selkirk returned to consciousness slowly. The first sound of which he became aware was the steady crunching of grain by the horses in their stalls. He realized then he was gagged, bound tightly. Strips of rawhide, of the sort found around a stable and used to fasten blanket rolls, packages, and such items to saddles, locked his ankles together and firmly joined his wrists behind his back. A bandanna sealed his lips.

He struggled to a sitting position. Except for the horses he appeared to be alone. He worked himself over against a nearby wall, managed to gain an upright stance. Then, by a series of short hops, he made his way to the runway, anxious and fearful of verifying a fact he dreaded to acknowledge. He looked down the shadowy length of the stable. His hopes sank. The three horses, prepared for escape by Shad Ross and Quint Fisher, were gone. He was too late.

He leaned back against a roughly hewn post and endeavored to think. His mind was still foggy but functioned sufficiently to get one thing through to him. He must somehow escape, start again to search for Fisher and Ross and Jude Wade, if Jude was the third man involved. He fought briefly with the rawhide that bound his wrists. There was no slack, no give. The hostler? Awaken him and persuade him to cut the strips that restricted his movements. On second thought he discarded that possibility. The hostler, afraid of Wade and the others, would hesitate to do anything that might lead him into trouble. Most likely he would summon aid from the town and Dan Selkirk knew he would be as bad if not worse off than ever.

But he must get free. Each passing moment put the outlaws farther out of his reach, plunged him deeper into a desperate situation. It could not be much after midnight, the hour the outlaws had set as their time of departure. He could not have been unconscious for too long after the fight with Ross and Fisher. If he could just manage to get his hands loose. . . .

He saw the barrel of water then. It stood near the doorway, a supply basin for buckets. His spirits lifted and he hopped quickly toward it. He halted at the door leading into the office first, however, caution laying its restraint upon him. He must take care to not arouse the hostler. The cot was empty—the man was gone. That failed to relieve him, served instead to disturb him greatly. The stableman was around somewhere, moving about; perhaps he had already gone for help.

Dan Selkirk wasted no time on speculation. He hobbled to the water barrel, backed up to it, and thrust his hands into the cool liquid. He began to work them immediately, chafing them briskly. At first there was very little give to the rawhide and then, as the water soaked into the strands, the leather began to stretch, to grow slick. He twisted his hands back and forth, placed them, palm to palm, prized them apart. He felt the cords cutting into his flesh but he ignored it; the rawhide had turned greasy, was giving way under his straining.

One hand came free suddenly. The dull aching in his shoulders ceased as he brought his arms around to their normal position. He ripped the gag from his lips, took a grateful, unhindered breath. He then removed the dangling rawhide from his other hand, bent down, and untied the bonds that hobbled his ankles.

He wheeled, rushed to the office in search of the time. There was no clock on the wall or the small table that stood in one corner of the room. He still did not know how late, how far behind the outlaws he was. He glanced at the holster at his hip. His gun was missing. He trotted to the rear of the stable where the fight had taken place. After a few moments he located the weapon, partly hidden in the straw that littered the floor. He checked it, slid it into its leather sheath. He would have to have a horse—and there was no time to go after the red gelding. He hurried to the first stall. A chunky little black stood dozing between the wooden partitions. He lifted a saddle and blanket from the bar, threw them onto the animal that came awake with a jerk. The bridle was handy and he slipped it into place. He backed the black out into the runway, vaulted onto the leather, and started for the door at a run.

He burst into the open, heard instantly a shout. The hostler, probably. He did not turn to look but, low in the saddle, raced on through the darkness. He swung along the edge of the settlement, came up to the jail from its rear. There was no necessity for care, he saw. The building was dark, deserted. Jude Wade had already gone. He walked the black around to the front, endeavored to read the clock. It was impossible. He could not tell if he were one minute or one hour too late. But he was certain of one thing—the outlaws would have struck southward for Mexico. Shad Ross had mentioned it and the proximity of the border made it a natural destination for any man seeking to evade the law. If the outlaws thought no pursuit was under way, they would likely be traveling easily, in no great hurry. And they could not have too good a start; he surely had not been unconscious in the stable for over a half an hour.

He left the jail at once, headed out into the street. He was gambling, of course; the bank bandits could have gone another direction, but he doubted it—and he had little choice except to follow his own hunch, anyway. He decided then it would be wise to have Marshal Corbin in on the deal. If the old man would listen to reason, he would release him, suggest he form a posse and follow. If he was still bull-headed about it all, he would tell him what had taken place, what his own plans were, and then let him sweat it out in the shed until someone happened by and opened the door for him. By that time, perhaps, he would have come to his senses, realized that Selkirk was sincere in what he was trying to do, and lend a hand. If he failed to overtake the outlaws and recover the money, Corbin could not say he had not been told of it and warned.

He swung the black off the street, rode in behind the building where he had imprisoned the lawman in the small shed. Before he reached it, he saw he was again too late. The door stood open. Corbin had managed to get out, either by attracting someone or by his own efforts.

Selkirk swore softly. It seemed nothing would work right. He pulled the black around, returned to the street. He could waste no more time; the bandits were getting farther away with each minute that passed. It looked like a job he would have to do on his own.

The lights of the Golden Eagle drew his attention. From the amount of noise flowing from its depths it would appear there was still a fair crowd inside. He slanted the black toward it, drew his pistol. He halted before the batwing doors, taking care to stay in the shadows beyond the flare of light. He held his gun overhead, fired twice into the night.

There was a sudden cessation of sound within the saloon. A moment later several men rushed through the doorway, pulled to a halt on the porch. Others crowded up against them shouting questions. Dan silenced them with another shot. "I'm Selkirk!" he called when they had quieted. "The men who robbed your bank have pulled out. I think they're headed for Mexico, and I'm going after them. Find Marshal Corbin. Tell him to get up a posse and follow."

"Hold on there a minute!" a voice ordered. "You're the one we. . . ."

Dan halted the man's threatening move with a bullet into the floor at his feet.

"Don't try anything brave!" he warned. "Most of the people in this town have me convicted and ready for hanging. I'm going to prove how wrong they all are. Now stand fast while I ride out. First man to make the wrong move is liable to get hurt."

He touched the black with his spurs. The horse broke into a run. "Tell Corbin what I said!" Dan yelled as he swept down the street.

He kept his gun leveled at the group on the gallery of the Golden Eagle. From the tail of his eye he saw several other men coming up the street at a trot. They had come from some of the smaller saloons, he guessed, attracted by the gunshots and yelling. One could have been Henry Corbin as there was a familiar figure in the group, but it was too dark to tell for certain. It made no difference anyway. To have stopped and waited for the old lawman would simply have meant more delay, more arguing. It was better the way he had handled it. Let Corbin form a posse and follow. If he could catch up with the outlaws, he would manage to hold them somehow, until the lawman could arrive.

He reached the end of the street, thundered past the last building, and strung out on the long, curving road that bore to the south. Now all he had to do was overtake the bandits.

XVIII

South—to Mexico. A moment of doubt again assailed Dan Selkirk. He could be wrong. Fisher and Ross and Jude Wade, if he were the third man involved in the robbery, could be smarter than he thought. He was going a lot on Clella's opinion of them; he was banking on their doing the expected, the obvious.

If it turned out he was wrong. . . . He shrugged. No point in thinking of that now. He had already committed himself, both to his own actions and to Marshal Corbin and the town of Apache Basin. If he had made the wrong move, then he could kiss McGowan's $1,000 good bye along with a good job and his own reputation. He would ride the Owlhoot Trail from then on.

He bent lower over the saddle, urged the husky black to greater speed. He wished he had the gelding under him. Few horses could match the big sorrel in both pace and staying power. But the red was back in town and there was no profit in wishing. The black wasn't doing too badly. At the end of the first mile he had covered the distance at a fast rate and wasn't breathing hard. At the finish of five he had slowed considerably but was maintaining a consistent lope that ate up the ground at a satisfactory average. Shortly after that point Selkirk caught his first glimpse of the outlaws, far ahead in the moonlight-flooded night. It was just a brief flash, three riders silhouetted on the crown of a hill, and then they were gone.

They had a considerable lead but that did not worry him too much. He was too relieved to see that he had been right. They were heading for Mexico, and, believing him to be securely trussed up in the stable and the town totally unaware of their activities, they were taking it easy. But that would change now. They would hear the oncoming black, speed up their flight. The chunky little horse would have to work hard to close the gap.

They rushed on through the night, swept around a flat-topped mountain in a wide curve. It was new country to Dan, unfamiliar in every detail. He saw that instead of the flat desert he had expected, they were in a land of short, choppy hills. It was not hard going; the road beneath the black's hoofs were solid and fairly smooth. He was running free and easily.

They broke out on the crest of a long ridge. Below, in a broad, gentle swoop, unrolled a shallow valley. Selkirk had a lengthy, unhampered view of the road—and realized at once the outlaws were no longer ahead of him. He slowed the black, wondered if the men had pulled off to the side and allowed him to ride by. He doubted that. There was no cover bordering either side in which three men with horses could hide. He drew the black to a full halt, listened. Faintly, coming from off to his right, he heard the steady drumming of fast-running horses. He knew then what had happened. The outlaws had simply turned off the main road, taken another that led westward. Selkirk put the black to a slow lope, his eyes searching the shoulder of the road. A quarter mile farther on he located the turn-off.

Immediately he spurred the black to a faster pace. He must make up the lost time. He was grateful for one thing—that he had been near enough to the outlaws to notice the change. Had he been farther back he likely would have missed it completely.

The trail began to grow rougher, steeper. The black was forced to slacken speed and occasionally stumbled on the uneven ground. It seemed strange to Dan that the bandits would forsake the hard surface of the main road for one that provided slow going at best. It was more logical for them to try and get completely out of the country and into Mexico as quickly as possible.

A half hour later Selkirk knew the answer to the puzzle. He recognized the area into which they were riding—the basin. The outlaws, slowed down for some unknown reason, or fearing they could not outdistance their pursuer, had swung back and chose now to enter the wild breaks area. Estimating their chances for escape, they apparently decided their best bet would be in the thick brush where it was fairly simple to elude anyone on their trail.

Dan pulled to a halt on the edge of the first dense outcropping. This was the southern lip of the basin but there was little difference in it and the opposite side where he had entered the previous day. It was no less rugged. The bandits would not be traveling fast now. No one could ride a horse through that maze of rock- and brush-littered land with any degree of speed and safety. That possible advantage was offset, however, by the lack of visibility that went with it. A man would have to rely mostly upon his hearing with, perhaps, an occasional, fleeting glimpse of movement the pale moon might reveal.

It was while he sat there on the rim, allowing the little black to recover his wind, that he heard the distinct click of metal against rock. It was all he needed. He knew now which direction into the basin the outlaws had taken. He moved off the low rise, set out at a careful pace for the sound. It wasn't much to go on but it was a start.

It resulted in little if anything of value. For the better part of an hour Selkirk drifted silently through the brush and rock, pausing every few minutes to listen. He heard a horse stumble once, was near enough to understand a man's explosive curse— Shad Ross, he believed. He had swung instantly toward the sounds only to find nothing. The hopelessness of his task began to dawn upon him. He recalled that, in daylight, he had been able successfully to elude an entire posse in the tangled depths of the basin. How could he, a man alone, expect to do better at night?

"Quint?"

The sudden, guarded query came from a short distance to the east of where Dan Selkirk had halted. It was the voice of Shad Ross.

"Quint? It's me, Shad."

Dan waited out the moments, trying to fix the man's location in his mind, hoping to hear the other outlaw's reply. For a time there was only the sly stirring of the birds in the warm hush. Then Quint Fisher's reply, low and angry, reached him.

"Cut out that yelling, Shad!"

"Not yellin'. Just tryin' to keep together. Where's the boss?"

"Over on my right. You hear anything more of that rider?"

"Not since we heard him on the trail. Who you reckon it was?"

Dan Selkirk kept the black moving quietly toward the sound of Shad Ross's voice. He was the nearer of the two. A thought was running through Selkirk's mind—a vague prodding, a recollection at something Shad had just said. He couldn't quite pin it down.

"Keep moving," Fisher said then. "Don't stand quiet. Still think we ought to have kept going," he added in a dissatisfied voice.

"We wasn't makin' no time," Ross answered. "And one man sure ain't goin' to pin us down here in the breaks."

"You keeping that horse on the move like I said?" Fisher asked.

"Sure. I'm walkin' him slow."

"Good. I ain't worried about one man, whoever he is, pinning us down in here. I'm worrying about a posse from town. I figure we ought to get out of here."

"Could be you're right. Never thought about no posse. Maybe we ought to catch up to the boss, talk to him about it."

Dan Selkirk pulled to a halt. It was useless to wander aimlessly after the outlaws. With luck, he might take one, Shad Ross particularly, as he seemed not far off. But he must have them all. And Quint Fisher had been talking good sense. They were foolish to hang out any longer in the basin. When—and if—a posse arrived, their chances for escape would be greatly decreased.

He swung the black around immediately. He knew now what must be done. The basin had two accesses—to the north, which led directly to the town, and to the south and Mexico. He hurried the black as much as possible through the rocks and brush.

Everything depended now on his getting to the mouth of the basin at its southern end, a sort of narrow, cañon-like entrance, he recalled. He was gambling again, he realized. Perhaps there was another way in and out of the breaks but he doubted it. He was certain he could depend on the three outlaws to take the easiest and fastest route in a dash to reach the border. They were already sorry they had not continued on in the first place. Now they would be racing time against the arrival of a posse, be rushing to correct what they considered a serious error. They would ignore him, believe him to be somewhere deep in the basin, and no source of danger.

It was graying in the east when he reached the rim of the sink, rode into the passage-like entrance at the extreme southern edge. The better light pointed up the area more fully and he saw now why he had paid scant notice when he rode in. There was scarcely any thinning of brush and rock; it was only a continuation of the rank growth and rugged fastness, lying, like a stubby finger, between two low and steep cliffs. Through it the trail wound to break, finally, out onto the smaller, smoother hills.

Near midway Dan Selkirk halted. He glanced about. This would be as good a point as any to intercept the three men. From behind a large slide of rocks, which formed a sort of abutment, he had a fifty-foot view of the trail. He could wait until they were well out in the open, then ride in on them. There would be no good cover for them to duck into nearer than a dozen yards. He prodded the black into a stand behind the butte, and positioned himself to where he had a clear view of the trail. He checked his weapon, saw that he had already replaced the cartridges spent in Apache Basin before he rode out. He was ready.

The odds were a little high—three to one: Shad Ross, Quint Fisher, and Jude Wade, if that was who the third man actually was. Who else could it be? Alone in the quiet, breaking dawn, Dan Selkirk gave it deep thought.

XIX

He heard the posse from Apache Basin first. The riders were coming fast, the sound of their horses a steady drumming on the early morning breeze. He swore softly. They could upset everything if they arrived too soon. That would force the outlaws to change their plans, perhaps wheel about and either again bury themselves in the tangle of the basin, or make a run for freedom out the north entrance. Such would take them away from the Mexican border, but it would be an avenue for escape.

He turned his attention to the narrow, corridor-like trail. If the bandits also heard the approaching horsemen, and were at that moment near enough, they would likely make a dash for the cañon's mouth. Once outside the limits of the basin, they could withdraw to one side, hide in the brush, and allow the posse to rush on by—thus go unnoticed. They could then resume their flight southward. The trio could not be far off, Dan thought. He had been waiting a good hour.

All speculation ended abruptly. Quint Fisher rode abruptly from the brush at the far end of the trail, his horse moving at a fast walk. He reached the center of the passage area where it was more open, half turned, glanced back. Shad Ross came into view then. He pulled up beside Fisher, halted.

"What's holding him up?" Fisher demanded in an aggravated tone. "We got to get out of here."

"He's comin'," Ross said.

The third man broke into the clearing—an old man with his right arm in a sling. Henry Corbin! Dan Selkirk stared, unable to believe his eyes. It was Corbin, not Jude Wade who, with Ross and Fisher, had robbed the bank. Explanations of many unanswered questions flooded into Selkirk's mind, chief among them being the reason why the outlaws had not continued on to Mexico but had doubled back into the basin. The old lawman was having a hard time of it in the saddle. His arm and leg evidently pained him greatly and riding, even at a moderate pace, was a terrible effort.

Fisher called: "Hurry it up there, old man! You hear them horses? That's a lynching party on the way. We don't get out of this sink before they close the gap, you're going to be the main attraction."

Corbin's seamed, leathery face was a mixture of disgust and agony. He spat. "If you're in such a blasted hurry, ride on out. I'll manage."

"Give me my third of that nine thousand and I'll sure do just that," Fisher shot back.

"Hold it right there and I'll just do that," Corbin answered.

Dan steeled himself for the job that lay before him. The posse was still too far off to be of help. He would have to stop them alone. Ross and Fisher would not be taken easily. Henry Corbin was the unknown factor; wounded, apparently sick of his deal, he might fight—and he might quit cold. Dan watched the trio draw up into a tight, small group. Corbin sighed audibly, twisted about, and thrust his hand into the left pocket of his saddlebags.

"We ought to wait till we're out on the flats for this," Shad Ross said. "Don't like this here waitin' around inside the breaks. Like bein' in a water bucket."

"Won't take long," Fisher growled.

Selkirk jabbed his spurs into the little black, plunged into the center of the trail. "Stand pat!" he shouted.

Ross's horse reared violently at the sudden interruption. The man yelled a curse, fought to keep the animal from going over backward. Dan saw Quint Fisher slap at his pistol. He fired quickly. Quint winced but seemed not badly hurt.

Shad Ross had his weapon out. The sound of it was a quick

echo to Selkirk's .45. Dan felt the bullet sear across his thigh, touch the black in its passing. He snapped a shot at Ross as the black shied and began to pitch. Fisher had jerked the white sack of money from the hands of Henry Corbin. Bent low over the saddle, he was circling wide, trying to by-pass. Dan threw a shot at the outlaw, turned him aside. At that moment Shad Ross cut down on him from almost pointblank range. Dan threw himself to one side, leveled his own weapon at the burly Ross. The outlaw fired first. The bullet struck the steel of the horn in front of Dan, ricocheted, thudded dully into nearby rocks. Through the smoke haze and churning dust, Dan caught Ross off the end of his gun barrel. Fisher was again trying to rush by. Dan could do nothing about that until he got Ross off his back. He squeezed the trigger. Ross snapped backward, sagged to one side. His gun blasted again. Dan did not feel any impact, or hear the whine of the bullet's passing. The outlaw's final shot had gone far wide. He gave Ross no further thought. He wheeled, started after Quint Fisher.

The outlaw had reached the edge of the brush on the far side of the clearing. Dan brought up his revolver for a quick shot. He held back. He was not sure if the gun was empty or not. It seemed there should be one, perhaps two cartridges left in the cylinder. The last moments had been so hectic he had lost count. He pulled the trigger. Quint Fisher was at that moment ducking into the brush. The bullet struck something, a branch, Dan guessed, veered off. Before he could shoot again, Fisher was within the protective screen of shrubbery.

The black thundered down the trail in pursuit. Selkirk fumbled with the cartridges in his belt, thumbed them into the .45's cylinder and wondered about Henry Corbin. He had taken no part at all in the fight. He had simply sat back and allowed his two partners to do the gun handling. Was it for a purpose? Did he intend to wait until it was all over with, hopeful that Selkirk would be either dead or badly wounded, grab the sack of money, and escape? Or was he backing down, sorry he had been a part of the robbery and ready to give up?

The answer to that would come later, Dan thought, as he finished cramming the last of the loads into his pistol. Fisher had the money now and Fisher was getting away. He must be stopped.

Up ahead there was a sudden spatter of gunshots. Quint apparently had collided with the posse. Dan muttered a prayerful hope that Fisher had not caught the oncoming riders by surprise and managed to get by them.

Suddenly a lone horseman was before him. He bore down at reckless speed through the rock and brush. It was Fisher. Evidently he had wheeled at contact with the posse, preferring now to take his chances with one man rather than with several. His gun went up. Selkirk saw it jerk in his hand, saw the puff of smoke. Pain bit through him as the slug tore into his leg.

The black slowed before the charging outlaw. Dan, knowing his life depended upon accuracy, steadied himself. He lined up Quint Fisher off the sights of his revolver, doing it deliberately, coolly. He was aware of the outlaw's second shot but the bullet missed. He fired. Fisher rocked on the saddle, slipped to one side, recovered, came racing on. Dan sent another bullet into him almost as they drew abreast. Fisher went off his horse in a headlong plunge.

A half a dozen riders burst into the clearing. Selkirk recognized Jude Wade in the lead. He was followed by the banker, Bishop, the man called Jonas, and others Dan had seen before but did not know by name. The men rode up and halted.

"Where's the others?" Wade demanded. "Somebody beside Quint there in on it, ain't there?"

"Two," Dan said. "You'll find them back there a ways." He swung his attention to Bishop. "There's your money," he said, pointing to the sack still clutched in Quint Fisher's hand.

The banker dismounted, retrieved the sack. He glanced at its contents. "Appears we owe you an apology," Bishop said then, looking up at Dan. "Sure hope we haven't caused you to lose out on that cattle deal. . . ." The banker paused, his eyes reaching beyond Selkirk.

Dan turned. Jude Wade was coming up the trail. He had his gun out and leveled at the slumped figure of Henry Corbin who rode slightly ahead of him.

"You mean the marshal . . . ," Jonas began, and halted uncertainly.

Selkirk said: "Quint Fisher, Shad Ross, and your town marshal. They were the ones."

"Great Godfrey," Bishop breathed. "I just can't believe it."

"Reckon he was kind of sick of the deal," Dan said then. "He probably would have pulled out of it if he'd had the chance. He could have thrown in with Quint and Shad back there when I jumped them. And with that kind of odds, I might not have been so lucky. But he didn't." Selkirk paused, waited until the lawman and Wade had halted before the group. "I'm obliged to you, Marshal."

Henry Corbin shrugged. "Habit, I suppose. Just not in me to side an outlaw."

"Why?" Oscar Bishop asked, moving up to the side of the lawman. "Why, for the love of heaven, Henry, did you do it?"

Corbin lifted his tired eyes. "Why? I'm sixty-four years old. I've been town marshal of Apache Basin for twenty-three of those years . . . at sixty dollars a month. I own this horse, the clothes I've got on my back, my gun, and nothing more. Now I'm all shot up, a cripple. Good for nothing . . . and about to be out of a job. That's why, Oscar. I needed that money to see me through the few years I've got left." In the silence that followed, Corbin turned his bitter gaze to Jude Wade. "And you want my job," he said. "You've been straining at the halter to take over. You're a bigger fool than I thought, Jude. Any man that wants to be a lawman is a fool."

Jude Wade made no answer for a long minute. Then he said: "Reckon we'd better get started for town, Mister Corbin. Couple of you boys lead up Shad and Quint's bodies." He swung to Dan. "Guess I ought to say I'm sorry about figuring you wrong and roughing you up the way I did. But a man's got to be that way in this business."

Selkirk grunted. "Take a little advice from me, Deputy. Change your ways right soon or you'll never live long enough to be a town marshal, anywhere."

Wade swept Selkirk with a cool glance, said nothing. He touched his horse with spurs and moved out, herding Corbin ahead of him. Oscar Bishop walked to Dan's side.

"He'll learn," he said, "if, like you said, he can stay alive long enough. Now, it just occurred to me. If you want to ride on, hop to it. I'll give you your thousand dollars out of the money here in the bag and you can be on your way. It'll save you riding clear back to town."

Selkirk grinned at the banker. "I'm obliged to you for the offer, but I've got to go back anyway. This is a borrowed horse I'm riding. I left my sorrel there in town. Besides I want to say *adiós* to a lady I met . . . and see if maybe I can get her to do a little doctoring on me again."

"You hurt?" Bishop asked quickly. "Sorry, I didn't notice. You ride on in, see Doc Wells. I'll take care of the bill."

"Never mind," Dan said. "Got my own private doctor. Anyway, there's a couple other things I mean to talk to her about."

ABOUT THE AUTHOR

Ray Hogan was an author who inspired a loyal following over the years since he published his first Western novel, *Ex-Marshal,* in 1956. Hogan was born in Willow Springs, Missouri, where his father was town marshal. At five the Hogan family moved to Albuquerque where they lived in the foothills of the Sandia and Manzano Mountains. His father was on the Albuquerque police force and, in later years, owned the Overland Hotel. It was while listening to his father and other old-timers tell tales from the past that Ray was inspired to recast these tales in fiction. From the beginning he did exhaustive research into the history and the people of the Old West, and the walls of his study were lined with various firearms, spurs, pictures, books, and memorabilia, about all of which he could talk in dramatic detail. "I've attempted to capture the courage and bravery of those men and women that lived out West and the dangers and problems they had to overcome," Hogan once remarked. If his lawmen protagonists seem sometimes larger than life, it is because they are men of integrity, heroes who through grit of character and common sense are able to overcome the obstacles they encounter despite often overwhelming odds. This same grit of character can also be found in Hogan's heroines, and in *The Vengeance of Fortuna West* (1983) Hogan wrote a gripping and totally believable account of a woman who takes up the badge and tracks the men who killed her lawman husband by ambush. No less intriguing in her way is Nellie Dupray, convicted of rustling in *The Glory Trail* (1978). One of his most popular books, dealing with an earlier period in the West with Kit Carson as its protagonist, is Soldier in Buckskin (Five Star Westerns, 1996). Above all, what is most impressive about Hogan's Western novels is the consistent quality with which each is crafted, the compelling depth of his characters, and his ability to juxtapose the complexities of human conflict into narratives always as intensely interesting as they are emotionally involving. *Against the Law* will be his next Five Star Western.